if you could haunt your house forever

a collection of odd stories

by

ETHAN RENOE

The freakin sweet author illustration by:
Casey Rooney @caseyruthrooney

Cover design by Ethan Renoe

Illustrations courtesy of The British Library

Other illustrations by Ethan Renoe

Other Books by Ethan

Leaving Weather
This first book began as a college senior project and ended up being a unique collection of essays, poems and photos.

The New Lonely (#1 Amazon best-seller!)
Today, everyone seems to be lonely, despite being more connected than ever before! What happened? Explore this phenomenon in The New Lonely.

Bad Timing
All the love, heartbreak and laughs a single book can hold.

Now Let Me Find A Stopping Place
Every night for ten years, Ethan wrote at least one poem. This collection takes the best of these poems from around the world, written between 2008-2018, and mashes them together

Time Kills All Things
The best 272 blogs from the first five years, published in this collection on everything from dating & sex to faith & death.

How to Understand the Entire Universe, part 1
Yes, really. How to understand it all. It's a mashup of philosophy, history, and theology, but FUN!

Open Hands
How to live. Easily my most powerful and easiest to read. 100 pages with a lot of illustrations!

All The Immortal Things that Live Inside of Us
A year of heartbreak, healing, and finding God all over again.

Dedicated to the 1830 boys
who will probably never read this
because they're little babies

Jerbear, Colito, Anderson Cooper,
Zasth, Nath, Seth,

but most of all Tipper.
May she be stoked for 14 more years,
too lumpy to be grumpy.

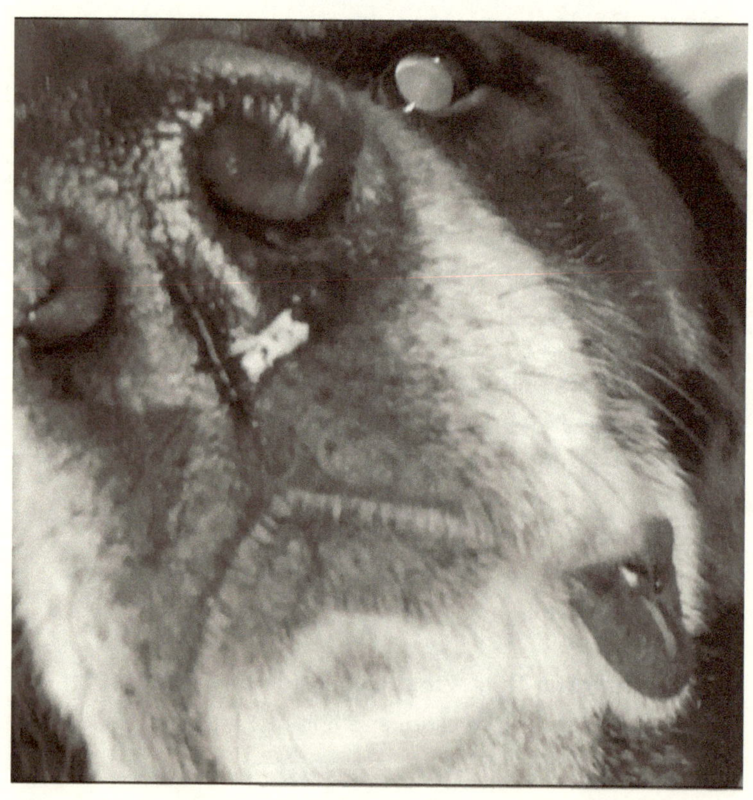

In the Winter

2011

Inside the houses, ghosts regard the bay with empty eyes.
From empty docks and empty boats, the phantoms start to sigh.
They exhale silence, move the waters—curtains in the breeze,
and with each swell, the quiet curls, the ghosts slip out to sea.

The summer homes sit still as stone, a throne without a queen,
and time to time, with vigil kept, a scamper can be seen.
Some movement here, a rustle there, a child's hand escapes,
and anything you thought you saw has drifted with the wake.

contents

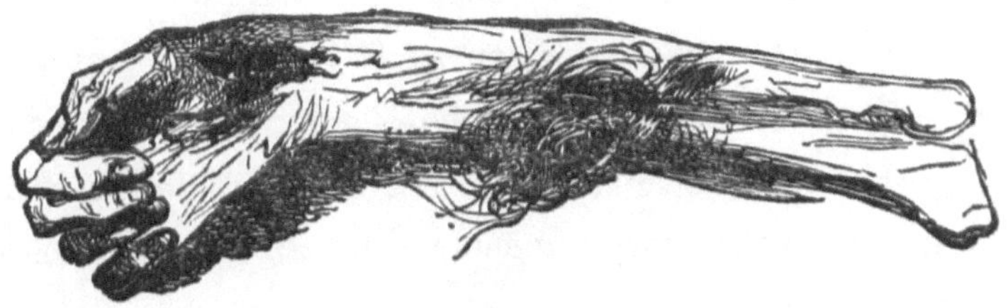

0. Intro

ost people, if you asked them, would say that they are pretty weird. I always chortle a bit when I hear a popular, normal person who shops at H&M say things like,

"Oh my gosh, I'm just so strange!"

Because inside, I'm always tempted to think *No you're not…You shop at the same places as everyone else and wear the same shoes. You watch the same shows as the rest of the world and quote them to your fellow not-weird friends.*

You want to be weird? Do something different.
Fill your mind with something the rest of the world hasn't.

That's who this book is for: The people who have grown tired of the same routine, whether its on Netflix or NBC. Those who don't follow the same YouTube channels or Instagram profiles as anyone else. And for that reason, this book will be a strange one. It won't make sense sometimes. The stories will often go where you're not expecting, and they will tend toward being far darker than your usual show or movie.

"Why can't you write something nice and happy for once?" my mom has asked me on several occasions.

The answer is, I have no idea. I don't know why my brain becomes far more fascinated with crafting an eerie mystery than a bright and sunny romance. There may be a few of those in here, but they're certainly the exception. The vast majority are NOT suitable for kids, or adults with sensitive faculties for that matter.

These stories' creation dates range from my ninth grade year of high school (2006ish) to today, 2020. They're not in any discernible order.

They don't have much purpose other than wild entertainment and adding a little more curvature to your otherwise normal mind. They may not make sense or exist in this universe, but they are, first and foremost, unique. And did I mention, weird?

Consider yourselves warned, weirdos.

1. The Tollman

Act I: Today I Buried a Man

I am the Tollman. I sit in this lonely lonely desert tollbooth and collect the tolls from people who pass by. In the night when it's quiet, I hear the voices of people arguing, but no one is nearby.

I can see for two miles to the West over the hot white sand, and to the East is a dune. I sit in my lonely booth and collect the tolls.

Today someone approached my booth. I could see him in the distance and as he drew nearer, I could make out some details about him. He carried a large backpack, and came from the direction of E-City. Or, The City. The E stands for Earring, but you don't want to know why. The City is a violent place. Years of moral decay have led men to devolve into a species of violent barbarians, ripping each other apart and wearing their bodies as adornments. I left the violent, violent city a long time ago.

This man approached my booth today and I could see he had walked a long way. He had a scarf around his face to keep the sand out, and shades over his eyes. He looked weary but strong. His gait was sound and each footstep seemed to happen on purpose. As this man drew nearer to my booth, he pulled down his scarf to speak to me.

Then he fell down dead.

I exited my booth through its only door in the rear and circled around to the man. He lay there on his face, dead as the sand surrounding him.

I studied the scene for several minutes, attempting to decipher what had happened to this man. With no sound answers, I dragged the man behind the dune to the East. It's only several hundred yards to the rear of the dune and I tugged him back there and put him near the others.

This is not the first time this has happened.

In fact, for the past several years, this has been happening. I will see someone—or a group of people, even whole families—approaching from the West, coming to pay their tolls, and they bridge the distance between the horizon and my booth and then fall down dead. I then take them behind the dune to Hinnom—that's what I nicknamed the place. The Valley of Hinnom. But it's not really a valley. I cannot figure out what causes it. I have searched the area around my booth, and have found nothing queer to speak of.

The problem is, I cannot leave my booth for too long—it's just a weird thing of mine. When I finished putting the man back behind the dune, I scurried back to my booth. I never look at the bodies.

And I'm never away from my booth for too long.

Act II: The Day My Father Showed Me His Booth

It was early on the morning of my seventeenth birthday when my father came into my room and stirred me from my sleep. He smiled as I resisted his invitation to emerge from my dreams.

"You're 17 today, my son," he said with his gentle whisper. "You're a man."

I moaned into my pillows, unwilling to rise.

"Today you will come to work with me." This caught my attention, I remember, for I had always wanted to see my father's booth. He was a city tollman. It was an entirely different career working a booth in the city. The city was violent and barbaric, and men had abandoned their roles as humans and taken up animalistic identities. Men wore other men's intestines as necklaces and used their shriveled, shriveled organs as coin purses. I had never been to my father's booth before, for it was in the center of the city. He was one of a few men brave enough to face The City and continue to do his job despite the enormous risk.

We lived on the outskirts of E-City, where people are relatively safe, but still within the dangers of the metropolis. My father and I sat on the train into the city. He was a large man whose figure commanded respect, though he was a warm and generous soul. As I sat in the seat by him, he asked me about my schoolwork and my interests. He asked what I had been reading, and the friends I had been spending time with.

The train ride went by quickly and soon we were walking through the streets to my father's booth. He walked near me as we strode through the ghetto. On the train, he had told me not to look around once we exited the train car; not to make eye contact. "Everyone you see today has murdered people," he stated with dire gravity. "That's why they're still alive."

We entered a heavy metal door that seemed to have been misplaced in a grimy alley. It opened to a rusty, rusty staircase where echoes ran up and down the tall metallic corridor. Paint peeled off of everything. I followed my father down about a dozen flights of stairs to another drab looking door. He pressed it open into the bowels of the city. We were several stories underground, where the most feral of men dwelt. They were those fearful of the sunlight, addicted to tranq's and hogs, and unwilling to make use of language. They would shriek or mutter nonsense to themselves in place of words. Many had never heard language spoken. They were animals given over to maddening darkness.

And this is why I admired my father. Few men were willing to collect the tolls from beings such as these.

My father looked back at me and gave a small smile. "Almost there," he assured me. I could see his booth now; it was on the side of one of the roads that ran through the underground. As I walked, I saw motion in my periphery, darting behind a pillar, or diving under a dumpster, though I did not catch a direct look at these underground men.

We stopped before the door of the booth and my father sorted through his keys, whistling as he found the one that fit the handle. He flicked on the light switch as we entered the booth and the buzzing fluorescent bulb sputtered out light before catching its consistent homeostatic buzz. Still whistling, my father slid open the window of his narrow booth and pulled a second seat near his chair for me. I sat near him.

It was glorious.

I was 17 and sitting in a tollbooth with my father in the city.

Act III: Today I Buried a Woman

It was three days ago when the scarfed man fell down before my booth. Today, I found a cut on my arm. Don't know how that got there.

I saw a woman approaching in the distance. I knew it was a woman because her long brown hair was free on the wind, blowing out like a raven trying to escape from her hood. I sat up in my old, old chair and paid close attention to what happened, anticipating a similar fate for this poor girl. I watched to see what happened as she drew nearer.

She closed in on the booth, coming to pay her toll. I could make out her face: slender and pretty. She reminded me of the woman I used to love. One hundred feet. Fifty feet. Twenty. Ten. Then she fell down dead.

I must have blinked.

I knelt by her body as her empty eyes stared into the pale, pale sky. Her hands were marred, as if she came from a fight of some sort. Her fingernails were broken and worn down. I would have wept for this girl, but I haven't been able to weep since the night I had The Dream.

I tugged the girl around to Hinnom as the purple, purple twilight gave way to night. Then I hustled back to the booth. It's getting chilly.

Act IV: The Day I Saw My Father Sawed

My father was a gracious collector of tariffs. Unlike other tollmen who grunt in exchange for the toll, my father would welcome the payer with a grand 'Hello,' and engage in conversation with all who were willing.

"Boy, it's so nice to have someone to talk to," I remember him saying to me that day. "Usually, I try to talk to the payers, but they're not big on dialogue down here. It can get pretty lonely being a tollman sometimes. In fact, if it weren't for your brothers and your mom and you, I'd probably go mad down here!"

I could not picture my father being mad. He had never really gotten angry with my brothers or I, but instead used everything as a teaching moment. My brothers and I knew we had done something crooked when he started out with: "I think there's a lesson somewhere in this looney episode..." and then his grand voice would expound on this point or that.

It was early in the afternoon (I only knew the time by the analog clock above the door, not the motion of the sun. There was no sunlight there.) and we were in the middle of a game of cards. I was winning. He had just given up a pair of Queens when a finger tapped on the window next to him.

"Give me one second, you dirty rotten cheater," he said to me with a smirk. He turned and slid the little window open. "Good af—" his big voice was reduced to a slur. I looked up to see an iron rod protruding from his stomach. It had been sharpened into a weapon by one of the underground men. The one who was shoving it into his belly, to be specific.

I froze in fear, clutching the playing cards like a shield before me. I watched as my father stumbled backward, trying to find the arms of his stupid, stupid chair that swiveled as he fell, casting him onto his stomach on the floor of the booth. The rod came all the way out the back of his midsection, tearing through the stitching of his uniform shirt thread by thread, like a straw poking through a plastic beverage lid.

I continued to watch in frozen shock as ten skinny, dirty fingers grabbed the frame of the window and pulled their owner up. I got a look at the man—or the boy. He was about my age, with white, white skin like I had never seen before. He had no hair on his body that I could see, and his clothes were rags held together by whatever he found to keep them on his body.

He hoisted himself up into the window, pulling his legs up and then stepping through. He looked straight at me for a second and I saw his eyes: big white orbs with no colored iris, just a burning black dot in the center of each. I tried to speak, still sitting and holding the cards, but no sound came out as my jaw moved up and down.

The boy seemed not to care about me as he snapped his gaze back to my father, who was moaning on the ground. The boy spoke to himself in his own invented language as he calmly knelt down beside my father's body and pulled a saw out of one of the many folds of his rags. It was a rusty and rancid old thing, with cracked and crooked teeth beneath a thin sheet of metal. He began sawing at one of the ankles. Blood filled the dirty floor of the booth, splattering onto the boy's rags.

He cut through the foot and placed it by the body. He moved onto the other one and set it by the first. I had slid to the floor and crawled back against the wall, never taking my eyes off what had been my father. He continued moaning and gurgling until the boy had completely severed both his legs and moved up to his shoulders. I had heard stories from the boys at school about people in The City doing things like this, but I had never accredited them into the account of plausibility in my head.

I remember sliding my way along the wall once both my father's arms were removed from his torso, and the boy was pulling a dagger out of his cloak.

Blood was everywhere. Everything was blood. There was no

distinction between this object and the other because it was all blood. Fleshy tissue lay about the floor, soaked in blood, and the boy leaned once more over my father's torso. He put the blade into the stomach, and I turned and floundered for the door. I realized that even as I fumbled with the knob, I smeared my father's blood about the handle. I don't know how or when it had gotten on me, but I later realized I, too, was covered in it.

I made it out the door, tripped down the step, and stumbled back toward the stairs we had descended.

Then my memory goes blank.

I never went home again.

I wanted to be as far from that city as possible. I know I became a tollman in the desert, but I honestly have no recollection of the process.

Act V: Today I Ran From My Booth

Today began the same way as many before it. I was in my booth waiting for someone to pass by, so I may collect their toll, or maybe figure out why people walk up to my booth and fall down dead. Gall, it's the creepiest thing.

Nothing was out of the ordinary, except I was dusting out the booth and airing out some clothes and saw some scratches on my shoulder. I don't remember getting them. They didn't hurt, just some short red streaks down my arm.

When I had finished cleaning up a bit, I sat. (This is what I spend most of my time doing...sitting). I sat and thought. I was enjoying the breeze from my faithful fan, wondering how something visible can propel invisible air forward, onto my face, when I saw a person approaching in the distance. They begin as a black mole atop the horizon and seem to slowly grow in size until they are about a hundred yards from me. I watched this play out once more, but when the person reached that point of descent from the horizon, something was pointedly different.

I stood up and ran out of my booth.

Act VI: The Days I was in Love

Five years ago, a woman came to my booth. I saw her approaching from the horizon and thought nothing of it. I slid my window open and held out my hand. Rather than put her tariff in it, she shook it.

"Boy, it's a hot one today," were her first words to me. *Small talk. We were in the desert. Of course it was a hot one.*

I remember that she wore baggy travelers pants, a tough canvas jacket, and a scarf around her head. She had long brown hair with a gentle wave in it that made her head seem like a waterfall of bustling liquid chocolate. She was beautiful.

She proceeded to ask me what it's like sitting in the desert booth all day. I listed off a few niceties, but I seemed to be boring her.

"No, what's it *really* like sitting in here all day every day?" she cut in. "What do you think about?" Her eyes were not solid objects, they were liquid pools of laundry detergent, because that always seemed to be the richest shade of blue. She looked at me without blinking as we talked. Her head seemed to tilt forward whenever she listened, and the corners of her mouth dug back into her cheeks in a sly grin. She leaned against the booth, and I remember thinking about how strange it was since I sat two feet higher than her. I guess her need for human contact was greater than her sense of awkwardness. In time I realized that she was lonely.

And a while after that, I realized I had been lonely too.

We were two lonesome souls who found each other at a desert tollbooth.

That first day, she leaned on my booth talking to me until the sun sank below the sand. I invited her into the booth for the night, and she stayed. She also stayed for the one after that, and the one after that, and the 716 after that.

She loved to talk, telling me the sad stories of her childhood on the outskirts of the city. We realized we had probably seen each other at least twice when we were kids. She shared her thoughts about the world, about the desert, about the road. She showed me her grandmother's old silver ring which she kept on her right ring finger and never removed. Her heart poured forth her weaknesses and exposed her desire for a home built in the heart of those that she loves, if not in a geographic location.

I told her I can be her home.

Almost more than she loved to share, she loved to listen. I told her about my father, and what a great man he was, and that he didn't deserve to die. Out of everyone in The City, he did not deserve to die. I never told her how it happened though. Or that I had seen the whole thing. I would tell her about my lovely mother and my brothers, and how I missed them all awfully. And she would sit and listen with that same head tilt, showing that she was eagerly anticipating the next words to dribble from my lips.

I loved her. And she loved me.

We would take walks around the booth beneath the effervescent ceiling of stars. She initially made fun of me for not wanting to stray too far from the booth. "Come on, take a risk, you chicken!" she elbowed me in the side. After a few months, however, she too came to realize the importance of staying near the booth.

And a few months after that, she didn't want to wander too far from it either.

Act VII: Today My Mother Got Her Wings

Although she was a bit more hunched over than I remember from years ago, my mother had the same unmistakable gait as the day I left home. She was quiet and gentle, the perfect companion to my father's eccentric warmth. She walked in a manner that was sure of what she did, though the age in her legs was now showing.

For years, I have been watching people approach my booth and fall down dead outside of it. And for years, I have not felt compelled enough to try and find the cause or actively try to put an end to it. There is something cursed about the land around my booth, and I was not going to let my mother go near it.

I ran out to her. I was running faster than I had since grade school on the playground. I waved my hands at her, desperately trying to stop her from coming any closer to the booth. I closed the gap between us. Seventy yards, sixty yards.

She stopped walking.

I ran close enough to see her well-wrinkled cheeks peeking out from behind her sunglasses. She seemed to be in good enough health. I kept my eyes fixed on her, terrified that at any moment she could become the next victim to the jinxed place. I even began muttering under my breath: "don't fall down, don't fall down, don't you die on me, don't..."

I ran to her as her sweet voice met my ears. "Honey, what's the matter?"

I panted for breath.

"What were you runni—" her voice turned into a gurgle and she was dead on the ground.

I fell to my knees next to her, still heaving for oxygen. My chest burned like an angry squirrel was running around inside of it, clawing at my organs.

This was the first time I had seen my mother since I was 17 and now her body lay dead before me. When my body began to receive air once more, my gasps turned into sobs and I collapsed on my mother's thin frame. We were a painting. Her blood spread into the sand where she lay, and I on top of her, mourning the enigmatic death of my second parent.

Many people had fallen dead before me in the past several years, but now my mother lies still beneath me. And I'm far away from the booth.

Act VIII: The Dream

The night before my lover left me, I lay down for the night and was instantly taken up in a dream I have still not forgotten. It began in the booth and my hearing was amplified. I started to wander away from the booth, and every crunch of sand beneath my boot sounded like a thousand needles racing down a metal door. The dune rose before me, thrice as tall as when I am conscious, and there was a purple haze all around it that contributed to an aura of eeriness. But I was not afraid.

I approached the dune and found a door at its base. I drunkenly stumbled through the door and suddenly the location changed. I was no longer in the desert near my booth, but was somewhere on the outskirts of the city. Not the nicer outskirts where my family had lived, but the run-down ghetto where crime was nearly as rampant as malaria. I was walking down an empty street, and now I was holding a gun. Then from the other direction down the street walked countless men in business suits. They looked like stars of films I had seen from before The

City had decayed. The men wore expressionless faces and black suits and ties and looked straight ahead. They walked in rhythm without distraction or hesitation. I bumped into one and then another. Then I was in the midst of them, still trying to walk the opposite direction like a slippery, slippery salmon swimming up a waterfall.

There is this tangible feeling of angst and worry, that I am supposed to be getting somewhere but the business men are pushing me back. I begin filling with this violent longing to get past the parade of men.

Then I remember the gun in my hand. I shoot one of the men in the head and suddenly they all stop walking. They stare at me, and now they are no longer men in suits, but the hairless animal who murdered my father. Their handsome eyes are replaced by his all-white eyeballs with a pitch black pupil in the center, each staring directly at me.

I shoot one, then another, but they do not die. They do not even flinch. They circle around me and close in on me. I run out of ammunition, and I am defenseless. The angst turns to fear and helplessness.

Suddenly the monsters freeze. Their unblinking white eyes stare at me for a second more, then turn their attention down the road where they came from. The road fades into blackness, and out of this thick, thick blackness comes an aqueous platform. It is a stage made out of water, but it is staying in a rectangular shape. As it fades from the darkness and its origin becomes clearer, I see that it is less like a stage and more of an altar.

Rather than ornate golden intricacies, the waves of the water seem to have splashed up and frozen into complex designs around the altar.

The white-eyed creatures part before it, and I sense an invitation to ascend the blue steps and look at the object upon the altar. It is glowing.

I am now full of curiosity as I ascend the steps and behold before me the ritual of the underground men.

My father's bloody, bloody body lays on the table, cut into ten pieces, identical to the last time I had seen it. I am stricken with the same feelings of fear, horror, and shock from the day of my seventeenth birthday, but also with a feeling of rage and anger. The angst fades away and becomes fury. I turn and am about to begin slaughtering the boys below me on the road, but I wake up before any sort of vengeance is had.

I still remember the details from this dream as vividly as the morning I rose to find that my love of nearly two years had vanished.

I don't know where she went, or why she left, but she disappeared.

As if she was never here at all.

Act IX: Today I Examined Hinnom

My mother's body is not like the others. It is not one I can merely drag behind the dune and think nothing of. She is my mother. And here is her corpse lying in the sand!

Familiar feelings of petrified shock blend with a growing sense of urgency to return to the booth. I pick up my mother's body as gently as I can. Her face has purple bruises on it now and her glasses hang loosely off her cheeks, smashed to pieces.

I felt tears stream down my cheeks as I walked back to the booth with my mother dripping from my arms. Her nose and mouth were bleeding, and it ran down onto my sleeve.

It was not until I was nearly back to the booth that I began wondering why, after all these years, she had come to see me now. Perhaps this was how long it took for her to find me.

I made it back to the booth and tried to open the door with my mother's thin body still in my arms. When that failed, I set her down on the sand and ran inside.

I was at a loss. I had no idea what to do. I wasn't sure why I felt such urgency to act, but I knew I had to find the source of this death. Standing in the booth, I looked down at my right hand. It had been bruised across the knuckles as well. I wasn't sure how that happened, but I returned my mind to my mother.

The desert was cursed, and I had to find the source. I resolved to return to the Valley of Hinnom and look for clues. In the years since these bodies first began appearing, I had made a habit of not looking at the older corpses. I would avert my eyes and rush back to the booth. But now, in honor of my mother, I had to go once more behind the dunes and scour the dead.

I exited the booth and bent once again to lift my mother's frame. She hung limp as a wet napkin across my arms, and I walked toward the dune. Each step carried closer the echoes of dread I had felt in my dream all those years ago. I felt as if I would discover something dark by looking at these bodies which I myself had placed there over the years.

I rounded the dune and before me lay the rows and rows of bodies.

For the last time, I set my mother down as gently as I could, and fixed her clothes to cover her properly. A bona fide ceremony.

I made a wide arc around to the far corner of Hinnom, where the first bodies lay. I looked at them from a small distance, expecting the decrepit limbs to suddenly start moving again.

Minutes passed and I deemed it safe to move toward the bones. I bent down next to the first body, it was clearly the oldest of the lot, and I brushed some sand away. I looked closely at the cartilage of the limbs. There was nothing unusual that I could see. I moved up to the head. It had patches of brown hair running like a chocolate river down into the earth. I scooped more sand away from under the head. My fingers scraped a thin cloth. I pulled it up and stared down in confusion. It was a silk scarf. I knew the pattern well.

Without thinking, I reached across the body and violently jerked the right hand out of the sand.

There was a silver ring on the third finger. Then I knew. This was a hand I'd held for many days and nights. And this was a scarf with whose scent I had become well accustomed.

These were the remains of my lover.

Act X: Today The Mystery Was Solved

I sat back in confusion. The amalgamation of emotions nearly paralyzed me. I looked around as if someone in the desert were playing a black, black joke on me. Then something stung. As I rocked back onto my fists, a small, small streak of pain ran up my hand and I remembered the mystery bruises on my knuckles. And then the scratches on my shoulder and arm. Some puzzle pieces in my head began clicking together and I walked back around to my mother's still body.

I knelt down beside her and looked at the bruises on her face. Her tender left cheek was bruised and her nose was broken. Bits of her smashed sunglasses were splintered into her temples and forehead. I looked once more at my now trembling hand.

Could I have beaten my mother? My hands quivered more and more violently as the reality set in. Then the still, dead hand of the woman lying next to her caught my attention. Her nails were scraped down to their beds, and she also had bruises on her face and body.

Is that where the peculiar scratches on my arm came from? I pulled back my sleeve and realized it was so. The woman had tried to defend herself with her bare hands against a crazed tollman in a flash of violent rage.

I looked beyond and saw the same was true of the man next to her, and the one beyond him.

My whole body began seizing as I looked out over the entire plot of bodies, hundreds laid neatly in rows, and I realized that I had killed them all.

I dismiss the entire idea as madness. I would remember committing murder. Wouldn't I?

Then The Dream comes to mind. I remember the emotion of waking up with a need for vengeance unfulfilled. I recall the bitter madness that set in as I choked my lover to death while she dreamed. It all flooded back into my head.

She never left.

I killed her.

And ever since that morning, my brain flashes hot white for a moment while I kill these people coming to pay their tolls. The ground is not cursed, except by an insane tollman disturbed by his past and too much time alone in the vast screaming hot desert.

I am the curse.

But now I'm feeling itchy. I need to get back to the booth. People may soon be coming to pay their tolls.

2. Lifeguard

My name is Lifeguard.

There is a lot of thinking that takes place atop the seat overlooking the pool. I spend most of my days there; watching others play, watching them have fun. I see grandparents bringing their toddler grandsons and granddaughters to the pool to splash around. Young parents bring their infants to adapt to the life aquatic. High school sweethearts hang on each other, faux-drowning and whispering the deep secrets of their hearts into the ear of the other.

Time on the stand passes slowly.

If you're not careful, you can waste a whole day and not have thought about anything. The day can slip away into an ebbing tide of lusts for the barely-clad swimmers your age, or you can simply retreat into the room inside your brain where nothing happens. No thoughts are produced, and no ideas are conceived.

Lately, I have entertained my attentive brain by imagining a man who follows me home after work each day. It's a twenty-four minute ride to and from work on my bicycle. I think about a man following me home in his turquoise sedan.

He rolls down the window, arm hanging limply on the door, and shouts, "Ey, Lifeguard! I know where you sleep! Open ya window tonight and I'll give ya a surprise!"

I think about how fast I'd have to pedal to outrun him. Of course, to eradicate all of his knowledge of my residence, I would have had to have done this from the start. I would need to pedal 9% faster, and lose him through the path behind Kum & Go, 4 minutes out of the way.

These scenes play out behind my eyes as I sit on the edge of the pool. It's not a huge pool. It has a straight slide with a weak drizzle of water creeping down its shoot. Rust grows from the base of the ramp and is progressing upward. The zero-depth zone is where the babies come and sit, joyfully splashing in the ankle-deep tide because they are unaware of how run-down this place really is.

The rec center was built in the seventies and has not been maintained well. Patrons pay a base price of two dollars apiece, or five for a family, and come splash around for a little while. I work with two other guards on a double rotation. There's Lindsay, the apathetic snob who clicks her gum loudly while her eyes are magnetized to her phone. Jerry is the other guard who lost his *real* job three years ago when the economy tanked. He lost his wife with his work, and has been obsessed with conspiracy theories and UFOs ever since.

"Hey, Lifeguard," Jerry says to me one slow day while the pool is empty and we were cleaning the deck. "You ever notice the license plate of that dude you think is following you home?"

I don't want to think about it, so I keep scrubbing at the scum line and pretend I didn't hear him.

"Lifeguard, hey, you hear what I said?"

I looked up and sighed. "I haven't noticed it, why?"

Jerry shrugged and went back to looking down at his cleaning.

The truth was, I can picture it. It's out of state, but I don't know which one. I only know the colors are different.

Today is a busy day here at the pool. My eyes have glazed over and I have lost myself once more in deep contemplation. I think the man who follows me home is working for a government of a different country. Or maybe I'm just making him up in my daydreams. Possible. It's happened before. These hallucinations always begin with a simple question, such as 'what if there was an old lady who became a serial killer because she was so afraid of dying she killed everyone who talked to her? Now *that's* paranoia.'

Thoughts like these lead to images in my brain that play themselves out. Often they become entire narratives. I have only shared a couple of them with another human, and that human has been Jerry. He is the only other one who understands the brain-numbing boredom of working at this pool. He reads books on the stand. I can't bring myself to, though, for fear that I'll miss someone drowning. At least if I *look* like I'm watching, they can't blame me for the oversight.

My brain thinks too much. Sometimes, it even makes up its own words. Like 'slentor.' That is, a being that can pass through walls. It originated one day while I was thinking about the concept of neutrinos, the sub-microscopic particles that travel so fast they pass through anything, and have only been seen twice. Or rather, the place where they *just were* was seen.

I'm now at home letting my brain wander and a slentor drifts into my bedroom as the television plays. It cannot speak, but it can point, and move metallic objects. It readjusts the antenna on my set and changes the channel to a ballet recital on the local channel. Piano sounds fill the room and I drift to sleep. The slentor leaves. 'What a crazy idea,' I think as I drift off. 'Things that can pass through walls...'

& & &

The pool has been busy in waves today—no pun intended— which makes the day crawl by even slower than usual. It fills up, then empties for an hour. The hands on the clock don't even look like they're moving. Maybe they're not. Broken clock.

Lindsay is working with me today. I picture an electric can opener that operates by slicing the can in half and pulling the two halves apart and pouring the contents into a bowl. It's all automated of course. It produces a knocking sound as it operates, like a knuckle on a giant, thin tin wall. The knocking continues and I realize that it's not the imaginary object in my head producing the sound, but someone standing outside the back door of the pool.

This door is never used. It was originally installed as a back door for taking trash out to the dumpster. However, the pool doesn't even generate enough trash to warrant a dumpster these days, and garbage is collected out front on Tuesdays. I don't even think I'd ever seen the door opened before.

Two parents were in the four foot section of the pool with their baby, who cried every time they tried to put her head underwater. I figured they wouldn't miss me for a minute as I went to open the door.

The knocking returned once more. It was very gentle still, but more urgent than the first round. I fidgeted with the lock and finally got it open. As I pulled it open, the rusty hinges creaked, and I looked at them. Before I could identify the knocker, my head was slammed with a drained tequila bottle and I fell to the ground, unconscious. I picture no one reacting, and the family of three continue cooing at their infant daughter.

I tell Jerry about the daydream the next day. He shrugs and tells me he doesn't know what's on the other side of that door either.

We worked the whole day and at closing time, Jerry asks me if

I've ever taken narcotics. I haven't. He says maybe I should talk to someone about these daydreams.

I tell him I'm not sure they're all daydreams.

I walk out the front door to where my bike is chained up. A turquoise sedan with a blue license plate is parked across the street with the engine quietly humming. I rub my eyes, look up at the sky, and back at the street.

The car is gone.

Figures.

I begin pedaling and ride to the edge of the town, down the shortcut path, about halfway to my flat. A slentor suddenly slides out of a tree to my right. It takes control of my bike and swerves the handlebars so violently to the right the I fly off and hit my neck on a baby tree to the left of the path.

I lie there for a while until I hear footsteps approaching from the street. I see old cowboy boots walk right up to my face as their owner inspects my busted frame.

"Nehh," the man sighs and turns and walks away. I try to reach up and scratch my arm to see if this is a daydream and I'm really back at work seated on the stand—neither arm stirs.

As my vision blurs more and more, and the setting sun fades the objects of the day into ambiguous dark shapes of the night, I hear a car come to a stop on the street, a baseball toss away from where I'm lying. The car door slams, but the engine stays on. In the dim light, I can tell it's the man who follows me. I thought he'd be here sooner.

"What took you so long?" I gurgle as my consciousness fades.

In place of an answer, he lifts a cigarette to his cracked lips and cups his hand to light it. Still not sure if this is real. I mean, I don't feel much pain. I just wish I could move.

I wake up in a basement next to a pool table with the green surface torn in several places. I'm seated in a metal folding chair. I can move my arms slowly and clumsily, but my neck is frozen in place, tilted severely to the left. I turn my entire torso from side to side and inspect the room. Old Playboy centerfolds pepper the walls, held up by tape over the corners. It smells like stale cigarettes and spilled beer. Empty booze bottles cover every surface. There are literally hundreds of them.

The place is spurdent—another word I invented.

Even in my crippled state, I still make up words. Incredible. Most people would be extremely afraid right now. But my name is Lifeguard, and I have to think. Fear would only interfere with that right now.

I hear footsteps descending the stairs.

"Lifeguard!" the man shouts when he has neared the bottom.

I turn my body to look at the man. His left arm still hangs limply by his side, just as when I see him in his sedan. He stares at me for a second, and my mind races.

My training prepared me for this.

He didn't bother to check me for weapons. No one ever expects an old lady to be packing heat. I pulled the 50 caliber out of my belt and blew a hole in his stomach. Another in his chest. His facial expression changed little, since the porn and drugs had left him looking dead and glazed over already.

A pitbull upstairs began barking at the sound of the shots, and as it raced down the stairs, testicles in full swing, I popped a hole in his side as well.

I went up the stairs and out into the bright morning sun. I got into the man's sedan, found the keys under the seat, and turned the ignition until it kicked to life. Driving back to my flat proved more difficult than expected, thanks to my now sideways neck.

When I got home, I made sure to reload the three rounds I had spent. I probably won't tell Jerry about this; I'll have to think of another explanation for my crooked neck.

My name is Lifeguard, and I just might be the old lady who is so paranoid she kills everyone else.

3. How to Have a Birthday
or, "Dave Gets His Just Desserts"

Birthdays are a strange celebration if you think about it.

You spend 364 days working your darnedest to grow and expand yourself into the universe, into the fabric of time itself, and then on one midnight a year, the switch flips and you stumble into the next year. A 6-year-old will spend all his energy for those 364 days focused on becoming 7 and then, all at once, boom. It happens.

Some of you may think that there is nothing you need to do in order to pass from one year to the next. You may think the natural flow of time will carry you along from 42 to 43, or wherever you are in your string of existences we call "years."

But this is simply not the case.

Take June 2, 2019 for instance. Dave and I were on a bus from Guatemala City north to Coban. In order for us to safely arrive at our next birthdays, the bus had to stay in its own 8-foot ribbon of road for hundreds of miles. Just think for a moment about how impossibly thin those dimensions are, and yet, the driver of our bus (despite chatting with his friends on the bus, texting his *novia*, and occasionally swerving for no reason at all) managed to keep us between the ditches.

Then we transferred from a bus to the back of a pickup truck, where the deluge of rain could have drowned us if we were lying in a shallow ditch instead of in the back of a truck.

But we were not, we were in the truck.

The precipitation also meant that the dirt roads were now squishy mud and the driver would have a significantly more difficult time careening us to our hostel than if the roads were dry. We then made it to our hostel in the middle of the jungle where any number of humans could have secretly gone off their rocker and stabbed, shot, bludgeoned, or drawn and quartered us, but once more, Dave and I narrowly escaped death and inched closer to our 28th birthdays.

On this one day alone, we survived the bus, the truck, the rain, the hostel and its guests and passed the year's finish line, also known as our respective birthdays. Have you ever thought about how wild it is that we survive such incredible odds every day and the mere fact that any of us have made it past a few months is an absolute miracle?

Microbiologists would point out that our bacteria-soldiers

managed to fend off hostile bacteria-invaders and pass them along the rails of our intestines rapidly enough for them not to harm our bodies. Engineers would marvel at how every bridge we crossed—even the sketchy ones—held up under our vehicles, and even the ferry we used to cross that one river didn't sink under the multiple tons of automotive on top of it. Meteorologists would mix in that we were not struck by a stray monster comet soaring from galaxy to galaxy on this particular day, nor were there any freak megastorms, tornadoes, inland hurricanes, lightning strikes (on us...we saw many from a distance), or chemical rain.

Indeed, June 2, 2019 was an incredible day, for the mere fact that we survived it and raged madly onward toward our birthdays. If you had asked me that day, or even the next, I would have thought nothing of it; after all, none of those bad things happened, and we did not narrowly escape the wispy fingers of death—even though we did, now that I really think about it.

My birthday is June 19, but it was supposed to be the 17th, if only my wicked best friend hadn't snatched it from me. You see, Dave was supposed to pop out on June 19, and I was due the 17th, but we switched and have been friends ever since, despite the fact that I have a heated grudge against him for stealing that birthday from me.

It was my right.

Presently we find ourselves roughly 4 months from our next

birthdays, and I will do everything in my power to reclaim those two days of extra-utero life Dave seized from me. I feel like the kid whose shoulders he stood on to climb up the waterfall while shoving my face underwater. Not everyone can be stepped on like that without expecting some sort of recompense. Indeed, many people are fine being stepped on so others may get ahead.

But not me.

Dave thought he could propel himself into the cosmos two days ahead of schedule—ahead of me—but that was the first in a long line of mistakes he would make throughout his life. Those additional two days of life have afforded him countless opportunities which should have been mine. Who knows how he spent those first blissful 48 hours before my body burst onto the scene??

So my act of vengeance has been hatched; my plan has been set in motion. I will reclaim the two days Dave has stolen from me, and it will be spectacular.

The best part is, Dave won't know it's coming for years—decades, even.

Assuming he survives the next 53 birthdays, which, again, would be a spectacular feat for his miserable little husk of a body, I will enact my plan.

Dave and I will end up in the same nursing home, both crippled beyond belief (because of an "accidental" honey harvesting accident I've orchestrated for us in Vietnam in 2027), where we will whittle away our days on *Jeopardy!* reruns and cottage cheese. I will sense my end nearing as my breath gets thinner and thinner until I am certain—beyond the shadow of a doubt—that my life has exactly two days left in it.

Two days before I discover the Great Mystery and step into the pool from which there is no swimming ashore, I will invite my friend—a young man I have discovered on the dark web who goes by "Mr. Ralph"—to come and pose as Dave's nurse. Mr. Ralph is only 12 years old right now, according to his profile, which means he will be primed and ready for his task when the moment calls. I will make sure of it.

Mr. Ralph will come in because Dave's usual nurse got "sick" for the day and could not show up for work. Through my cloudy vision and gargly breathing, I will watch with glee as Mr. Ralph swaps out Dave's oxygen tank with a fish tank. I have instructed Mr. Ralph to put exactly four fish in this tank and to customize it to have the same dimensions as his oxygen tank, so, aside from the glass housing and the fish swimming around inside, it will be indistinguishable.

Then, as Dave tries to breathe through the oxygen tubes, water will come up rather than purified air. In that moment of glorious victory, I will rise from my wheelchair, an act I saved up energy for for a week, and stand over Dave as he tries to breathe the fish water.

"YOU CAN'T BREATHE FISH WATER!" I will yell as I tower over the conniving old coon, white gunk and saliva spraying from my cracked lips. "YOU BREATHE AIR, NOT FISH WATER! DON'T

YOU KNOW THIS??"

As Dave continues trying to extract oxygen from the poopy fish water, I will enjoy the two days of life I was robbed of 81 years prior.

Of course, Mr. Ralph will skedaddle and the real nurses will come rushing in because of the yelling and sounds of Dave drowning. They will ask him why there are fish in a glass tank connected to his nasal tubes, but he will be coughing and unable to speak. They will pump the water from his chest and I'll watch with glee as he comes to, makes eye contact with me, and knows deep in his soul that I didn't kill him—but I could have.

I want him to know that, at any moment, I could reclaim those two days of existence which he stole from me. As long as he knows that and is spooked by the fish water incident, I will be satisfied.

It will all be worth it.

Then, two days later,

I will die.

4. In the Morning I Will Die

I. The Depths

"I'm ready," said my father to the room full of elders and tribespeople gathered around his bedside. They've come to see him off, to witness his departure from our tribe; from the world. His long braids lay on either side of him, running silver and black along his body.

He was not ill, but his strength was failing and he was not able to lead in the way he once did. One by one, the families slid out of his presence, starting with the young children and their parents. Then the youths and the rest of the women.

When only a few of the strongmen remained, my father reached from his bed of stacked pillows and grabbed my forearm. His strength surprised me as his fingers clamped my wrist and pulled me closer to him. He then spoke as if to me, though loud enough for the rest of the men to hear.

"Is the boat ready?" he asked me intensely, as if the world would splinter and divide if it were not. I was accustomed to this intensity in my father, but tonight the subject was more difficult than ever before.

I nodded, "The boat is ready, father. What do you—"

"Tonight I will be with my family," he cut me off. "You will stay by my side until I rest. I have completed the work of my land, and I have led my tribe as well as possible. I can honestly say I have led my people to the best of my ability. Not perfectly, but to the best of my ability." His voice thundered through the room and I sensed that my eyes were not the only ones brimming with tears.

My father continued, "I will rise in the morning and go down to the water. There at the edge I will say goodbye to you, my son. To my tribe. I will get in the boat, and there, tomorrow morning, I will die." He must have sensed my arm trembling because he—still holding it—gave it a squeeze that said *be still.*

I sniffled and stood up straighter.

"I have done what I have needed to do, so tomorrow morning I will die."

I didn't want to imagine the waters just a few hundred feet from where we were. Those waters which I had stood beside hundreds of times with my father, as he explained that the waters are chaos, pure. The waters are the womb from which the entire world rose.

One time, when I was a young boy, he led me through a whipping storm down to the water's edge. The waves roared triple the height of my father, and he pointed to them. "See this, son? This…this is the fury of the gods."

And indeed, the fear of that tempest never fully left my bones. I never set out very far into the waters the way the fishermen did, nor did I ever desire to quest beyond the horizon. In all my years, I don't think I ever went as far as the crest of the horizon which is visible from shore. It always frightened me to see how the earth bent there the way it did no other place. The forestland prevented me from being terrified of the depths because you can only see so far in every direction.

The prairie gave me whispers of terror if I ever stood on the shoulder of the world and beheld it as it yawned out toward the sky, an awful span of space wide before me. The prairie land was flat and wide on this edge of our settlement and you could dedicate a lifetime to pacing every cubit of all this visible land and never cover all of it.

The breadth made me dizzy. I was scared of staring across the prairie too long, but it was the water I truly could not bear.

Whenever I went out on a boat with the other men, they displayed no fear or hesitancy to place their feet on the thin boards separating them from the chaos, but I gripped the mast for my life or wrapped ropes around my fists just in case of a capsize.

Beyond boyhood I could not even look over the edge of the vessel into the water because to look down may be to glimpse that which is greater than I: that which can withstand the chaotic deep.

The other boys would invent stories of what dwelt beneath our tiny ships, our pathetic attempts to tame the depths. They would tell me of monsters, and of the dead who, much like my father in the morning, make their way down into the darkness of the waters but never fully die. According to legend, if you fall off of a boat or swim down too deep, you could feel their fingers reaching out for your own. They have been in the frigid depths so long, they just want to feel the warmth of the living again. You may feel a palm of their hand graze your back, but at such depth, you can never be sure what you're really seeing or feeling. The boys sometimes have contests to see who can swim down the deepest, but of course I never participate.

I imagined my father's hand—which still gripped my arm now—graying beneath the water and floating lifelessly, reaching out for any passing fish or swimmer or monster. I pictured his eyes pecked out by the lipless fish as he made his bed on the ocean floor eternally.

"Tomorrow I will die," he said, but he did not say how. He simply told me to hitch the smallest boat in our fleet on the dock near our settlement and the rest would unfold exactly as it needed to.

I didn't know if I would see the life of my father end or if he would sail away and die past the horizon. I wondered if I would know when the moment had come, when he had fully surrendered to the deep.

I feared for my father though. I was afraid of him descending into the water. I was petrified to think of a storm rolling in again and the waves casting his decayed body back upon our shore, a blatant sign of what happens to those who give in to the chaos.

My father showed no fear as he lay in his bed presently. He did not weep like the rest of the men surrounding him, nor did his voice waver like mine does when I think about the waters, or when I fought another man…

Last week—my father did not know this—I challenged another man my own age to a fight because he had stared at the woman I admired, and we decided to fight with our hands to find who would earn the right to pursue her. As I approached the place of our battle, my stomach spun and rattled within me like tent flaps with wind blowing through them, and I only hoped that my exterior did not betray such insecurity.

I won the fight of course—there was never any question about that. Even as I approached the location, though my stomach fluttered, I knew I would have her.

It was her.
It has always been her.
I never doubted for a moment that she would be my witch.

I know many of the surrounding tribes use that word to mean someone who devours infants and casts spells on her enemies. In our tribe it stands for something different: Woman into the Chaos. WITCh. I forget that not everyone is familiar with the language of my people, but the origin of the word, as it has been passed down, is just that this woman will be with you forever, until you step into the chaos of the deep. The two of you spend your lives together until the waters swallow you, at which point you are literally *in* the chaos together.

And the men are the HITChes. The Husbands into the Chaos.

There was never a question who would be my witch—it would be her, and it could be no other. I knew it since I first laid eyes on her small form, pulling crops from the fields even though her head barely rose above the heads of the plants. Her black hair fell along her back in two neat braids and I couldn't take my eyes away, even after she looked up and caught me staring at her.

And that was the moment when I first saw her eyes. They were as black as her hair, laced in almond brown skin which rose gently and folded around her sharp features. I knew that to look into her eyes for the rest of my life may send the same shivers down my spine as the black waters themselves, but that was a thrill I was willing to embrace.

And there was no one for her but me, so I knew that I would win this fight, or I would be as good as sunk into the waters. Losing wasn't an option, I would simply win.

He stood a full head taller than me, but I knocked the man out in under a minute. He did not have the same desperation for this woman that I did; he had the passing attraction of a gentle breeze while my longing for her was the furious gales of the gods themselves.

I then walked directly to the home of my woman. When I arrived, I wrapped my arms around her neck and kissed the top of her head. I stepped back and held her shoulders in my hands.

I asked her to be my witch, and, even though she knew I hated the waters, to be with me until I sank into the chaos. Tears were already running down her face and she nodded. Her father came to the door behind her and smiled. He opened a case of the hardwater and we shared a swig. The burn bolted into my stomach as the fire ran down my throat and blossomed into a warm ember.

I held my woman beneath the stars for many hours that night. We talked and we sat in silence and then we talked and then we sat in silence.

It was always her, there was no question.

My father never found out about the fight, but he did rejoice with me for my woman. He smiled and placed that firm grip on my shoulder, but when I asked him if he could postpone his voyage to the deep, the corners of his mouth dropped and his voice lowered.

"My son, the day is set. I will be surrounded by my people in the evening, and then in the morning I will die. I will set out into the vast waters and be swallowed by her entirely. I will join your mother in the ancient chaos."

Upon hearing this, I lost control of my body and slunk to the floor like a hollow puppet.

Neither my mother nor my father would be present for the happiest day of my life, when I would become one skin with my woman. They would not get to see her adorned with the rare flowers of the prairie, or me standing tall in the garment of my home (That garment is a special tradition among my people. We compile our garment in just the right way such that it weaves together our childhood bed sheets, our adult bedsheets, certain flaps from the entrance of our home, signifying that we have *passed through* each necessary stage of life, and then a new patch of fabric which we create from our mother's loom. This has a new design which we create and it's presented for the first time at the ceremony). They would not know my children or help raise them.

I knelt on the dirt before my father, pleading with him to witness my union with my woman, but he held my head and told me it was just not possible. The voices of the deep were calling to him and he could not alter the course of his future any more than he could tell the gales to stop their blowing.

We would rise in the morning to find, however, that my father would be late to his appointment with the waters.

II. Lights on the Horizon

When my father had closed his eyes and drifted into his dreams, I left his room and went to find my woman. It was late, but she had said she would stay awake for me. I made my way to her home and whispered her name at the entryway.

She came out and didn't say a word, she just wrapped her arms around me. I could tell she had been asleep before I came, but it was the sort of sleep which was light as she waited for me to arrive.

Her arms remained wrapped around my waist for a long time, and it was here, in the safety of her presence, I could finally let out the tears which I held for so long beside the bed of my father. They ran down into the hair of my lover and she kept her head tucked into my chest. Her ear was against my heart, as if listening intently for something.

I had always been drawn to this woman, and there was something about her small size which drew me in. I always found that the warmth and size of her presence was inverse to her physical size. I could wrap my arms around her and feel the entirety of her being fit within mine. But the comfort she brought my body; the way her nearness seemed to relax every molecule of my muscles, was far bigger than her stature.

I found that even before I met her and adored her, I was always drawn to smaller women. In many ways, they contrast the unfathomable vastness of the water. The water is an untamable void, black beyond comprehension and mysterious to the point of agony.

This woman—the end of all things—is equally mysterious, but at least I can comprehend her dimensions. I can measure her small, brown shoulders and hold all of her at once. This small woman is the antidote to my fear of the deep.

I held her outside her home for what felt like hours. My tears ran dry eventually and her grip around my waist loosened and she took a step back, letting her hands slide to my sides.

She looked up at me and said, "you will get through this." Even in the darkness I could still sense the intensity of her big eyes looking up into mine. "You've been a good son and you will get through this."

I could have stood on the ground outside her home all night, just holding her close to me, but that's when everything changed.

Her home was only several hundred feet from the shore, and that moment is when I looked up and saw something out on the water I had never seen before.

It was a light.

No, it was multiple lights, all very close together, as if they came from the same place.

I had never seen lights so bright. It was like they had tied miniature versions of the sun together and bound them to the horizon. Fire was not so bright, not at this distance, and I couldn't take my eyes off of it. My woman saw my eyes and turned to see for herself.

"What is that?" she asked, as if I could possibly know.

I didn't answer, but I took her hand and began walking toward the shore. Even being so close to the shore sent a shiver down my spine. The mysterious lights on the horizon only added to my quiet terror—after all, could this be a creature risen from the chaotic depths? Are those hideous beasts capable of radiating such bright lights, visible at this distance?

I tried to hide the quivering of my body from my woman, but I'm sure she still felt it in my palm. If she did, she didn't say anything about it. She already knew about my fear of the water, despite my efforts to appear brave. My mind raced and I contemplated running to my father and waking him so he could see the lights. I made that decision inside of a second and, turning to gently pull my woman by the hand, made my way back to my father's home.

She understood and followed me silently toward our home, both of us constantly turning to watch the horizon and see what the lights would do. When we made it to my home, she waited outside the door while I went in and gently touched my father's arm.

"Father," I whispered. He didn't stir, so I pushed harder and repeated it louder.

"Mmm, what is it, son?" he then jerked his entire body but then looked up and saw me, his mind still deciphering dream from reality. "Mmm what? What is it?"

"Father, there are lights on the horizon. They are brighter than fire and they are all grouped together, like a home made of suns resting just on the horizon of the water."

Suddenly my father sat up and paced to the doorway. Without pausing to put on his day clothes or shoes, he tore down the trail that led to the water so he could see the lights for himself. It was as if he knew what was happening, like it had happened before. Like a pack of wolves was back and was tearing apart the children.

He paused when he came to the clearing of the beach and looked out. His eyes were weaker than they once were, but he was far from blind. He stood there, staring out over the water for no longer than five seconds before turning and running back into our settlement. He went to several of the homes where the strongmen lived and called their names.

The lights from the deep remained exactly where they were every time I turned back to look at them.

My woman and I, our fingers still tied together, followed my father around at a distance but his crazed haste was nearly dizzying as he zigzagged from one home to another. Eventually, he slowed enough for me to approach him and ask, "What is it, father? What are those lights?"

He looked back into my eyes and at first said nothing, letting the smoldering burn of his gaze burn the gravity of the situation into my mind.

"Is it something from the water? Are they coming for you?" I asked.

"No, son," he answered firmly. "This is far worse than a sea creature. It's—" before he could finish his explanation, some of the other men had come out of their tents and were coming to him for instruction. He turned to them, leaving our conversation in the air, and began delivering orders. I watched his back, with his two long braids running down his back, as he ordered these men who had known and obeyed him all of their lives.

I turned and looked at my woman, still holding my hand in the darkness, and she turned from the movement of the men to meet my eyes. My hand impulsively squeezed hers and neither of us said anything.

III. A Ship Without Sails

Hours later the lights had descended from the horizon as the thing got closer and closer to shore. We could now see that it was a gigantic ship—one bigger than I ever thought possible, and the lights aboard it were mesmerizing. I couldn't believe such a vessel could even exist, it seemed more like a dream than reality.

My father had told the men to take up their arms and keep watch on the shore. Meanwhile, he had gone down to the small boat where he would die and from which he would eventually sink into the deep.

I met him there, where we were finally away from the other men and the women and children who had also woken up from the commotion. I asked him what he knew about it.

My father hesitated—something I had never seen him do in all my years—and kept working his hands along the small ropes in his boat. Then he did another thing I had never seen him do: he spoke to me without looking at my eyes.

My father always maintained an intense gaze whenever he spoke to someone. He said that to look away from someone while speaking to them shows weakness and men should not be weak. At other times he had told me that men who cannot look you in the eye are often lying.

That thought passed into my head and for the first time in my life, I wondered if my father may be lying to me. He had never lied before—at least, not that I knew of. Now I began to question everything.

"Father?" I asked hesitantly, hoping he would look up and meet my eyes with his own.

But he did not. He kept his eyes down on the ropes where his hands worked.

"What is that ship, father?" I asked again.

"This is my fault," he replied without looking up. "I brought them here, so I will go out and meet them."

"No!" I instinctively shouted before I could think. "I can't let you go alone!" I continued to speak without thinking, but as the words came out of my mouth, I felt my throat sink down into my stomach. "I will go with you."

"No, my son," he replied. My resolve to accompany my father to the larger ship hardened. Inside my head, I determined that if he rowed out alone, I would take one of the other small boats and follow him.

The sky's blackness began to crack and give way to a gray morning. The sun had not yet breached the horizon, but it was getting easier to discern shapes and people. The ship didn't seem to have gotten any closer, though I'm sure it had. The horizon is a long way off.

My father had finished preparing his boat and turned to the rest of the tribe gathered on the shore. In a loud voice, he yelled, "I will go out to these lights on the horizon and find what they have come for. I will not let them harm you. If I do not return, it was an honor leading you, my people, and dying on your behalf. Goodbye."

He promptly stepped into his boat and used the oars to push off from the beach. No one moved, they simply watched him paddle off into the water. Ten yards, then twenty. I waited until just the right moment to run for one of the other boats and follow him. It had to be a long enough time that the other strongmen had dispersed, but not so long that I couldn't catch up with my father.

Eventually the moment came. I didn't want to draw attention to myself, so I slowly walked to where the other eight boats were overturned on the shore. Then I began moving quickly. I flipped over a small craft and lugged the oars inside. Then pulled it to where the waters were lapping at the sand. I didn't look behind me, but I heard some of the men talking to me. They were not angry, just confused and asking what I was doing.

I pushed the boat out into the water and once the hull left the sand, I hopped aboard. It oscillated beneath me as I found my way to the bench and got the oars into their rings. It was only now that I was facing the shore and saw some of the other men had run down to the edge of the water. They were not coming after me, they were primarily just watching me row out away from them, toward my father and toward the large ship.

After several minutes of pulling at the oars, I could hear my father yelling at me. It was so faint I couldn't understand the words, but it was clear that he did not want me to follow him.

We continued this way for a while. Every time I glanced over my shoulder, I seemed to be the same distance from the ship, as if I was going nowhere. The shore in front of me continued to get smaller though.

This reinforced my hatred of the water: it didn't seem to align with the laws of land and math and sense that the rest of the world obeyed.

And as much as I tried not to look beneath my vessel, I couldn't help it from time to time. Each time I looked down at the black waters holding up my craft, I had to remind myself to breathe. I was sitting atop the chaos and for some unknown reason, it continued to hold me afloat. For now.

At one point, I glanced behind me and noticed the ship finally appeared to be closer. It was marginally larger than before. My father stayed a steady distance behind me. He occasionally yelled out for me to turn back, but I kept rowing after him.

The skin on my hands burned but every time the blisters rubbed the handles I pushed the focus on them from my mind. I glanced behind me again and the ship was closer. I could now make out multiple levels of the ship. It had lights and poles sticking up from it, and as I slowly got closer, I could detect humans on board.

Suddenly it hit me: why the ship seemed so strange to me. It did not have sails. Nor did it have oars—though they would have to be massive to propel a ship that size anywhere, bigger than a tree trunk even. I wanted to just stop and stare at the ship, but I couldn't look at it and continue rowing at the same time.

The waves tossed me back and forth. It was not a choppy day on the waters, but with such a small boat, even miniature bumps in the ocean would toss me back and forth. Even when the boat rocked violently from side to side, I tried not to look down into the depths. I knew what awaited me there: death and chaos. I knew there were things living beneath my small craft which could withstand the might of the water without being sucked down into its stomach. Perhaps I feared these faceless creatures more than the water itself. The mystery was the worst part.

I was now close enough to the ship to see the faces of men and women on board. They looked nothing like me. They didn't look like anyone from my tribe—or any of the surrounding tribes for that matter. They had light skin and their clothes were dark blue and bright white. I had never seen cloth so white in all my life. It was like they were wearing a cloud, but it was cut so precisely.

I saw the men throw a rope down to my father. He was now only a few lengths from the massive ship which was as tall as a tree. Taller, perhaps.

"Father!!" I yelled. I paused my rowing and watched to see what would happen.

My father took the rope and hitched it to the boat. He looked at me, then began climbing up the rope along the hull of the impossibly large ship. The men on board looked down at him and watched as he made his way up the rope. The strength of his arms still surprised me, as just yesterday he was on the edge of death and now he was climbing up a rope to a foreign ship.

I rowed my boat next to his as quickly as I could, and despite being terrified, intended to climb up the rope behind him. When I came alongside his boat, I threw the oars into mine, grabbed the rope at my feet and tied our boats together. Then, as quickly as I could—which was difficult in two flimsy boats in choppy waters bouncing in the wake of a massive ship—I stepped from my boat to my father's, and then grabbed the rope leading up to the deck of the ship.

My arms were not as strong as my father's, but by putting my feet on the ship's hull, I was able to slowly walk and pull my way up after my father. He was already standing on the deck with the men, but I could not see what he was doing—or what they were doing to him. He had stopped yelling at me to turn back and had apparently accepted me coming after him.

I finally crested the deck and what I saw amazed me. It was even more incredible up close than from a distance. There were poles, boxes, and wheels, as well as all sorts of colorful tools made of materials I had never seen before. I could not believe my eyes. I was stunned for a moment such that when my father spoke to me, I was still staring in disbelief at the machinery.

All my life I had only seen wooden shafts and poles and weapons made of sharpened stones. We cooked food with fire and lived in tents made of animal hides. My brain could not even comprehend the complex technology I was now trying to take in and figure out all at once.

"Son," said my father, holding his hand toward one of the other men on the deck, "This is Captain William."

IV. "I had seen them before"

The man next to my father smiled and said something to me in words I didn't understand. He had all of his teeth and they were as white as his uniform. I was still stunned and couldn't say anything. I looked to my father standing a few feet from Captain William and waited for some sort of understanding to descend upon me.

My father took a step toward me and finally began to speak. "My son..." he paused once more. He never hesitated when he spoke. *Hesitation is for the weak,* he would always say. "I have lied to you, and to my tribe. I don't expect any of you to forgive me, but I want to explain."

When he said these words, I felt my throat sink even further into my stomach. The past several hours had upended my entire life. Suddenly I had an impossible desire to hold my woman and let my tears fall into her hair again.

"It started two years ago," my father continued. "These lights—this ship on the horizon approached the back side of the island, beyond the prairie. Some of the strongmen came to me and told me that foreign men had come to the back side of our land—you know, where the prairie meets the far waters. I went to meet them, and one of those men was Captain William."

"Wait—" I spoke before my father had finished. "You knew these men before today? You've seen this ship before?"

"Yes, my son. Captain William and his men come from a place called Ah-Mer-Ick-Ah, and they came in peace. When myself and the strongmen approached them before, we had our spears and weapons raised. We were ready to kill them or die defending our tribe."

I was holding onto the rail of the deck as my father spoke. My legs felt weak beneath me. Captain William stood near us, smiling although he did not understand what we were saying.

My father continued, "Captain William and his men came in peace. They have weapons far beyond what we can imagine, and they would have easily destroyed us and our tribe." Then he paused to clarify, "'Captain' is his title. He is the Chief of this ship. Captain William and his men communicated with us, and after much discussion, I agreed to help them."

"What could they possibly need help with?" I asked suddenly.

My father continued as if I had not spoken: "They are called Ree-Sur-Churs, and they work for a tribe called Sye-Ents. They want to learn about our tribe and our people, but they cannot come in. They communicated to me that if they came to our tribe, many of our people would die. I could not understand why, but they told me it would be bad. There would be a sickness or a curse of some kind. Captain William said I should come with them and tell them about our people and in doing so, I will help the future of my tribe."

I was still feeling queasy; the combination of the rocking sea, my outsized fear of it, and the mind-shattering news my father was giving me. I never imagined there could be tribes like this in the world. Up until this point, all the other tribes we knew had the same tools and weapons as us: sticks, stones, hide and fabric. This ship, however, had lights contained in jars, and some of these lights were even brighter than fires.

"So," I spoke carefully, "you were never going to die today?"

"No, my son," my father now looked directly into my eyes and spoke plainly. "I was going to go away with Captain William for the good of our people. They told me that they would be back in 25 moons, and that day is today. They were not supposed to come within sight of our people though. I intended to row out beyond the horizon and meet them here. But now our people have seen the ship and I must decide what I will do."

I slid down the rail onto my backside and sat on the deck of the ship, the lower rail pressing against my shoulder blades. I thought again about my woman and if me being here would affect my return to her. Could I see her again? Would this mean my father *could* come to our ceremony? Hundreds of questions ran through my mind at once.

Captain William walked toward me, knelt down beside my legs, and put his hand on my shoulder. He began to speak slowly, though I still couldn't understand a word he said. When he realized this, he turned and called some words to another man on deck. This other man approached and knelt down beside Captain William. He was older than me but younger than my father—like Captain William—and smiled in a friendly way as he looked into my eyes.

He put his palm flat on his chest and said, "Pat-Rick. Pat... Rick."

I stared at him, understanding but unable to respond. He pointed his hand toward me and I knew he was asking for my name, but all of the new discoveries had put my body and mind into ice water so it moved very slowly, like when your joints are in the snow for too long. Everything I had known was upended and I suddenly realized how little of the world I really knew.

I looked at my father, then back at Captain William. All three men stared at me and no one said anything.

"F-father," I said. "What will they do to us?" I felt tears creeping out the corners of my eyes.

Pat-Rick began waving his hands around in a flurry of movements, touching his chin and laying both palms open before me. My brain and body were too exhausted to attempt to interpret his motions.

My father spoke, "I do not know, son." His eyes were on the deck of the ship, rather than looking at me. I didn't know what to think. Out of the corner of my eye, I saw motion and looked along the rail to see other men pulling my father's boat and mine out of the water. They were carefully pulling them up with the ropes and hoisting them over onto the dock.

Sudden terror filled my stomach and I felt it fluttering the way it did before I fought that other man. I thought of my woman and suddenly a mad impulse drew me up to my feet. Without thinking or looking over the edge of the ship, I held the rail and threw my legs over the edge.

Then I was in the air.

My stomach elevated up into my throat and I was weightless.

I looked down into the black waters as they seemed to dance in a movement slower than time while my body flew toward them.

I had time while I was falling to think several thoughts—that's how high the ship's deck was.

I began to wonder how long it would take me to swim back to shore, to my woman.

Then suddenly I was underwater, submerged by the object of my deepest fears.

V. The Mother of Worlds

The cold shock ran up my feet and paralyzed my spine. My mouth was jarred open from the surprise and my lungs instinctively tried to suck in air, but only received a mouthful of salty water. My throat burned and I felt the weight of the water move down my throat to my chest like a frigid stone going down my neck.

For several moments I was frozen underwater. I felt the motion of the waves and they both comforted and terrified me. I was being moved by something exponentially larger and more powerful than me; something so chaotic and vast that I could do nothing to possibly affect it. That thought brought a momentary cloud of rage into the back of my skull, rage so red and so black that every particle of my body tensed in anger, but it passed as I realized my need for air.

My limbs jumped back to life and began thrashing. I had not swam in water since I was a little child. I began to transport through time to when I was a little boy. My mother's hands were beneath my back as I floated in the shallows of the waters. She was teaching me to swim.

"Relax your muscles," she said. Her strong arms held me close to her breast and I felt safe despite my entire body resting atop the dark depths. I looked up into her tan face and she smiled down on me. The waters were calm on that day in my boyhood, and I remember the feeling of the waves rising and falling, gently lifting and dropping me. My mother slowly lowered her hands from my back so I was freely floating on the surface, but I still felt her fingertips keeping contact with my skin.

Not long after that, my mother would be taken by the waters herself. The strong arms which had once supported me in the water were now swallowed by it. My mother was dragged into the chaos. A terrible storm tore through our coast, producing a rogue wave which rose from the deep without warning. The swell of water hit the land shelf several lengths from our beach and roared into the sky. My mother was tying up a boat with another woman from our tribe and neither of them saw the wave. Both were immediately drawn out into the waters.

That day was one of the few times I saw my father cry.

Now, after leaping form the ship, I hoped to remember the correct movements of swimming, but my muscles seemed to rebel against me. They just thrashed wildly with no calculated rhythm or order.

I was not sure which way the surface of the water was, but I seemed to only be sinking deeper. My spastic limbs were taking me further into the heart of the chaos. The water got colder the further I sank from the top, and I felt the weight of it pressing into every ounce of my body.

My ears exploded within my head and sharp pain ran from my ears into the center of my neck. Everything inside my skull felt like it was about to burst out of my forehead. My throat made a desperate gurgling sound which was curbed by the lack of air, *ng nngguh.*

As I descended, I imagined the hands of the dead reaching up to grab my ankles. I kept expecting to land on the bed of decayed limbs and twisted bones, but never did. I only sank deeper into the fluid abyss as my body raged against it, unwilling to give up.

The pressure weighed on my chest like I was a doll and a massive man was pressing my torso between his palms. My arms and legs continued to beat against the indifferent water, barely affecting it. The salt water I swallowed filled my lungs. They impulsively tried to cough it out, but in doing so, sucked in more. It burned my throat like cold fire and I felt the acidic flame streak down my chest.

The air I so badly needed seemed further and further from me as the light from the surface dimmed.

At once my body relaxed and a sudden calm came over me.

I felt the fingertips of my mother on my back. They did not lift me; they simply touched me and I was comforted. My lips parted and I suddenly stopped caring if more water came in, or if air did, or if anything did ever again. My fear of the dark and chaotic deep suddenly vanished as I was engulfed by it. Had I conquered my fear by becoming it? Or at least, by allowing myself to give in to it?

Growing up, the other boys would stand in the shallows, with the water at their waist, and punch the waves as they rolled in. I would watch and notice different things about all of them. Some would beat the sea as if their lives depended on it. Others turned and put the breaks of the waves on their shoulders and rode the waves in to the shore.

But there was a third option. There were those boys—the ones I admired the most—who waded into the shallows and when a tower of water yawned leagues above them, they simply went limp. They let their bodies be thrown hither and yon by the chaotic force. They always ended up with scrapes from the stones on the bottom, or rashes from the sand, but they enjoyed the feeling of letting the dark liquid throw them around like a leaf on a breeze. These boys were the most honest. You could not defeat the sea, no matter what levels of anger you achieved.

When I fought the other man for my woman, I knew I would win. Because the rage inside of me was much, much larger than the rage in him. His passion for my woman was lacking and I was able to defeat him despite his physical grandeur.

With the ocean however, no amount of rage or passion could affect that mass of water. It's too big. You're useless against it whether you are a boy splashing in the shallow surf or a man channeling the fury of a jilted lover.

Nor could you tame the chaotic void. You may be able to ride the smaller waves, but what about when the storms —"*the fury of the gods*"—rolled in? What good could your skill and precision do against those black towers? No, the sea cannot be tamed or conquered.

The only option is to surrender to the chaos; to go limp in her cold and dark grip.

My body was presently limp as it sunk deeper into the void, letting the currents swirl it back and forth like an infant being rocked by his mother. As much as the sea had terrified me my entire life, it presently comforted me with its gentle sway.

As I fell further from the sun, darkness came over me. It was both physical darkness from being far from the light, but also a physiological light as my vision clouded and my mind was calmed. My life was running through my mind at an incredible speed. It ran forward from my earliest memory—just my mother and father smiling down on me as I lay on the ground—to the present moment. Then it ran backward and as I ran through the entirety of my existence, I realized how very small I was.

I saw that my life was a grain of salt in this eternal ocean.

Nothing I did would affect the world. The past few hours alone had revealed just how little of the world I really knew. I longed to see all of it. I wanted to take my woman by the hand and lead her all across the world.

I wanted to feel her head in my chest again as we cried beneath the moon.

I felt so utterly small as the water swallowed me, and at once my mind seemed to break free from the restraint of thought and reason. I suddenly relinquished my desire for anything—good or bad things—and I was immersed in the mere fact that I exist.

I saw a light so bright it violently stabbed my eyes. I squeezed them closed, but the light persisted. A moment later they had adjusted and I was floating above the world. I was in the blackness of the night sky and saw the sun in the distance. It drifted toward the moon and the two merged into one eternal light that burned brighter than the lights of the ship without sails.

The stars drifted magnetically toward the New Sun and joined in the chorus of its brilliance. It was not simply white light, but the brilliance of every color displayed vibrantly at once. My mind couldn't comprehend the amount of colors I was beholding.

Then from deep within my fractured ears, I began to hear the singing. At first it was one voice, quiet and small. It was like a child's voice singing a simple melody which rose and fell like the motion of the water on a calm day.

This voice was soon joined by more, until a full choir sounded inside my head. The sound was both inside and outside of my head. I was submerged into the sound like my body was in the water.

My eyes continued to watch as one by one, more stars were absorbed by the sun and it grew not just in brightness, but in colorful brilliance.

The sound of the choir grew until the chant was overwhelming. It was nearly intoxicating like my tribe's hardwater. If I still had eardrums, the voices would have burst them again. At first the voices were simply singing a melody, but now meaning emerged from the syllables.

They were singing in a language I had never heard before; it did not sound like a human language—it was unlike anything I had heard before—yet I understood the meaning. My mind did not understand it, but something deeper within my being did. My spirit knew.

The song's rhythm continued to match the motion of the water and I understood it all at once.

> *I know your name,*
> *I have seen you.*

The voice called me by a name I had never heard before; a name which fit me more precisely than any hollow human word conceived in syllables and glottal stops.

> *Your fear is fitting;*
> *only a fool does not fear this chaotic abyss.*

> *I am the Ancient One,*
> *the Mother of worlds*
> *and the Father of suns.*

> *I am the movement and the stillness.*

> *I am the terror and the calm.*

I am the bottom of the dark void
and the source of eternal light.

I am the wheel which will not be broken,
you are a spoke within my turning.
You matter because I know you.

The tune rang on, not in words, but in feelings and intangible thought. I understood that the creature of the depths was speaking to me, imbuing truth into my brain in a way language never could. It was altering the way I understood all of reality.

Follow the ancient paths,
Find rest for your soul in the land of your fathers.
I will meet you in the blackness of the water
and the expanse of the prairie.

You will not make your bed in the depths,
you will be lifted by the arms of your mother
and hold your woman once more.

The stars continued to slowly be sucked into the New Sun and the brilliance became overwhelming. I closed my eyes but the light persisted. My limbs felt heavy as they were pulled in every direction at once; gravity crushed my body while simultaneously pulling it apart. I felt the fabric of my skin begin to drift apart. It was the opposite of what was happening to the stars and the sun: while the little points of light were being sucked into the larger body of light, particles of my body drifted away from me and into the darkness.

I felt incredibly small but suddenly important.

If something as small as me mattered, then everything mattered. In that sense, I felt connected to the entirety of the cosmos. I no longer feared the depths or the prairie.

I was at one with creation.
I had encountered the Creator.
And the Creator knew my name.

The light grew and grew until my body began to violently seize and my limbs flailed, slapping the wooden deck of the ship.

I coughed and spewed water from my mouth, which cascaded back down on me as I lay on my back. One of Captain William's men knelt beside me, hammering at my chest.

Through blurry eyes I saw my father staring down at me, crying.

VI. You cannot go back

As my mind descended back into the reality of my body, I realized that what I had seen was not real...or was it?

Was it the most *real* thing I had encountered in all my life?

Just as the coming of Captain Williams' ship had expanded my knowledge of what was possible in this physical world, my experience in the water had blown away any notion of what I knew about the invisible world, that horizon across which there is no return. I had crossed it and returned. I had come within a mere whisper of existence Itself.

What had I known before? What did I think I knew?

I now realized I knew nothing but fear and my tribe's small settlement on the edge of the world. The water had brought me closer to *life* than any experience I had on this side of the abyss—the dry side above the water. I smiled at the irony and my father rushed down to my side, yelling a word he had called me all my life: my name. But it wasn't really my name.

I knew that now.

I knew I wouldn't be at home any longer until I was once more engulfed by the chaos and sunk inside her frigid womb. Not even my woman's arms would be enough for me after this taste of eternity. Yet as my mind reeled from darkness into the light, I knew I would spend several more decades with her before permanently joining the dark waters.

I slowly pushed my body up into a sitting position and looked around me.

"One of the men had to dive in after you," said my father. "He saved your life." My father pointed to one of the men circled around me, and sure enough, he and his brilliant white clothes were dripping wet.

Just yesterday I would have marveled at the bravery of a man who could dive into the waters, fearless. Now, however, I envied him. For a moment I felt the draw to heave the rail again and jump back into the water myself.

Finally, total coherence brought me to myself and I looked at my father. The only words I could say were, "My woman!"

He put his hand on my shoulder and delivered the news: "You cannot go back, my son."

The words didn't register inside my head for a moment, then I felt the same sinking feeling in my stomach again. "What? But father—"

"You will endanger our entire tribe if you go back," he said gently.

"But how?" I asked, bewildered. I felt the floor of my torso fall away and all my organs tumbled down through it. Unforced tears rolled down my cheeks before I even realized I was crying.

"I don't know exactly," said my father, "but Captain William and his men explained that there are very small dangers that they carry. So small we cannot see them. They will make you sick and you will carry these dangers to our people."

I took in the news, even though it didn't make sense to me. How could something be a threat to me if I couldn't even see it? I began shaking my head violently, "No father! I must go back to her! She is all I want!" Then my chin finally dissolved into uncontrollable sobs. I had to tell my woman what I had seen in the abyss, tell her I was no longer afraid of the sea or even the prairie.

It was then that I looked up to the other men and examined their faces. I also became aware that the ship was moving away from my land. I scrambled to get up, but my father and several other men grabbed me and held me back, fearing another jump into the water.

Captain William made his way to the front of my vision and held his hands up, calming me down.

He pointed to the boat I had rowed out in, still sitting on the deck of the massive ship. Then he pointed to me and made a rowing motion toward land. But then he held up his hand and pointed to the sun with a finger.

This way he slowly communicated to me that I could row back to my land, but I needed to wait ten days before returning to my people. Otherwise I risked making them sick with the dangers of the ship's men. I nodded as I understood and the plan became clear to me.

Captain William made it clear that if I became sick in those ten days, I had to stay away from my people until long after I was well. The sinking feeling in the pit of my stomach began to elevate. I excitedly looked at my father, but as soon as I did, I realized what this would mean.

"Father..." I began. "You will not come with me, will you? You will not see my ceremony with my woman?" My mind raced all over again. "You will not see my sons grow strong or play with my beautiful daughters."

For the second time in my life, a tear fell from the eye of my father. He went to speak once, but choked on a high note. "You will return to our people and you will lead them well." He looked intently up and down my body, as if the outcome of his observation would determine what he said next. "You have now faced the waters. You are ready."

I was shocked for a moment because I had not told my father anything about what I had seen under the water. The way he looked at me communicated that he too had encountered the ground of our being beneath the waves.

I nodded then, suddenly understanding the meaning in our moment.

"I will go back—" I began, but I too was swallowed by more sobs. My father nodded knowingly and put his big, solid hand on my shoulder. Then he embraced me for a long time.

By the time he had finished embracing me, I looked up the ship and saw that other men had turned over my boat and attached it to ropes in order to lower it to the water again. I saw them putting packages of some kind into the hull, and I would later find that they had given me food and water—enough to survive the ten days apart from my people.

I knew my father and I had said enough words to one another, so I walked toward the boat and waited for the men to finish preparing it. When they had, I stepped over the edge into it. A giant metal arm lowered me by metal ropes down into the water with my food. As I descended back to the water, I felt no fear of the sea. I felt only deep sadness over leaving my father, blended with uncontrollable joy to see my woman again.

It had only been a few hours (and one eternity underwater) since I was with her, but I realized as I began rowing that I never wanted to be away from her this long again. My rowing was fueled by this combination of excitement and grief. I laughed alone in my boat, and as I did, tears flooded my face. The laughter turned from joy into sobs, and eventually back into laughter.

My father stood on the deck of the ship the entire time I rowed away from him, watching me as I pulled my tiny vessel further from him until the waters bent us over the horizon and we could see one another no more.

5. The Tiniest Human Ever (A Parable)

The island was small but the men were all good. The men never fought and they all shared their food. The island was quiet, not subject to noise. Perhaps it was how they loved life's little joys.

The men lived in peace with no reason to fight. They were not very loud but they weren't very bright. The island knew peace, that's how it was arranged.

Their lives were quite simple but one day that all changed.

A human appeared, not more than three foot. They had thought *they* were quiet, but this one was mute.

Said Ralph, "Why, I've never seen a human so small. Most humans are strong and most humans are tall."

"I've heard of this kind," said Ralph's little brother. "They live in the tropics and eat one another."

"No, no," said another, "that can't be correct...because this one looks harmless. He has no effect!"

The men were confused; all tripped up in wonder. Their isle had been breached and the men torn asunder. They argued and fought about what they should do without talking directly to the one who was new.

He stood to the side and watched all the commotion, and all the while wondered why the sudden explosion. He watched as the men conversed louder and louder, until one was a yeller, the other a shouter. And all of the noise and all of the cries caused him to start whimpering in soft little sighs.

But nobody noticed, at least not for a while, the new man felt alone on the small crowded isle.

But after a minute, or maybe a few, the little one's sobs did come into view. So Ralph and his brother and a handful of others approached the small man and oh, how he shuddered. To be surrounded by all of these gigantic men, it gave him a scare from his bones to his skin. So he cried even louder and louder until, all the men spoke more kindly and they softened their wills.

"Now what is your name?" said an old man drinking rum, "and how did you get here and where are you from?"

"But now wait half a minute," said Ralph's brother Edmund. "How did any of us get here? And just where are we from?" Then a long silence fell upon all of the crowd. For no one knew where and nobody knew how. They all just appeared there, they awoke as a man; nobody asked questions and life just went on.

But now there was this one, so small and not strong. He was not like the others; his size was all wrong.

"Well, if we attack him I'm sure we would win," said one of the grown men, now rotten within. "I mean look, he's defenseless! His arms are so weak. I think we could take him, his chances are bleak."

"But what is the point, what have we to gain? I know we'd defeat him, but why inflict pain?"

"Because this one is different, he's so filled with fear! Our island would be better if he were not here."

So they bickered and fought about what they should do, all because this small little human, to their minds, was new.

For no one had told them how they had arrived—that at one point all of them were this child's size. No one had told them they were from somewhere else, and then shipped to the island to fend for themselves. All these men were imported from far, far away just to see how they'd fare without systems in place.

But there'd been a mistake and a child got sent, and his presence got all the men rather upset. Some were in favor of killing the boy, because he was a nuisance just there to annoy. "He's just a mistake!" some selfish men said, "We never planned for him, he's better off dead!"

But others defended the helpless small child. "We need to protect him and teach him the wild." But they were outnumbered, twelve hundred to one, so they took the small human and punctured his lungs.

"He was just a mistake, he's not full-grown like us," and they went back to their lives and forgot all the fuss.

6. Chris & Mary

I can hear the frogs in the alleys screaming about the rusty spoons they have to use to prep their H. Not real frogs, obviously, but that's what the addicts sound like to me. I rolled my taxi slowly around Detroit, waiting for a customer to hail me down. Last month, Mayor Snyder declared bankruptcy over the whole city. Did you know a city could declare bankruptcy? I didn't either.

My name is Chris.

I've been a taxi driver here in Detroit for as long as I can remember. Or at least since I could reach the pedals.

I've enjoyed the life. Since the city's decline, the skyscrapers have hollowed out and gone dark. It's like living in a big forest where all the trees are dead. People always ask me why I've never left Detroit and gone somewhere safer, but the truth is, it gives me a rush. Way more than those frogs get by scooping needles out of dumpsters behind the Little Caesar's.

I turned onto Mckinley Street and patted under the passenger seat one more time to make sure Mary was still there. That's my nickname for my buck knife. She's twelve inches of hardened steel with a leather wrapped handle. A customer gave her to me.

Well, he didn't really give her to me. He sort of left her in my car.

It's funny, every time I get into my car, Mary yells "I call shotgun!" and I say, "No, you stupid girl. You're a knife!" Well, I think it's funny. Mary used to laugh at it but doesn't anymore.

I see a guy walking out from the Marathon Gas station. He waves so I pull over.

"Alright girl," I muttered to Mary, "you just stay quiet down there."

The back door opened and the man got in—I'd guess he was in his mid-twenties but looked much older because of this neighborhood—and then he just sat there.

"Well...?" I asked.

He looked up from the belly of his hoodie. "Oh, my bad," he mumbled. "Renaissance."

I flicked off the cab light and started the meter. I eased away from the curb and headed downtown.

"Yo, can you drive faster?" the passenger shouted from the back seat, more animated than before. "Jesus, gotta get somewhere."

I pressed into the gas a little more, but evidently not enough to satisfy the kid. A handful of minutes later, he leaned forward once again so his mouth was inches from my ear.

"Ey. Let's go." He then jiggled something in his hand. I saw in the rearview mirror that he was pulling the handle of a glock out of his sweatshirt pocket, rattling it against some coins.

I pressed a little harder into the pedal and he leaned back. "Why you out here ackin' like you a banger, child?" I asked him, casting a glance into the rearview again. He said nothing. "If you knew what was good for you, you'd throw that piece of trash into the river and start living right."

He brooded for a while before saying, "Mannn, shut *up!*" He clicked his tongue and then, "I don't let no one talk to me that way. I should ventilate you righ'now for that."

I smiled and almost said something to Mary but reminded myself we had a guest.

He was still agitated, clicked his tongue again and shook his head while he looked out the window. Suddenly I didn't like his attitude anymore. I pulled over right in front of Slows and he began looking around.

"This ain't the Renaissance."

"Get out," I warned him. "I don't like your attitude."

"Whaa? B, you making a mistake," he said as he yanked his gun out of his pocket and thrust the tip into my temple. Without thinking, I grabbed Mary's leather handle and drove her through his hand until I felt the tip hit the metal of the gun. I dodged my head forward just in case he twitched and squeezed the trigger, but he didn't.

He just screamed profanities and dropped the gun, staring at his hand as it began to bleed.

"Yo, what kind of old lady are you??" he shrieked while squeezing at his hand to try and stop the bleeding.

"Now," I said, "Please get out of my cab before you bleed all over it."

With his other hand, he scrambled to retrieve his gun from the floor, *and we just can't have that, can we Mary?* He had left his back exposed so we took advantage. Mary dove in headfirst.

Minutes later, I had dragged him into the alley next to Slows and started the cab again. "Well now, Mary, we have a new friend left by another customer!" I looked at the glock and said, "My name is Christine and...what shall we name you?"

7. "Thinking of you, Danny!"

I rubbed my eyes and looked up from the screen. I often get so sucked into my work as a programmer that I can go hours without looking away from the screen, much less getting up and moving around.

It doesn't help that I live in a basement apartment and can't even tell when the day slips down into night. I wandered over to the fridge, flicking on the light as I entered the kitchen. It's almost embarrassing how much my refrigerator highlights my singleness. The faint smell of weeks-old produce emanated from somewhere in the back. I'll take care of it later.

Finding nothing edible, I closed the door and looked around the messy counters of my kitchen. Not even a bag of chips. I swore and muttered to myself that it's no wonder I can't get a date with a woman. Still stretching my legs, I aimlessly wandered over to my bedroom and, although I didn't want to, glanced at my reflection in the full-length mirror as I passed by. My stubble had nearly evolved into a verifiable 'beard.'

Had it really been that long that I've been down here?

It got worse when I looked on my bed and saw my phone. I picked it up and the screen ignited into a bouquet of notifications and missed calls. Half were fantasy football, some were news and sports updates. Mom texted twice saying, "Love you," followed by a "Thinking of you Danny!" There was a missed call from my friend Louis as well as one from an unknown number. I looked again at the missed call from Louis and it said it came yesterday. *Is it really after midnight already?* I mused. I had sat down to my computer around mid-afternoon.

I yawned and arced my chest up to the ceiling in a catlike stretch. Without looking behind me, I fell backward onto my bed and stared at the ceiling until I drifted off to sleep no more than a minute later.

I awoke feeling rested in the exact same room. Nothing had changed. Not having windows makes me feel like I'm in an underground bunker, or perhaps a circadian-rhythm testing chamber. As my eyes relearned how to focus, I grabbed for my phone beside me on the bed and checked it. The usual flurry of news and updates greeted me, followed by another missed call from the unknown number. I rolled my eyes at the tiny hassle of having to block another spam caller.

My stomach was rumbling. I stood, grabbed my wallet from the dresser and headed for the door of my apartment. After undoing the chain lock and turning the knob, I opened the door into the hallway only to find it completely dark, save a flickering light over the emergency door at the far end of the hall. I pulled out my phone and tapped the flashlight button to make my way to the elevator.

When I had made it halfway down the hallway, there was a piece of paper taped to the silver doors. 'Out of Service.'

No apology or anything, I muttered to myself as I reached up to my chin. Rather than finding my chin, however, my fingers found a beard nearly an inch long. I was stunned for a moment and figured it must be the morning grog making me think differently. I ran my fingers over the beard a few more times to make sure I wasn't imagining it. I muttered to myself something about needing to get out more as I guided myself by phone light over to the stairwell.

It was then that something stood out to me.

I live in downtown Chicago on the outer west edge of the city—the third biggest in the country—and I suddenly realized that it was quiet. Alarmingly quiet. There were no sirens or horns blaring on the street just outside, and no yelling from my dysfunctional neighbors. No babies were crying and no teenage drag racers were peeling out.

My phone screen illuminated suddenly, informing me that my phone battery was under ten percent. Of course. That's what happens when you pass out and don't plug in your phone.

I approached the stairwell door and pushed the bar. It opened two inches and stopped. Something on the other side was blocking it.

I closed it and tried again. It went two inches and stopped once more. Something just outside the door was blocking it. I shone my light through the crack and looked down. There was something there. I bent down and saw through the two inch slit that it was cloth of some sort. A jacket.

Someone was lying on the floor. Probably some bum who wandered in and fell asleep. The jacket looked familiar. I looked closer and realized it was just like one I had in my own closet.

I shut the door then slammed it into the body on the floor again to wake them up.

I waited. Nothing. No movement.

"Hey!" I yelled through the crack. I was shocked to find how strange the sound of my own voice sounded. My throat felt stopped up by days of inactivity.

I tried to slam the door into the body a few more times with the same result. Nothing. Silence. I let the door glide shut and that's when my phone died. My eyes hadn't adjusted, so the world went black for a few seconds before slowly fading back to see in the dim hallway. I could barely see enough to make my way back down the hall to the door of my apartment. Now I was getting mad—at myself, at the bum, at the crappy apartment maintenance.

I grabbed the handle to my apartment but it didn't turn. It must have locked behind me. I patted my pockets and dread sank in as I realized I had locked myself out of my own apartment. I had a dead phone and no way out of the hallway. I resolved to knock on my neighbor's door. Christine was perhaps the least friendly elderly woman I had ever met, so the thought of disturbing her at…what time was it? Regardless, she wouldn't be happy. To be honest, I don't think I've ever even seen Christine, I only know her through the passive aggressive notes she periodically leaves on my door.

I knocked firmly and waited. Nothing.

I waited at least a minute and knocked again.

Still nothing. Not even the shuffle of movement behind the door. I waited a bit longer and balled my hands into fists as I realized I'd have to knock on a stranger's door next. My frustration rose.

I went down the hallway to the next door and knocked. Again, silence. After one more round of knocking on the stranger's door, I decided that my only remaining option was to go out the emergency exit and set off the entire building's alarm.

I put my hand on the wall and began walking down the hallway. There were six apartments from mine to the elevator, then six more to the emergency exit. It was so dark at this end that something could be on the ground and I'd trip right over it.

With my hand on the wall, I began traipsing down the hall. My hunger was becoming more sharp, and my hands were even starting to shiver a little.

I hadn't gone ten feet when I heard the knocking. It was coming from the door behind me I had just knocked on. I stopped walking and froze. Seconds passed.

Then someone knocked again. I slowly turned and walked back to the door, confused. When I stood before the entry, I looked down and noticed no light coming under the door.

I jumped when the knocking returned, much louder now that I was directly in front of the door. I wasn't sure what to do, so I knocked back.

> *tap tap tap tap*

I made sure not to pound too hard so as to come off angry or aggressive.

Time passed.

Seconds.

Then a minute of silence.

I gathered up my courage and turned the knob, not sure what I would find. In the back of my mind I was disappointed in myself for not knowing my neighbors better after living here three years. Surprisingly, the handle turned so I eased it open. The entryway was as dark as the hallway, but no one was there.

I slowly pushed the door open more and still saw no one. And nothing. Just black.

I pushed it until it was all the way open, rubbed my sleepy eyes again and stepped forward through the door. There was no one there, and as I stepped through the door, it closed behind me before I could turn and catch it. I was now in a stranger's apartment without even knowing who or where they were.

"Hello?" my voice piped up, still sounding strange after hours of disuse. I stepped into the apartment which seemed to have a similar layout to mine. I was in the small front hall which leads to the living room ahead on the right and the kitchen on the left.

I took another step into the apartment and it happened again. Someone was knocking on the wall, only now they were further into the apartment around the corner near the living room.

"H-hello?" I tried again, still with no response. "M-my name is Dan and I got locked out of my apartment...Do you have an iPhone charger I could use?"

Silence.

With my hand on the wall, I continued slowly into the apartment. It had that faint old-person smell of old objects and stale bodily functions, but I couldn't see well enough to make out the decor. I came to the end of the short hall and now the kitchen was to my left and the living room to my right.

There was a sound in the kitchen. Some pans rustled and clanked against each other. I jumped and turned my head, but in the pitch blackness I couldn't make anything out. I reached behind me to the wall where there should have been a light switch. I found it and flipped it up and surprisingly, the lights came on, blinding me for several seconds.

When my eyes had adjusted, I found that the apartment was very similar to mine. No, it was more than similar. It was identical. They even had the same furniture and television as me. Some of the wall decorations were different, but I could have walked into this apartment and mistaken it for my own. I looked in the kitchen and it was empty. It had many of the same pots and pans as mine, but some of the pictures on the refrigerator were different. I walked over to it and examined them more closely. A shiver ran down my spine.

They had photos on their fridge which appeared to be recreations of pictures I had on mine. There was one of some people in front of Mount Rushmore, just like I had on mine, except the people were different. The photo was taken from the same spot, same angle, everything, just with different people.

There was a Save The Date just like one on my fridge, but instead of "Andy and Caroline," it read "Randy and Carolyn." The people in the photo looked like my friends with minute changes. Their eyes seemed different—different colors, maybe—and slightly altered haircuts.

My chest jolted when an iPhone on the counter vibrated and lit up. I looked at it and for a second thought it was my own. It had just received a news update, but I glanced at the screen and noticed that it had a few new text messages as well. One was from "Mom," and it read "Thinking of you Danny." Then the screen went dark, so I pushed the button to bring it back. I scrolled down past a few more news notifications to the next text, also from "Mom," which read "Love you."

I had become so absorbed in looking at the phone I failed to notice that someone had come into the kitchen behind me until they knocked their knuckles on the countertop. My heart jumped into my throat and I instinctively ducked. When I spun around to face the person, my heart nearly stopped. I was looking at myself, only years older. His beard was nearly down to his belt and his eyes had sunken down into his cheekbones. He was at least twenty pounds skinnier than me and had a slight quiver running through his whole body. His shirt was identical to one of my own, only with more wear and holes. He beheld me with confusion through eyes made sad from years of loneliness.

I was completely frozen and he seemed to be the same. I didn't know what to say.

Then he tried to talk but only glottal gurgles emerged from deep in his throat. It was as if he hadn't spoken in a decade and his vocal cords had cemented together. Then one of his skinny arms shot toward me and I reeled backward, slamming into the refrigerator. Several of the magnets clattered to the linoleum.

Without thinking, I shoved him into the counter and ran past him back toward the hallway. The older version of me was slower, but he began chasing after me, still making gurgling sounds. I grabbed the handle of the front door and tried to turn it, but it seemed to be locked from the outside.

I suddenly realized why he had been knocking from the inside of the door. He was locked in here.

The other person—the other me—grabbed my shirt and pulled me backward with his old, weak arms. I turned and looked at his face. He didn't seem to be grabbing me out of anger or aggression, but out of sadness and desperation. He had the look of a prisoner who had been locked up for years without knowing why. His sunken eyes pleaded with me as they searched my face. *What were they looking for?*

I pushed him away and ran back to the kitchen, looking for anything to break through the door. The only thing I could find was a pan, so I grabbed it by the handle and went back to the front entryway. In a fit of rage, I struck the door knob. Then again. And again.

Eventually it bent and with one more hit, it fell to the floor. I pushed the mechanism out the hole and pulled the door open. The old man had watched me quietly the whole time and now he followed me back into the dark hallway. I looked back at him and noticed how timidly he stepped through the threshold. It was as if he hadn't left his apartment in years. Or ever.

I decided to go to the next door and knock to see who or what lived there. I walked down the hall with the older me behind me and knocked on the door. This time, I heard movement in the apartment. Footsteps coming to the door.

I still held the pan in my hand and I squeezed it, ready for anything on the other side of the door. The handle jiggled, but again it seemed to be locked from within. Once more, the inhabitant knocked from inside their own door so I turned the knob.

I was shocked to see a familiar face. My own. But this one was different. Rather than being older, it was my face as it was a couple years ago. Beardless and smooth. He looked at us and froze. Confusion and near disgust crossed his face.

"Wh- what?" he muttered, unable to look away from our faces. "Who are you?" he eventually got out.

I went to speak, but had to clear my throat once more as it was stopped up by phlegm. "I don't know," I said. "We've gotten trapped in this hallway."

A few minutes later, we had resolved to walk to the emergency exit together. The younger version of myself still had a working phone, so he led us to the far end of the hall. We approached the door and I gingerly pushed the red bar to open the emergency exit. I was prepared for a blaring siren, but to my surprise, no sound or flashing lights came.

We opened the door all the way and rather than an exit of any kind, found a small concrete room. There was a desk directly in front of us with filing cabinets lining every inch of wall space. On the shelves were papers, folders and books haphazardly thrown all about, and at the desk sat a small bald man with his back to us.

The younger version of me stepped forward and addressed the man, "Hey!"

The man at the desk turned around, surprised.

"Who are you?" the younger me demanded.

The small man searched his brain for a response before nervously mumbling, "Oh, I, uhhh. Well, I, uhh." He stopped talking, stood up, and walked toward us. He wore an untucked button-up shirt and glasses which kept sliding down his oversized nose. "You aren't supposed to be here," he chattered. "Oh, you aren't supposed to be out. Hmmm, oh man, you're not supposed to be out."

The younger me and I looked at each other.

"Okay, so you are all..." the small man continued. "You're all drones. We made you. You're not who you think."

My heart sank down to my stomach.

He continued, "You're workers. We made you to work. You do your jobs on your computers, and..." he drifted off.

"Wait," the younger me interjected. "You're saying we're clones?" He laughed. "I'm not a freaking clone. I got two texts from my mom this morning." He fished his phone from his pocket and pulled up the messages from his mother.

Before he could read them aloud, I put my hand on his shoulder and told him I received the exact same texts this morning as well.

"So, wait a minute," the nervous little man said. "How did you get out of your rooms?"

I told him I left like I always did and he shook his head, saying something about maintenance leaving a door unlocked or putting the handle on backward. My mind drifted as the reality of my existence began setting in. Then I remembered something.

"Wait, if this building is full of us clones, who was that in the stairwell?"

"Stairwell?" replied the little man. Then he muttered, almost to himself, "Ahh, we must have lost A469." He rubbed his chin and then remembered the three of us were still standing before him. "Oh, right. So you see, clones don't live as long as humans. They are created, we get a few good years of work out of them, and they—uhhh—expire. I'll have to get that out of the stairway."

I could see the little man's mind racing. He suddenly turned back to his computer and clicked and punched in a few commands.

I walked back to my apartment door and turned the knob. After checking the kitchen and finding nothing to eat, I cursed at myself for not having more food in the apartment. I'd have to get it later; I was in a bit of a hurry because I had a lot of work to catch up on.

This story, nearly in its entirety, came to me in a dream while I was living in Guatemala. I woke up, so stirred by the dream, and cranked out all 6+ thousand words at a nearby coffee shop. I still don't know if it makes any sense to anyone beside me, but it's still a wild ride nonetheless.

8. Crum Hill

"Ok, but I don't get why we have to give up our weekends for this," whined my sister Margaret.

"We think it's very important for you and your brother, Maggie," said my mother from the passenger seat of our old minivan.

"I don't even get what it is," Maggie replied.

"It's hard to explain…You'll understand when we get there."

It was the late 80's (I forget the exact year) and the five of us were on our way to the middle of the Berkshire mountains, a small town called Crum Hill, where our parents had a 'surprise' for us. Maggie and I sat in the bucket seats in the middle of the van, mom and dad were up front, and Maggie's twin sister Valerie was alone in the back seat. Valerie and Maggie were polar opposites. Maggie was loud and obnoxious while I rarely ever heard Valerie utter more than a syllable or two. They were two years older than me; Maggie rarely let me forget it while Val never seemed to care.

The two of them always seemed to have different health problems as well. Val went through everything silently, while Maggie just complained more and more. Currently they're undergoing thyroid issues and always vacillate between being too hot to too cold.

I turned to look at the back seat and as usual, Val was sitting in the center seat, hands in her lap, staring straight ahead.

The sun was setting as we pulled into a parking lot in front of an unmarked building. It looked like an old office of some kind, but there were no signs or anything. We exited the van and stretched after six hours of driving.

"We're here!" said dad in a halfhearted tone trying to get us excited.

The rest of us mumbled incoherently in response. Suddenly a light turned on in the small office building, and some shadows moved behind the closed blinds. We walked over to the door just as it opened, and I was surprised to see a familiar face. It was Miss Aylor, who used to go to our church, but she'd stopped attending years ago. I just assumed she died, since she was pretty old. As she opened the door, I examined her face, and she didn't seem that much older than I remembered— maybe even younger—but she did look tired.

"Hi," she managed to utter while tugging up the corners of her mouth. "Come...in." She slowly pulled the door open so we could enter. I looked sideways and saw Maggie roll her eyes at the thought of spending the weekend with old people.

As we entered the office building, I was surprised at the interior. From the outside, the building appeared to be from the early 1900's, but the inside seemed as modern and high-tech as any building in the 80's. The design made my hopes rise at the prospect that there may be some cool things in here after all.

"Dr. Brown..." Miss Aylor said from in front of us without turning her head. Every syllable she spoke seemed to exhaust her. "Will be...so excited to see you."

"Well we are excited to meet him as well," my mother replied courteously. Miss Aylor opened an unmarked white door and stood to the side for us to enter. As I looked around, I saw three older men seated on velvet couches in the small room. There was barely enough room for all of us to sit comfortably, but the kids squeezed onto the couches.

I looked at the three men again and noticed that two of them appeared to be twins, and just like Maggie and Val, one seemed to have bright and focused eyes while the other sat there staring into space, removed from reality. I figured this must be some sort of twin study and my hopes sank again because the focus, once again, would be on the girls all weekend.

The man who was not a twin leaned forward and spoke first. "Hello, children," he smiled a warm smile beneath a fluffy white mustache. He caught me off guard when he looked my way and spoke directly to me, "Timothy, I'm very excited to meet you. You are 13 years old, is that right?"

I nodded, becoming more confused by the second.

He continued, "That's great! Well, we have some big news for you."

I looked at my parents but they were focused on Dr. Brown as he continued. "Have you heard the term 'cloning' before?" I nodded again. "Well, what we do here at the Crum Hill Research Center is similar to that. We like to think of ourselves as 'life extenders.'" At this, the lively half of the male twins chuckled and nodded. The three of us children sat in confused silence.

Suddenly, Dr. Brown hopped to his feet, startling me. He took two steps toward one of the twins on another couch. "This is Mr. Henry," he said, motioning toward the livelier twin. Mr. Henry smiled at me and gave a little wave.

"Mr. Henry," continued the doctor, "is a real, organic human being, made the old fashioned way." He winked at my parents. All this time, Mr. Henry's twin sat beside him, staring into space like a rag doll. "And next to him is his clone…have you given him a name, Mr. Henry?"

"Umm, Louis? Mr. Louis?" replied Mr. Henry.

"Great!" replied Dr. Brown. "So, Louis—Mr. Louis—is Mr. Henry's clone. He's been created in this chamber behind me from Mr. Henry's DNA."

I looked at the mysterious door he had mentioned behind him, and then at Maggie who looked back at me. For once, she didn't have anything to say. She and I were both thinking the same thing as we turned to look at our sister Valerie. Valerie sat in silence as always, looking straight ahead.

"Now," continued Dr. Brown, "I know this may be hard to hear, but fifteen years ago, your family was part of an earth-shattering experiment which has allowed us to give hundreds of people hope." He motioned to Valerie. My parents listened, expressionless.

"We took your sister Maggie here and made a copy of her. You've always known them as twins, but actually, Val—is it?—is her clone." I looked at Maggie and her jaw sagged agape in shock. Val did nothing.

"The reason this gives us hope is simple. We will all grow old and die, right? Well, when that happens, we can take your brain and move it into your clone, allowing you to go on living, just in a fresh, new body. Right now, these clones have a barely-functioning brain, like a blank video tape." He smiled when he had finished explaining this like he had just won the Super Bowl.

"So," I spoke up after the reality had set in. "I don't have twin sisters? Val is a..." I didn't want to say it out loud, as if that would make it more real. "Val is a clone?"

"That's right," Dr. Brown nodded.

"And honey," my mom turned to face me. "We brought you here because Dr. Brown has been very kind and offered to make us another clone since we let him experiment with Maggie...and Val."

"Yes, we have had tremendous success with this! Just this year we cloned the daughter of a wealthy family from California. Are you familiar with the Olsens? No? Well they now have a beautiful pair of 'twin' girls." He chuckled at his own cleverness. After a moment of silence, Dr. Brown piped up again. "Well! I'm sure you are all tired from your trip! Let me show you to your rooms and you can get some rest."

We all stood up and filed through the door. Miss Aylor and Mr. Brown led us out to the lobby and down a hall lined with doors. They opened three doors for us—one for mom and dad, one for the twins—or, clones—and one for me. I got my own room! I walked in and found that the room looked like a hotel, but there was no TV. I was sad about that, but jumped on the bed and turned on the light. I opened a notebook and began to write in my journal about what I had learned that night. It actually made a lot of sense, since Val was always so lifeless and Maggie was more lively.

Wind rustled the branches just outside my window and a chill ran down my spine. When we were driving here, it was obvious that we were in the middle of nowhere and that was scary. I ran over and yanked the curtains closed.

Fifteen minutes later, I was finishing writing and drawing in my notebook when a pounding came on my door. It scared me half to death and I jumped in my bed before I realized it was probably just Maggie. I bounced over to the door and opened it. I was surprised to find that it wasn't a family member, but one of the older men who was in the room earlier. I instantly realized he was the clone, not the 'real' one.

I was so surprised I stood there for a moment, looking at him before he stepped forward and I impulsively pulled the door open more for him to enter. He dragged his feet into my room and began grunting and moaning. It was creepy, like a zombie from a movie. I didn't know what to do, so I went to get my parents. Before I made it to the door though, I felt his hand grab the back of my t-shirt. I yelped, but he yanked me back and put his hand over my mouth. I panicked and thrashed back and forth, trying to escape.

"Zzzz…..shhhhh," he said, trying to calm me down. A few seconds later, I realized he was communicating that he didn't want to hurt me so I settled down and sat on the bed with him.

"Ayyyeee," he began, trying hard to speak coherently. Each word clearly caused him terrible pain. "I ammmm in paiiinnnn." I was confused.

He slowly bent down and pulled up the bottom of his pants to reveal a massive sore of some kind on his shin.

"Owwww," I said when I saw it. "How did you get that?"

He moved slowly and put his pant leg back down. "C— clooone," he drawled.

"What?"

"Don't...clone," he managed to get out. He then lifted up his left hand and showed me his fingers. Once I noticed it, it became obvious. His ring finger looked different than the others. With his other hand, he lifted it up and it slid right off, revealing a skinny nub that only went to the first knuckle. The rest of the finger was just a plastic prosthetic.

I began to get scared by what he was saying. What if cloning was really bad for you? Maybe that's why Maggie and Val both seemed to have so many health problems!

Just then I heard a voice calling in the hallway. Dr. Brown was yelling, "Louis! Louis, where are you?"

Louis turned his head to the door and his lifeless eyes got a little wider. He looked back at me before standing up and repeated, "Donnnn't...c-clone." He dragged his feet over to the door and opened it.

Dr. Brown ran over to it and said, "Oh, there you are!" He then looked over Louis' shoulder and saw me on the bed. He walked past the clone and approached me on the bed, forcing a smile beneath his white stache. "He shouldn't have been in here. Did he just wander in?" I nodded. "Did he do anything to you? Are you okay?"

I nodded again, then summoned my innocent-little-boy voice and asked, "Mister Brown, is there anything that can go wrong with cloning? I don't know if I want to do it!"

"Oh, don't be silly!" he smiled and continued. Through the door I could see Louis standing in the hallway, staring into the distance. "There is nothing to worry about! It will give you a nice long life, and then another long life! Ha!" His chuckle stirred some of the long white strands of his mustache.

"Well, it's just that…Mr. Louis showed me his finger. And his leg —"

"Oh, he did? He should not have done that! He'll scare you kids! He's not the brightest of clones. He can be a little clumsy." Dr. Brown smiled again before standing up and saying, "Whelp! I'll let you get your rest. You have a big day tomorrow!"

He left and shut the door behind him. I crawled under the covers and tried to sleep, but I couldn't. I heard the branches outside the window scraping the glass, and kept thinking about being cloned. I thought about how all this time, Val wasn't really Maggie's twin, but was just a lifeless copy of her. Did that mean she wasn't a real person? I didn't want to believe it.

It felt like I lay there thinking for over an hour because I couldn't sleep. I was lying on my side facing the door because I didn't want to face the window when suddenly I saw two shadows come and stand in front of my door—two feet. I heard people whispering just on the other side of it and slammed my eyes shut since I was supposed to be asleep.

I heard the door ease open and one person—probably Dr. Brown—whisper to someone else, "Good, he's asleep. We can take him now and do it before he wakes up and tries to fight us."

Another shiver ran down my spine. I wasn't so sure I wanted to be cloned anymore, even if it would make me live longer. Their footsteps drew closer to my bed and I had to make a decision. I shoved the covers down and looked up, seeing a momentary shock on Dr. Brown's face. I ran over to the window and yanked it open. I reached out, grabbed a branch and climbed onto the tree. After shimmying a few feet away from the window, I looked back to see Dr. Brown leaning his head out the window with his hands on the pane.

In a soothing voice, he called to me, "Where are you going, Tim? What's all this about?"

"I don't want to be cloned!" I yelled back. I saw a light in the next room turn on.

"Well why don't you come back here and we can talk about it?"

"No! I don't want my body to fall apart!" Dr. Brown turned to look at the other person in the room, whom I couldn't see. At that, I crawled further along the branch and climbed down the tree to the ground. It was fall, so the temperature wasn't freezing cold but I was chilly in my pajama shirt and shorts.

I started running away from the office building back up the road we had come down.

Behind me, Dr. Brown yelled, "Timothy! I assure you, there is nothing to fear! Timothy!"

I was surrounded by a dark forest on all sides and I heard a door slam open behind me. I was terrified of the woods, but didn't have an option. I turned to the right and ran into the forest. I went about twenty feet from the road and dropped to the leaf-covered ground.

A moment later I watched Dr. Brown and Mr. Henry run past me, saying something about me running back to town. I didn't know how far the town was, but decided I had to get there and find someone to help me. Even my own parents wouldn't help because they were the ones who brought me here to be cloned in the first place!

A few minutes later, the adults jogged back to the office building and I heard them talking about getting a car to get to the town.

Minutes after that, Dr. Brown's MG sped past me and I came out of the forest. I followed in the direction of the car to the town. I was barefoot on the pavement and kept hoping I wouldn't step on anything sharp.

It felt like forever, but the running warmed me up. I wasn't cold after ten minutes, and lights from the distant town slowly came into view. I went down a hill and up another one, and over the top of the second hill, I could make out buildings in the darkness. As I got closer, I found most of them to be homes where people were asleep.

I ran a few more blocks and found the main street. I looked around for the police station, and eventually found it. There was a light inside, so I ran over to the door and pushed. It was locked, so I knocked and breathed a sigh of relief when I heard footsteps behind the door.

A chubby middle-aged cop opened the door and looked down at me. "You must be Tim," he said in an annoyed tone of voice.

"Yes I...wait, how did you know?"

"Did you run away from Dr. Brown's office?" he said flatly.

I hesitated.

Dr. Brown must have come here first looking for me. Before I could respond, the policeman grabbed my arm and pulled me inside. He dragged me over to his desk and picked up the phone, still squeezing my arm.

"Dr. Brown?" he said into the receiver after a moment. "Yah, he's here. I have him...uh-huh...bye." The fat policeman then turned to me and angrily said, "You little brat. You don't know how lucky you are. My wife and I have been waiting for years to get in with Dr. Brown. We just don't have enough money, and on top of that, the waiting list is huge. Why did you run away from him?"

I was still trying to catch my breath after running more than a mile, but didn't want to say anything to this cop. He was on Dr. Brown's side and wanted to give me back to him to be cloned.

Rather than answer him, I yanked my arm out of his chubby fingers and ran for the door. Before I could open it, he was after me and grabbed me around the torso. I kicked as he picked me up and carried me back to the desk.

"It's gonna be like that, huh?" he grunted. He held me with one hand and reached into his belt pouch with the other, producing his silver handcuffs. They obviously hadn't been used much in this small town. He put one link around my wrist and the other through a ring screwed into his desk. I couldn't go anywhere now. I would be cloned and there was nothing I could do about it.

Eventually Dr. Brown came through the door, looking less friendly than before.

"Thanks for grabbing him, Ted," Dr. Brown said to the officer.

"No problem," replied Ted. Suddenly he was a lot nicer to the doctor.

Back at the offices, my entire family had been woken up by all the commotion. When Dr. Brown and Miss Aylor walked me in, once more squeezing my arms, my parents gave me a very disappointed look.

"What was that all about?" my dad asked angrily. Then, to the doctor, "I'm so sorry about this, Dr. Brown. Thank you for your help."

"It's no trouble really," said the doctor wearily. "Why don't we get him in the chamber now so he doesn't have time to pull another Harry Houdini? He's a bit worked up about the procedure so let's get it over with."

"Sure, doctor," replied my mother, "Whatever you think is best."

"Great, let's head back to the chamber and I'll get things in order." We all walked back into the room with the couches, but this time Dr. Brown went past them and opened the blank white door at the far side of the room. Inside looked mostly empty; there was a control panel and a carpeted floor. The patient was expected to simply go in, stand in the closet-sized room, and emerge with their new clone. Dr. Brown went in and I watched him make some adjustments to switches and panels and knobs.

A few minutes later, he reemerged and looked at me, standing with my entire family. "Okay," he said, "everything is ready. Once you shut this door, you'll be on your way to having a clone of your own! You won't feel anything and it'll just take a couple minutes. Go ahead and step on in."

I was on my way to a lifetime of pain and who knows what else, in addition to making a clone who would be in even worse pain. This whole cloning thing was brand new and I didn't want to be a guinnea pig.

I thought quickly.

Val was standing right next to me staring vacantly into the white room. I grabbed her arm, pulled her forward, then shoved her back so she tumbled into the chamber and I slammed the door behind her. It happened too fast for my parents or the doctor to react. Under the door, I saw flashes of light. I turned back and saw the faces of my parents and Dr. Brown in shock. They didn't know what to say or do.

Seconds later, we heard Valerie begin to moan behind the door. At first it was a low groan, but it grew into a panicked shriek.

Then she screamed several times, horrid, toe-curling screams of agony.

Then two full minutes after it had begun it was done. The lights under the door were off and Val was silent. I looked at Dr. Brown and he broke the long silence.

"We...we've never cloned a clone," he stammered. "We don't know what it would do. It's like making a copy of a blank video tape. I-I don't think anything would happen."

"Do they always scream like that??" my mother asked, panicked.

The doctor quietly looked at his shoes for a moment, then replied, "No...no they don't."

He then stepped forward and opened the door. My sister Valerie was lying on the ground. She lay on her side, facing away from us, breathing shallowly in her nightgown. Dr. Brown walked in and bent down next to her and helped her sit up.

I almost fainted when I saw her.

Her skin was gray and flaky, like dry ash clinging to a log after a fire. Before, she had looked like a normal 15-year-old girl, but now her face was aged and wrinkled like an old woman. She had long, curly gray hairs mixed in with her brown hair and eyebrows.

The worst part, though, was her eyes. They were pale gray like her skin and seemed to be unseeing as she stared out into the distant void. Suddenly I regretted shoving her into the chamber.

Even though she was just a clone, she was still a part of our family.

Valerie suddenly started groping around like a dog who just caught a scent, seemingly unaware the doctor was beside her on the ground, holding her. She crawled forward toward the rest of our family. No one moved. We hadn't seen her this animated in her entire life. She seemed to be terrified of something none of us could see. Or maybe it was the doctor she feared.

Valerie paused, looked back over her shoulder at the doctor, and continued crawling toward my parents. They were scared now too, and took a step back from her. Even Maggie was silent. Valerie reached my parents' legs and collapsed again on the floor.

"Where does the clone come out?" my father demanded.

"Normally," replied the doctor, "we open the door and both of them are in here. I've never seen this before. We've never tried to clone a clone before..." He was still on the floor of the chamber room, looking deflated and trying to think.

Val continued lying on the floor at the feet of my parents. Her body rose and fell in short, shallow gasps like an ashen fish lying on the beach. Then she began to speak. Her voice was now lower, raspy, glottal. She sounded like a human if you sucked all the moisture out of its body.

"Stop...them," she gasped. Her tired muscles hoisted her up so she lay prone, resting on her straight arms, and she turned her head back toward the chamber, as if a bear were coming out of it and she couldn't get away.

Then, before our eyes, we saw sores begin to materialize on her legs, just like the ones on Louis'. She screamed again, as if her legs were being burnt with an invisible hot iron. Her body convulsed and she seized. No one in the room knew what to do.

She was still for a second before pushing herself up the rest of the way and stood on her feet as if nothing had happened. The sores were still sitting on her gray skin, but she was suddenly calm. She looked around her, making eye contact with everyone in the room like a normal human being.

"You can't see them, can you?" she asked my mother in a newly calm voice. It was utterly unlike the Valerie I had known all my life.

"S-see what, sweetheart?" asked my mother.

"*Them*," replied Valerie, pointing toward the cloning chamber. We all looked, but still saw nothing in the room except the doctor—but she wasn't pointing at him.

A shiver ran down my spine. I got the urge to run again, but I didn't know where. The police were essentially governed by this doctor, the cloning magician, and no one here could help me. I could run into my room and lock the door, but that wouldn't last long. Regardless, I couldn't rip my eyes off the new Valerie. Her gray skin continued drifting off of her like ashy dandruff, but she didn't notice.

Suddenly, she looked at Maggie.

"Maggie," she said slowly, clearly. But Maggie didn't even look at her. It was as if Maggie didn't even know Val was in the room with us; she was staring at the open cloning chamber, looking confused.

"Maggie," Valerie said again.

"Are you going to answer her??" I yelled at Maggie after another long pause.

"Answer who?" replied Maggie.

I looked at my parents, hoping someone could make sense of what was happening.

"Valerie!" I said. "Are you going to answer her?"

"What do you mean?" Maggie asked. "Where did she go?"

"She's right in front of you," our father said. "Don't...don't you see her?"

In that moment we all realized that Maggie couldn't see Valerie. Everyone else could, except Maggie. Another cold shiver ran down my spine and I tucked my hands into the sleeves of my sweater.

I looked at the doctor, who seemed as baffled as the rest of us.

My father turned to him and demanded, "What is going on here?"

Dr. Brown had risen to his feet and now stood with his hand on his chin. He rubbed it and then said, "I don't know. I have never seen this before. I'm thinking through…" his thought trailed off.

Maggie observed what was happening and began to get more panicked. "Wait," she started, her eyes wide, "what's going on? Where is Val?"

Dr. Brown spoke up again, almost to himself. "Well, cloning is essentially recreating the body but without the soul…cloning a clone must have sucked out even the little soul that was in Val… but why can't Maggie see her?"

I watched in horror as Valerie took three small steps toward where Maggie was standing and reached her hand out to touch Maggie's arm.

Dr. Brown saw this happening, but spoke up too late, "Wait! Don't—"

Maggie suddenly screamed in pain and jerked her body backward, as if she was now the one being prodded with a hot iron. She grabbed her arm where Valerie had touched her. When she pulled her hand back, she saw a sore just like the ones on Val. She looked fearfully at my parents, searching for some type of answer. Her eyes were begging, *Who hurt me? Why am I hurt?*

Then she collapsed, unconscious from the pain.

"Maggie!" my mother surged forward and wrapped her arms around my sister's unconscious body.

Valerie then turned her gray eyes toward me, no longer looking innocent, but malicious. She began slowly walking toward me and I instinctively took a step backward. Then another as she got closer.

"What happened to our daughters??" my mother screamed at Dr. Brown. The doctor shook his head as he began slowly taking steps backward toward the front entryway. Three steps later, he turned and ran out the front door. Miss Aylor ran after him, and it appeared that they would not be coming back.

This left my parents, my sister and me with the *thing* that used to be my sister Valerie. Was she a ghost? Was I seeing a phantom?

Valerie had been distracted by the departure of Dr. Brown and Miss Aylor, but she now returned her attention to me. She stood two yards from me, and began speaking in the eerily calm voice. "Timothy," she said.

"Wh-what?" I managed to get out, on the verge of also running away.

"Do you see them?" she responded. She was still calm. She seemed to be asking out of curiosity, not panic or fear.

"See who?" I asked.

"All of them...all of us," she answered, seeming to speak in slow, poetic stanzas.

> "They are everywhere.
> They are beautiful."

"Who are you talking about, sweetheart?" my father asked her.

"All of us.
We are all here and we are golden,
sparkling like the stars."

My fear was momentarily replaced by confusion. I looked at my father's face, which seemed equally puzzled. Maggie was still unconscious.

Valerie continued:

"We are all the ones from the machine.
We drift out of you."

"Valerie," my father asked her directly, "are you saying you're a...a ghost or a spirit?"

"We are the pieces you've left behind.
We are the tunnels left by the worms;
the footprints of your souls."

"Okay...so what can we do for you, hon?"

Valerie was silent and looked around at her family. Her gaze went from me, over to my father, then to my mother who was still holding Maggie's unconscious body.

"Meet me in the deep," Valerie said plainly.

"The deep?" I asked.

"The others are coming for you.
They are not happy about

what you've taken from them.
Shells of husks
and husks of shells.
Even air has mass.
I now weigh 21 grams
but I'm gaining fast..."

My father and I exchanged another puzzled glance, and before we could respond, Valerie turned and walked back to the cloning chamber. She grabbed the door as she entered it, closing it behind her. Now my father and I instinctively took a couple steps toward the door, curiously waiting to see what happened. The same lights flashed beneath the door, but this time there were no screams from the chamber. It was almost silent, only emitting a machine-like hum.

The lights stopped and the room fell completely silent. We were frozen in time as a minute passed. Then nearly another one before my father stepped forward and opened the door. He eased it open with his body angled as far away from it as possible, as if a tiger would leap out and tackle him to the ground. He peeked inside and his body seemed to relax. Then he pulled the door open all the way.

The room was empty.

Right then Maggie screamed.

My father and I spun our heads toward her as she screamed a second time from my mother's arms. Maggie was holding her head as if a hornet was trapped inside her skull, jerking her back and forth.

My mother looked at my father and yelled, "What is this?? What did we do??"

My father knelt next to Maggie and put his hand on her shoulder. "It's okay, sweetheart. We are both right here."

She continued writhing in pain and turning back and forth. I wondered where Valerie had gone. Did she return to Maggie? Did she finally reverse the cloning process?

Maggie screamed for several more minutes before gradually calming down. She was crying, but no longer hysterical.

If you were to walk into the room at that moment, you wouldn't find anything too peculiar. You'd see two parents and two children; both parents comforting the one crying child while I stood a few feet away.

And that's how life would be from then on: two children and two parents living out a normal life.

At least, that's how it appeared from the outside.

We drove home that night, not wanting to spend another night in Crum Hill. The doctor and Miss Aylor never returned to the office, which was abandoned as of that night. I heard that the building was shuttered and descended into disrepair. I never found out where they absconded to, but never bothered trying to find out.

We never saw Val again either.
At least, my parents and I didn't.
It was Maggie who had the dreams.

For months following our visit to Crum Hill, Maggie woke up screaming every night. Often multiple times a night. They were so frequent that I eventually got used to waking up to her blood-curdling wails and then falling right back asleep.

She would often tell me about the dreams.

She was deep underwater. Or, that's the closest comparison she could make. Wherever it was, it was deep and weightless and dark. The air—or water, or whatever it was she was submerged in—was all-encompassing.

She could try to swim to the surface but there was no surface in sight. Rather than fish swimming around her, there were people. Except they didn't seem like bodies; they seemed like the absence of bodies. They were human-shaped shadows floating in the depths all around her. They were pockets of air, or the absence of matter, shaped like people.

> Shells of husks
> or husks of shells.

At the end of every dream, said Maggie, she saw Valerie. Val was floating near her but facing away, and Maggie would call out to her. Every time, when Valerie turned around, it was the gray, ashen face that she saw. The same eyes with their flat, gray surfaces met Maggie's and Valerie began 'swimming' toward her.

Suffocated and claustrophobic by the deep, Maggie tried to get away, but could barely move through the suspension. The substance didn't seem to affect Val like Maggie; she cut through it like a knife.

As Valerie moved closer to her, she reached out her sore-ridden arms and said,

> "Join me in the deep.
> You'll sink and become golden
> like us."

Maggie woke up screaming at the same time every night—right when Valerie touched her forearm. Right where her scar persisted, no matter how she and my parents tried to get rid of it.

Years passed and Maggie's nighttime screams spread out more and more. It reduced to once a night, then to every other night, then once a week.

Now we're adults and Maggie still has the dream.

"It's strange," she told me at coffee one morning when we were in our thirties. "I get older but Valerie stays the same age. She hasn't changed. Nothing about the dream has changed.

Maggie took a sip of her latte, accidentally showcasing the wound which still looked as fresh as it did 20 years ago.

"Does that hurt?" I asked her, nodding to the sore.

"Only at night," she answered. "Only when she touches it."

We were both silent for a moment until Maggie said, "You know what the strangest part is?"

"What?"

"I think that when I first had the dream, I was closer to the surface. I think we get a little deeper every night, Val and I... There are always a few more people—or shells of people [she chuckled at this]—above us than below. We are always getting deeper and deeper. Farther from the surface. Eventually I guess I'll have to join her at the bottom."

I was silent and looked at my sister as if she was a homeless person spouting off drug-fueled nonsense. She didn't notice, but continued on as if it were completely logical and coherent.

> "We're becoming golden, Tim!" she smiled.
> "We really are.
> Val and I are really close now.
> We're almost there."

9. The Thinkers

The Thinkers, they think.

That is their job,

and that is all they do.

They never move

or have ideas.

Never do they speak,

and never do they sleep.

The Thinkers think,

and that is all.

They never eat

or drink.

Never do they make merry,

laugh, cry, or excrete.

The Thinkers, they think.

Thinking is their job,

and they are good at what they do.

The Thinkers, they think

and that is all.

10. The Price is Right

The Careys had spent months searching for an apartment in the city. After sleeping on friends' floors from July through the beginning of September, they were ready to have a home of their own. Their friends had been more than welcoming, but the search was growing tiresome.

"Hon..." said Owen from the couch one night as he scrolled through the online listings once more, "Hon, there's one in Lakevi-...oh wait, nevermind." The white glow of the screen lit up his glasses as he sat in the near darkness of another friend's apartment.

"Owen, let's go to bed," said Mal from the doorway. She looked endearingly at her husband and sighed with a sympathetic smile. "Come on, you've been looking for hours."

She crossed the wooden floor to sit on the couch by him. The old boards creaked beneath her bare feet. Mal put her chin on

Owen's shoulder but his eyes remained on the screen.

"Just one more..." he muttered, half to her and half to himself. "Mal, what do you think of this one in Wicker? It looks really good on here, but..." His voice trailed off as he scanned the glowing page. His eyes were sore. "But the price—that can't be right?" His thick brows elevated.

"That looks nice, Owe. Come, let's go to bed." She reached across his lap and slowly pulled the top of the screen closed.

"Alright," said Owen. "That last one looked really good. Let's check it out tomorrow."

"Oh, I have that thing with Beth tomorrow, but you go! Go look at it for us." Then, as she stood up, almost to herself she added, "hope I don't have that dream again tonight." They rose to walk to the guest room. Owen rubbed his tight neck; he didn't realize he had been hunched over so long.

Owen and Mal had moved to Chicago four months after they were married. Both were from Arizona, he from Flagstaff and she from Phoenix. Their wedding was beautiful and lush. They were beautiful. They had moved to Chicago so his web design business could finally get off the ground, and she could connect with the fitness community in Chicago.

Malorie was a marathoner. She was the fastest female at Phoenix U, but nowadays running was just a hobby. For a brief time before meeting Owen, she had tried to launch her own line of snacks for runners that replaced electrolytes and boosted energy called Malorie's Calories.

When the idea failed, she went by Mal.

The next day Owen and his friend David drove to Wicker Park to look at the house. It was situated just four blocks north of Six Points, Wicker's central hub, in a beautiful lane of multi-styled homes lined with green trees and brick sidewalks. Every house appeared to have been designed by a different architect, presenting the eclectic appearance of a giant mosaic. The house was in the center of the block, edged on one side by a very postmodern glass house, and a tall brown brick home on the other.

The house itself was nice enough. It boasted no spectacular features compared to the rest on the block, but it was beautiful in its own humble respect. Whitewashed wood paneling fronted it, with green trim and a red brick base.

"Wow," said Owen, looking over the building the way a child stands before a bakery window with his finger on his lip. "I seriously can't figure out why the price is so low."

Dave had accompanied Owen on a number of house hunts since he had arrived in the city. "Let's look at the inside," he sighed. "Maybe that'll explain it."

They ascended the steps and knocked on the green door. Getting a closer view of the house only made it more appealing to Owen. A relatively well-kept garden sat just below the front windows on either side of the front porch where a smattering of colorful flowers were in late-summer bloom.

The door opened and a woman in her northern sixties appeared behind it. She smiled gently as her bright green eyes welcomed the men.

"You must be Owen," she said, extending a small shriveled hand. Her skin was soft and cool. When she smiled, her lips dug deep into her cheeks. She told them her name was Ava.

"Please, come in," she said, stepping back from the door and opening it wider.

"Oh, thank you," said Owen.

"Can I get you anything?" she asked over her shoulder as she walked back toward the kitchen.

"Uhm. No ma'am, we're fine," he called back as they entered, scanning the interior of the house. It was small enough to be cozy but large enough to host substantial get-togethers. Dave and Owen both took turns throwing out courteous questions to show their interest, but Owen had already made up his mind. The worn white walls and hardwood flooring added character, and the location was ideal.

"It's all so great," said Owen after Ava had shown them throughout the entire building, "but if I may ask, is there a reason the price is so low? I mean..."

Ava looked at the ground and for a moment, her warm

demeanor dropped. Half a second later, she looked back up and smiled wearily. Her eyes suddenly seemed like they were a foot inside her head as she spoke through the forced grin.

"No reason," she nearly whispered, pushing her well-worn dimples back into her cheeks. And after a moment, "I'm just ready to move on, get somewhere quieter. Out of the city." She turned and walked back to the kitchen. "Please, look around all you want, gentlemen," she called back through the door.

The next day, Owen parked the car in the nearest spot he could find, two blocks away, and he and Mal walked to the house. He hopped alongside her, still reeling with disbelief that he had finally found their home. They were three houses away when Mal's pace slowed.

When Owen looked at her, her eyes were wide and her feet were dragging.

"Mal?" he said, "Everything alright?"

She paused for a moment. "Owe, this may sound crazy, but you have to believe me."

He nodded, encouraging her to go on, thoroughly confused.

"You know that dream I've been telling you about? The one I have a couple times a week?"

"Yah." He wished he had listened better when she had described it.

"I think this is the street from my dream. I know it sounds crazy, Owe, but I've seen this street before. Exactly like this, as it is today. Sometimes it's night, but also like this."

Owen was nodding sympathetically.

"And, I always walk up to that house over there."

Owen froze.

She was pointing to the house.

Their house.

"What happens then?" he asked.

"Well, I knock on the door, and then wait. Right when the door begins to open, I wake up."

Owen felt his neck tense again as a dozen invisible spiders crawled down his spine. He tried to brush off the whole thing, hoping it was mere coincidence.

They eventually walked to the door, knocked, and Ava answered with a big, wrinkled smile.

"You must be Mal!" she cried, reaching up to embrace her. Ava exhaled, realizing there was nothing to fear behind the door.

It must be a coincidence.

Ava and Owen walked Mal through the whole house, with Owen showing her every unique feature and special corner of the building. He was excited as a boy showing off the features of his new bike.

By the end of the tour, Mal had nearly forgotten her dream and had been swept away by the whimsical interior of the property.

On the drive home, Mal asked why the price was so low.

"That's exactly what I asked her," replied Owen. "I guess it's just her time to move on and she's in kind of a rush to get out of the city." He chuckled, "I guess at that age, you need to make decisions a bit quicker."

His wife elbowed him while he drove.

The next weekend the papers were signed and they moved in. By the first night, boxes littered every room and their bed was a bare queen sized mattress lying on the ground. They were exhausted.

Mal went to the bedroom while Owen got some work done on the computer. He had already made a few connections in the city, and business was quickly picking up. He was good at what he did.

About an hour later, a knock at the door punched through the stillness of the night. Owen looked at the clock in the corner of the screen and shook his head. It was almost eleven. Muttering under his breath, he pushed himself up onto his feet and walked to the door. He fidgeted with the locks. When he got it open, he looked out on the porch and no one was there. He leaned out the doorway and looked up and down the street.

He shook his head and closed the door. "Kids," he muttered to himself. And then, "old lady couldn't take a joke."

The next morning Owen told Mal about the prank.

"It's no big deal," she said, smiling and smacking his arm. "They're just welcoming the new people. We're like the new kids! We'll meet them soon and it won't happen again! Lighten up!" She laughed. Mal finished her breakfast and left for an interview with a gym a few blocks from the house.

The next few days blurred together as the two of them unpacked their belongings and filled in the barren places in the house. Mal got the job and Owen began catching cabs down to the Loop several days a week to meet with new clients.

Two weeks later, they were both asleep when there was another knock on the door. Neither one stirred for a moment until the knock came again, louder.

"Mm-I'll get it," slurred Mal as she threw her long legs off the bed and stood up. After wrapping her robe around her pajamas, she shuffled to the door and looked outside.

No one was there.

Mal froze as she fully woke up and remembered.

She had been having the dream again.

11. The Event

The city began preparing for the event months in advance. They didn't know what to expect, but they knew it would be big.

In the weeks leading up to it, I saw porta-potties hauled in by the thousands to line the streets which would soon be filled with people. The city called for street vendors and food trucks to come from everywhere in a 500-mile radius to ensure there would be enough food to feed the masses. Security was assigned and I saw men armed with giant assault rifles sweeping the street days before the event.

In a way, the event began before the scheduled date because so many people had come to the city early. Food trucks opened their windows and the streets were swarmed. The mayor had instructed people to avoid congregating on the street until it officially began, but when police officers tried to enforce this, the masses won. They couldn't fight the crowd.

The Saturday after the event began (It started on a Friday night) I was in the street enjoying the festivities. Street performers gathered crowds around themselves and smells from the exotic food trucks filled my nostrils. My mother had been sick for many years, so she remained back in our small apartment while I wandered the streets. She used to worry about her middle schooler wandering the streets alone, but that was months ago. She doesn't bat an eye when I head out the door now.

When I came upon the scene, a sea of unfamiliar faces met me. There were so many of them it was nearly impossible to discern one from another without intensely focusing on one at a time. With a general sweep, I just saw thousands of dotted eyes and noses and mouths, moving braille dots, all walking and breathing and looking around at the city streets I'd known my whole life.

They were not all walking in the same direction, however. Some walked toward me from the North, others from the South. None of them seemed to be heading toward one main event, so I wasn't sure exactly which way to go. *Where is this thing?*

I looked up my street and then down to try to see where the event was, but neither direction proved more interesting than the other.

I decided to walk North to try to find something unusual happening. As I passed by the blocks, it seemed to neither get more crowded or less crowded, just the same continual sea of people moving with me. Some walked up to food trucks and vendors to make purchases. Some stopped to watch street performers, and others kept on moving at the same steady pace.

As I got further from home, I decided to turn around and see if the South would be more eventful. I walked on the other side of the sidewalk in the opposite direction. I passed our apartment building and kept walking.

The South proved to be the same as the North. People continued walking, looking, stopping, and buying without thinning.

I tapped the arm of a man walking next to me. "Where is the event supposed to be?"

He looked back at me. He was a middle aged man with a white mustache.

He smiled and shrugged, "I wish I could tell you. That's what I'm looking for too! They didn't do a great job of directing us to it!" He turned and resumed walking and I soon lost him in the crowd.

I walked further South, thinking it surely must be in Hyde Park. Although if this many people tried to fit into that park, it would soon overflow. The mayor had promised that this event would fill the city, so maybe it was bigger than a single park could fit.

I decided to walk to the clearing anyway to see if maybe there was a smaller event happening there, and at the very least, to get into more of an opening and feel less walled-in by these buildings.

I continued a half mile to the park, and along the way had a realization. It was odd to me that there were this many people, yet no one was pushing or shoving each other. Everyone moved at a reasonable pace and the number of pedestrian traffic jams was far lower than I would have predicted. The crowd just flowed along.

The park came into view from atop a gentle hill and from my slightly elevated position, I could see down into it. It was full of people, just as the sidewalks were, only none of them were moving. The people in the park were all standing still, waiting and looking around.

As I got closer though, I noticed that none of them were looking in the same direction. They faced every possible direction and looked, up, down and straight ahead.

When I entered the park, I found some children playing around a tree. I watched them for a second. After a few laps of chasing each other around the tree, they ran over to their mother and tugged on her shirt. "When will it begin?" they cried up to her. "We're booored."

The mother looked down and put her hand on their shoulders. "Soon, guys. Keep playing." The kids ran back to the tree and began to climb its limbs.

I once again surveyed the crowd in the park and tried to find a unified focus when some movement caught my eye. A boy about my own age was passing through the crowd, so I tried to follow him. He wove a dizzying trail through the standing attendees and it was hard to keep up with him.

Eventually I got close enough to call out to him. "Hey," I called. "Hey, wait up!"

The boy stopped and looked over his shoulder. Seeing I wasn't a threat, he paused and turned to face me. As I got closer, I saw that he was probably a few years older than me—high school, maybe college.

"Where are you going?" I asked him.

"What do you mean?" he replied.

"The event. Are you going to the main event?"

He chuckled and shook his head. "The event," he muttered under his breath.

"What?" I asked. "What does that mean?"

"Just..." he looked me up and down, then said, "follow me. And keep up."

He turned again and continued weaving the same haphazard trail through the standing people. I tried to keep up, but he moved quickly.

From time to time, he glanced back over his shoulder to see if I was keeping up, though I don't think he would have stopped if I wasn't.

We came to the far side of the park, and I could see the same stream of people coming and going down all the streets on that side of Hyde as well. He turned left to head East on State and I followed. As we hurried through the streets and sidewalks, I noticed people turning to look at us since we moved faster than the flow of pedestrians.

I didn't know where I was going, who I was with, or what we were up to, but I followed. He seemed to know something no one else did.

A few blocks East on State, we made a right then a left then another left and I soon lost track of where we were. He eventually turned down an alley between two buildings and for once I was out of the swarm of humans. My guide finally slowed to a walk and went halfway down the alleyway. Then he abruptly stopped and turned toward me.

"How do I know you're not one of *them*?" he grilled me.

I was lost. "One of *who*??"

He reached out and grabbed my jacket with both hands and slammed me against the wall. It happened so quickly I didn't realize what had happened until I was pinned against the cool bricks.

He barred my neck with one forearm and fished in his pocket with the other. He pulled out a drivers license (it was from out of state but I couldn't tell which one—or if it was his) and jammed it in my mouth. The wide edges of the plastic cut into the corners of my lips. He squeezed my cheeks so I felt blood peek through the broken flesh.

His face was inches from mine.

"Who are you?" he said.

I was shaking, more from fear and confusion than from pain. "Riley," I said through parted lips. "M-my name is Riley."

He kept looking straight into my eyes, breathing heavily through his nose. His eyes studied my own, bouncing back and forth from eye to eye.

After a few minutes which seemed like an hour, he pulled the card from my mouth, slicing my lips more, and pulled his forearm away from my throat.

He took three steps backward and said, "You can call me Carr." He put the license back into his pocket. "What are you doing out here?"

"I live here," I answered. "A few blocks North of Hyde. I just came out to see what all the buzz for the event was about." I paused and he was silent, as if encouraging me to keep speaking. "But...it seems like no one is going anywhere specific. No one knows where the event is. Or when it starts, or even..." I trailed off.

"What it is?" he finished my thought.

I guess I had been scared to say that out loud, mainly because I hadn't wanted to look dumb in front of my friends. But thinking back to it, no one seemed to know anything about the event, they just acted like they did.

"Yes," I said. "Do you know what it is?"

Carr breathed deeply and didn't speak for a few seconds.

"No," he finally said. "But I know whose idea it was."

The way he said it heightened the enigma behind the event. My brain flooded with questions. How could something unknown draw such enormous crowds to my home city? A city whose sidewalks were typically littered with a couple pedestrians, a few pigeons and a bum picking through the trash. How did they get so many people to flock to this town without sharing any details about the event?

"But I can't say any more here," he said after another long pause. "I never know who's listening." He looked up and down the alley. No one seemed to be paying attention to us as they passed by us on either end of the corridor, an endless flow of humanity.

Carr silently walked back to the street we had come from and I followed. He turned right, back toward Hyde Park, and began running again. I began running too. This time, however, he seemed to maneuver more deftly and quickly than before.

Five feet were between us.

Then ten, then twenty.

Then I lost him in the crowd.

"Carr!" I called out, slowing to a walk. I yelled his name again, but amidst the voracious crowd it seemed hollow and puny. I looked for him in all directions, but it was futile. The sea of faces continued rolling in every direction as people looked for the event, and Carr was gone.

I touched my hand to the corner of my lips and looked at it. The little bit of blood had already dried and sealed the wound. I decided to try to find my way back to my apartment, but didn't remember all the turns we had taken to get to the alley. I asked a few strangers how to get back to Hyde, but everyone I asked was from out of town and didn't know, sorry.

I tried asking a few more people where and when the event would begin but got the same confused answers.

I eventually found my way back home and checked on my mother. She asked me why I had blood on my face and clothes so I told her, in as few details as possible, about Carr and the myriad people walking about aimlessly. She didn't let me leave the apartment again until the event had ended.

It took at least two weeks for our city to begin to resemble the one I knew before. Trash was everywhere, and people lingered for days after the event was scheduled to end. Whatever it was, I only got to experience it from inside my apartment. When school resumed, we all tried to act like we knew what the event was, but I never really got any solid answers. Eventually the city was back to normal and life floated on as it always had.

12. The Pig Farm

The website promised 80 acres of free range woods for the hunt. The Pig Farm was located in western Pennsylvania, removed from most of the state's civilization and miles from the nearest highway.

"You kill 'em, we fill 'em" was the motto for the taxidermy portion of the farm ($500 extra per head. Not included with price of hunt).

Mac and his son Wilbur, who went by Will, arrived on Friday afternoon, per their lodging instructions. They had paid nearly two grand to come take their crack at two of the best boars in Pennsylvania. The 80-acre plot was pumped full of the finest European boars, with a minimum weight of 200 pounds.

"I haven't been to this farm since my college days," said Mac as he plopped his duffel bag and rifle on his bed. *You and what friends?* Thought Will sardonically. He had never met any of his father's college friends despite how often Mac raved about their wild weekend at the Pig Farm.

They were standing in the upper room of the wooden lodge in the northern corner of the farm. "It even still smells the same!" exclaimed Mac.

Will was a big boy, at about six and a half feet tall, he towered a full foot over his father. He had just graduated from Penn State and this was his first hunting excursion. His father had always tried to get him to go up to Pennsylvania's back country, but Will always refused. Now that he was out of college, he figured he had no excuse and agreed to come to the Pig Farm for his first experience. He figured somehow, it was more humane to kill animals bred to be hunted on the large swath of land. Or at least less dangerous for him.

A knock sounded on their thin wooden door.

"Heya, fellas," the elderly groundskeeper Marney poked his head through the open doorway. "Just wanted to let you know dinner's about ready. Head on down after you make yourselves at home," and he hobbled back down the staircase.

"That's the same guy that was here when I was here last!" exclaimed Mac. Will rolled his eyes. "He looks about the same age as last time too! They must have something in the water that makes 'em live forever here! Haha!"

"Yah, only about the 400th time you've made that joke too," Will muttered under his breath.

They went downstairs for dinner and sat with Marney and his wife Gil. Marney was explaining that they would need to be out of the lodge by 6am to get the best shot at the boars.

"Well we don't want them to be sleeping," said Mac with a mouth full of potatoes, "that would just be too easy!"

"Oh no," replied Marney. "They're up with the sun but move much slower in the morning."

An hour later the lodge was dark and quiet and Mac was making a joke about early birds and boars and worms as the two climbed under their covers.

Sunrise came much faster than Will expected and he felt several minutes of intense hatred for his father who stood beside his bed prodding him into consciousness.

After a cold breakfast of biscuits and gravy that had been left out for them, they were out in the misty morning. The translucent gray fog lay low on the tree line as they crossed from the lodge into the thick woods. It only allowed for about a ten-foot visible radius in every direction.

They crunched over the leaves and twigs on the forest floor, still damp with the morning's dew.

"You want to split up or stay together?" whispered Mac. "Your old man could give you some tips when we spot our first boar."

Will thought for a moment and replied, "Split up, maybe?" He wanted to concoct a believable reason to get away from his father for a while, so he added, "We'll have a better chance at finding one if we split up."

"Good point, Willy!" said Mac. "I'll head this way and you go that way!"

They began walking in different directions. Will dragged his feet and slowed to nearly standing still. He aimlessly moped about and wondered if his bed in the lodge would still be warm by now. He thought about how nice it would be to pull those thick wool covers back over his head and get out of the dense fog.

Will and his father had not discussed where or when to meet up again, and Wilbur was okay with that. He kept thinking about the bed in the lodge and slowly his mind began wandering to what Gil would make them for lunch. Even though they were cold, the biscuits and gravy had been delicious.

How early must they have gotten up to make them so they got cold? And where were Marney and Gil? Did they go back to bed?

Will became so lost in his thinking that he didn't realize how much time had passed until his stomach growled.

He kicked a rock and then a stick.

His stomach growled again and he looked up to realize the mist had lifted slightly. He could now see roughly 20 feet rather than 10. He had not been paying attention to where he had been walking and was not sure which way he had come from. He didn't know which way his father had gone.

"D-dad?" he croaked into the fog. Despite the few hours that had passed since sunrise, the gray Pennsylvania brume had kept the atmosphere dim, as if it were stalled at twilight for a full 14 hours.

A streak of fear trickled down his spine as Will realized he did not even know the way back to the lodge. He felt his hands slip along the rifle as his palms began to sweat.

A twig snapped several yards into the mist.

He spun and pointed his rifle toward the sound.

"Dad?" he tried again. Nothing answered him but silence and the hollow *wooshing* sound of the forest which had been present since daybreak.

He heard more footsteps in the direction of the broken twig. A moment later he could clearly make out the rapid trot of a boar. His chest quaked, which rippled out to his arms. His rifle quivered as he held it in the direction of the animal.

Suddenly he remembered he hadn't switched off the safety, so he looked at the side of the gun and fumbled with the weapon until he slid over the small lever. When he looked back up, the boar was less than ten feet in front of him and charging.

He fired without aiming and the rifle punched him in the shoulder so hard he tripped and fell backward over a small fallen tree. He had skimmed the boar along the side but it continued at him. His rifle lay five feet from him. Will scrambled for it and right when his fingers grazed the barrel, the boar bit into his calf. He kicked his legs and continued scrambling for the gun.

He got it into his hands and grappled it against his shoulder.

He took aim and fired.

The bullet went into the boar's skull but it kept tearing at his calf.

Will cocked again and fired another round into the animal's head.

It kicked violently and released his leg. He cocked once more, fired, and the animal went still.

The muffled hum of the forest returned.

For a few moments, Will wished he had listened when his father taught him about moving an animal once he'd killed it.

Then the pain set in as the shock wore off.

Will curled into a ball and slowly reached down to touch his shredded calf. He flinched and recoiled his hand when he felt his finger go inside his skin where the teeth had pulled the flesh back.

"Daaaaaaad," he called out in a low guttural moan. "Daaaad."

Nothing in the forest moved. Will could only see a small collection of trees and the dead boar lying bloodied next to him before the fog swallowed the world.

He looked around but nothing moved. There was not even a breeze to move the limbs of the trees.

"M...Marneyyy," he cried. Not a second later he heard footsteps in the fog. "Hello?" Will stammered.

"Heya, Wilbur," came a voice from the fog. It was Marney. He materialized from the wall of mist with a walking stick in his hand.

"How did you find me so fast?"

Marney ignored the question and said, "Oh, he got you!" when he saw Will on the ground. He was barely concerned or enthused. The old man walked closer and bent over to look at Will's leg. "Yeh. Same thing happened to your father."

"M-my father?" Will felt the blood in his veins stop.

"Oh yah, your dad got bit too. I found him a bit ago not far from here. In fact..." Marney reached over and lifted the dead boar's ear from its shattered skull. He ran his hand along the boar's side and examined its hide. "I think you may have got 'im!"

Will froze. His pain had gone from fear to confusion. He went to speak but only a low snort came out.

"Oh, look, you're turning too! Ha!" The old man slapped his knee and stared at Will's face with half a smile creeping onto his face. "Oh yah, it's a-comin'."

With some of his last remaining human thoughts, Will realized why he had never met his father's college friends from this hunt.

They must have been bitten as well, only to be killed by more successful hunters. Maybe even by his own father.

"You know," said Marney as a mist began to roll over Will's eyeballs, "I overheard what your father said last night. There *is* something in the water here. It's kept Gil and I kickin' for forever! An' it means these here boars ain't your every day boars neither. They's special. One bite from them and they'll turn you into one of them! Your daddy was one of the few dumb ones who didn't even realize what happened to his pals! And you know what else?" he smiled and leaned close to Wilbur whose hoofed feet had healed and begun to kick. "We don't feed our hogs here. That's why they's so hungry all the time!" He sat back on his feet and laughed.

Marney hoisted himself back up with his walking stick. He began dragging Mac away by his hind leg and as he hobbled away, he said over his shoulder, "And you's a big one too! Whoever gets you's gonna be one happy camper!"

Then he vanished into the mist.

Wilbur kicked until he rolled his fat tubular body onto his hoofs and trotted off into the mist.

13. Bed of Towels

1. Bed of Towels

I woke up before the dawn because my feet were cold and damp. The pile of towels on top of me kept sliding off rather than falling into place, meaning parts of me were too warm and others were too cold.

The bed I sleep on is towels too. Everything is towels and everything is damp.

"Hey."

I looked down at my toe and said hi to it. Not all of my toes, just the one sticking out of the hole in my sock. I'm alone down here so I often need to speak to things to keep from going crazy.

As the sleep drifted off of my eyebrows, I sat up and listened to the day. Just like every day, I saw the green splotch on the wall where water always slowly runs down it. The walls are concrete and the floor is concrete and I don't know what the ceiling is made of, but I have a long fluorescent light to illuminate my room.

There used to be two light bulbs next to each other, but one has died so now it's just her sister that gives me light. It always hums and there are always little shadows running up and down the tube like an army of ants. I don't know what they are. Sometimes I wish the light would just be solid because the flickering gives me a headache sometimes, but it also gives her a little personality.

I'm on my pile of towels and there is a door without a handle and also my books. I keep them on the far side of the room so the green splotch water doesn't ruin them. One night I fell asleep reading a book and it fell to the floor and got ruined by the water over night. Now I make sure not to fall asleep reading anymore so I don't lose any more books.

Mr. White tells me not to cry.

He is the one who brings my food and takes my potty bucket and also gives me helpful rules for living my life. He says I have potential and if I am disciplined and work hard and, most importantly, follow all his rules, I can do anything I want in life.

I sit on my towel bed a bit longer, enjoying the dripping sound on green splotch and looking around my room. I don't get as lonely as I used to. It used to hurt a lot to be alone so much. I eventually got used to it though and came to appreciate the silence. Mr. White tells me that outside, a lot of kids my age are glued to their music and TV shows and can't just enjoy the silence and their own thoughts.

I never know when Mr. White will show up, but I feel my stomach gurgling within me and hope he comes soon.

There are always footsteps upstairs. Throughout the day I often hear voices, but can't make out any words they are saying. I hear the static sounds of machines, but I don't know what they do.

I was young when I came here. I have hazy memories of the world outside my room, but I lose some every day. I remember my mother holding me, and I also remember her yelling a lot. I don't remember my father. I asked Mr. White about this one time, and he said I am your father now, don't worry. Then he told me not to cry.

He always says that, even if I'm not about to cry.

Finally, I hear footsteps coming down the stairs and then I hear the clicking of the door.

"Good morning!" said Mr. White with a smile. He had a brown paper bag in his hand, and he brought it over to my towel bed. "I have some rolls and Pop-Tarts for you," He reached into the bag and pulled out a clear bag of rolls and a box that said TOASTER BRAND on it.

"Why do you call them Pop-Tarts if the box says something different?" I asked him.

He didn't answer, he just ripped the bottom of the box open and shook out two of the foil-wrapped packages. "It's, uhh..."

he started. "These are better than Pop-Tarts! Yah, these are the nice ones that everyone wants. Pop-Tarts are the cheaper, more common ones so that's what everyone calls them."

This made me excited. I knew Mr. White always took good care of me.

"What are we going to do today?" I asked him. Some days he took me out of my room and we got to do fun things outside. One time we walked in a forest, and another time we went to the city. For some reason, he always blindfolds me when we leave the room until we get where we're going. Then he takes it off. He says it's because he doesn't want me to see where I live. He didn't really say why though.

"Well," he said, "unfortunately, I am busy with work today. The machines are running a lot today and we have a lot of guests coming in upstairs. So I need to take care of them."

He said that most days. I still got my hopes up every day, just in case we did something different.

"Sorry, Sam," he said quietly. He knew it had been a while since I had gone out. "But I tell you what! Maybe I'll go out and get you a new book today...if I have time."

That *did* get me excited! I love new books.

Mr. White stood up as he folded the brown paper bag. "I'll see you in a few hours, Sam. And remember, no crying."

"Okay," I said.

He paused at the door and turned back. "And Sam, today let's not sing either. Or talk to anyone. These floors are thin so people can hear you. I don't want to disturb my important guests today." He smiled, then quickly turned and walked out the door without a handle.

2. The Special Day

"Hi, splot—" I started to talk to the green splotch but then caught myself. Mr. White had told me not to talk to anyone today and I always followed his rules. I got up from my bed of towels and took a few steps to my book pile.

I decided to look at the one with the trees and the dog on the cover, I liked that one. I liked to look at the pictures, but don't know how to understand the letters around them. I carried it back to my bed and put two of the white towels over my legs, then the book on top of the towels, then opened a bag of Pop-Tarts to eat while I read.

I liked this book because the dog goes through a bunch of different places, and it reminds me of when Mr. White takes me out to go to different places. I ask him a lot of questions when we are out, but then he tells me not to ask questions.

The lightbulb flickered and made it hard to concentrate on my pictures. I normally can concentrate just fine, but today my mind kept wandering upstairs and I wondered what was happening today that was so special.

Mr. White said today is a special day. Soon I began to hear more voices upstairs. I also heard the machines in the ceiling start to run more than usual. They turned on, making their loud solid noises, and didn't stop like they normally do.

I stood up to finish my Pop-Tart, pacing around my room and eating it. I was thinking in my head all of the things I wanted to say out loud to the things in my room. There are some pipes on the ceiling that make a lot of noise. There is also a dead plant in a pot in the corner. I think Mr. White was trying to make me feel like I was in the forest with the plant, but it died after a few days. There are no windows down here, and that's why I like to go outside with Mr. White so much.

I wait until Mr. White comes back with my lunch. My brain just won't sit still today, so I paced around my room for a long time. I listened to the hum of my fluorescent lightbulb and the voices of men upstairs and the booming and clicking of the machines.

But then, when I expected Mr. White to come back with my lunch, he didn't come. Instead, I heard the voices yelling louder than they usually do and then I heard even louder clicks and booms. They didn't sound like the normal machine sounds, so I began to get scared.

The yelling went on for several minutes and didn't stop. I ran to my bed of towels and pulled several over me. I didn't take the time to cover myself neatly either, I just plopped them on top of me and I'm sure some of my toes were sticking out.

Finally, as the yelling continued, I heard footsteps coming down the stairs. And just in time! My stomach was gurgling again. I saw the shadows of Mr. White's legs beneath the door, but then there was a bang louder than any bang I had heard before. Then two more quick bangs, and I heard something slam into the door.

More footsteps on the stairs, and soon after, the voices stopped yelling.

Then it was just the machine sounds and no voices.

Then the machines finally clicked off, the mechanical whoosh fell silent, and all I heard was the flickering of the lightbulb and the dripping from the green splotch.

When it was silent, I realized I had been staring at the ceiling for a long time and I finally "snapped out of it," as Mr. White always said. I looked down from the ceiling and scanned the room. There was a lot of light from the door, and not just the bottom of it.

Then I realized the door was open.

3. Five Sleeping Men

"Mr. White?" I said. I suddenly felt scared because this had never happened before. The door was only opened when Mr. White was coming in or out of it.

I listened and still only heard the fluorescent lightbulb and the water dripping on the green splotch. It was dripping a lot today because the machines had been running so much.

"Mr. White?" I asked again. He must not have heard me the first time.

I rose to my feet, holding the towels still wrapped around me because I was scared. I walked toward the door quietly and peeked through the crack where the light was coming in. I didn't see anyone on the stairs, but then looked down. Someone was there!

I pulled the door open a little to get a better look. It was Mr. White!

He was lying face down at the bottom of the stairs like he had fallen down them and hit the door. His face was still resting on the door and there were some holes in his clothes. He wasn't moving, but a lot of red water was all over his body.

I wondered what type of water caused this, and how different it was to the water that made the green splotch. The red was the same type of red as the green is green. I'd have to figure it out later.

"Mr. White!" I yelled. I could tell he tripped and fell asleep and I had to wake him up. I poked him with my finger and eventually turned him over. His eyes weren't moving and neither was any part of him. He just looked up at the ceiling where the pipes were.

The red water kept coming out of him, and I had never seen so much of it before. It was all over me now, since I had been touching him. I looked up the stairs and suddenly had to cover my eyes. It was so bright up the stairs and it hurt my eyes!

I remembered that it always hurt my eyes when I went places with Mr. White. I opened my eyes again and slowly the brightness became less bright.

"Hello?" I yelled up the stairs. No one answered.

Suddenly, an awful thought came to me. What if someone pushed Mr. White? What if they poked those holes in him and pushed him down the stairs? And what if they were still here, waiting to poke holes in me and push me down the stairs?

Suddenly I was really scared again and wanted to go back to my bed of towels.

However, my stomach was gurgling and now that Mr. White wasn't waking up, I would have to get my own food. I didn't know how, but I knew I had to go up the stairs.

I wiped the red water off my hands with a towel and started going up the stairs.

I went slowly, in case the bad person who had pushed Mr. White was still there. There was a doorway at the top of the stairs, but the door was left open. That's why it was so bright. As I went up the stairs, it got a lot warmer and even more damp. Everything in the basement was cold and damp, and now upstairs, everything was warm and *really* damp.

I put one hand on the door frame and looked around. It was a steamy room. A little bit in front of me there was another man lying face down. He didn't have any clothes on, just a towel that was scrunched up around his waist. He also had some holes in him with red water all over him. I was scared for a second and almost ran back to my bed. I looked at the room a little longer, and no one else came in. I thought it was safe to enter.

I walked across the room, went around the man on the floor and approached the other door. This one was shut, and there was no window to look through. I pushed down on the handle and pulled it open slowly.

I just opened it a crack and tried to peek through, but it was unlike anything I had ever seen before. My eyes burned and I coughed. That next room was even *more* damp and hot than this one. I slammed the door shut and stood back, still coughing. I looked at the man on the floor and wondered why he was there too.

When I had stopped coughing, I turned the handle again and opened the door all the way.

There were really hot clouds in the room. After a minute I got used to the clouds, and walked in. It was hard to see at first, but eventually I could look around the damp, hot room.

There were tiles everywhere. They were white, but most of them were really dirty. There was a bench made out of tiles that went all the way around the room.

There were also two sleeping men in this room.

One had a towel around him, but the other man's towel had fallen off so he didn't have anything covering him at all. I had never seen such a big man without any clothes on. A lot of their red water was all over the floor, and one of them was still clutching a small black thing. I thought I had seen a picture of this thing in one of my books, but in the picture, the person is hurting another person with it. I wondered if he had hurt the other men and Mr. White. But who hurt him? Who put him to sleep?

I moved to the next door and opened it slowly. It was not as hot and damp, but there were more men on the floor. Whatever had happened, a lot of people had hurt each other and I could see why they were all yelling.

This room had tiles everywhere as well, but there were big pools of water — deeper than me. They were hot with clouds coming up from them, each with red water from the men mixing in with the clear water in the pools. The tile floors were slippery, and even more slippery where the red water was. I was careful as I made my way around the men and the pools and to the next door. This one had a window on it, and I could see light coming in from outside.

I knew it was outside light because light from outside looks different than light from inside. I remembered that from my trips with Mr. White. I wondered if he would ever wake up and if we could go on any more trips. Or if he could give me more rules to live by.

When I came to the window in the door, I peered through and saw another room, but this one didn't have tiles on it. There were white walls and cloth floors. And across the room were windows and I could see outside! On the cloth floors was one more sleeping man, but he had all of his clothes on. His red water was leaking out of him and getting into the cloth on the floor. He was lying on his side against a table with papers on it. He also had a small black object in his hand and it was pointed at the ground.

I opened the door and walked through.

It was cold in this room. I had become used to the hot, damp rooms and now a rush of cold air hit my body, especially my toe that stuck out the hole in my sock.

The room smelled sharp and smoky. I decided to just run out the glass doors to the outside. I pushed through the door and stepped out into the light. It was even brighter than I remembered.

As I stepped out into the warm, sunny day, I saw a lot of cars pulling up to the building. They had bright flashing lights on their cars that were blue and red, and one of the men got out of a car and ran to me. He bent down and asked me what had happened.

I didn't know what to say. I didn't know if he would understand my description of the sleeping men and Mr. White and the green splotch. My brain felt like it was making the loud whirring noises like the machines in my room and all of a sudden I couldn't think of anything.

So I started to cry.

The man in the black clothes put his hand on me and told me it would be okay. Then he asked me where my parents were. I couldn't stop crying at that point, so I couldn't tell him.

Next thing I knew I was wrapped up in a blanket and in the chair of one of the cars with the flashing lights. I was trying not to cry because Mr. White always told me not to cry, but now Mr. White was asleep and I don't know if he'll ever wake up.

When I stopped crying, I sat up and looked out the window. I didn't see any more of those men in the black suits, but I started to hear more of those loud bangs coming from inside the building.

It was the first time I had ever seen the outside of the building. It had pictures of clouds on a sign, and words I couldn't read, but they looked like this:

STEAM & SOAK

I don't know what they meant, but apparently it was the name of my home. After a minute the loud bangs stopped and it was quiet again. I sat in the car with the flashing red and blue lights, and waited for the nice man to come back out. But he never did.

So I decided to get out of the car and go on a trip by myself.

4. The Barrel Man

I pulled the handle of the car and as I slid out, my stomach gurgled again. I remembered how hungry I was and decided I should go look for some food. Mr. White had always brought me my own food so I didn't know how to find it myself.

I walked on the black street and looked around. There were no pictures of food or anything, so I would have to walk around until I saw one—or found someone to ask. The streets were deserted. I left the cars quietly flashing their red and blue lights behind me, keeping the man's blanket wrapped around my shoulders because it felt good.

After I walked to another street, I looked to my right and saw a car coming. I stepped out in front of it so it would see me and it slowed down, but it made a loud sound like *WAHHHH*. The car was big and blue and only had front seats. The back was open and had ten barrels in it. It came to a stop in front of me and the front window rolled down.

"Kid! What are you doing??" the driver asked me. He looked at his watch and then asked me, "Where are your parents?"

I don't know why everyone kept asking me that. Didn't they know I haven't seen my parents in a long time?

I told the driver I don't know, and he angrily punched the steering wheel and said a lot of mean words.

"Ok, get in, I'll take you somewhere."

I walked over to the door and pulled myself up into the truck. I remembered it was called a truck, not a car, because I had seen one in my books and Mr. White told me that's what they are called.

"It smells like a garden in here," I said. The man was silent when I said this. "What's in your barrels back there? Do you have garden supplies in them?"

"Umm. No, kid," he answered. "It's not for gardening."

"What is it then?" I asked.

"It, uhhh..." the man hesitated.

"And what are these tubes running from the back of the truck to the front where your feet are?"

"Look, kid. You gotta stop asking questions, okay?"

"Well, where are you taking me?"

"I was going to...uh, the Federal Building. But I gotta figure out where to take you first." He looked at his watch again. He seemed to be in a big hurry.

"Do you know where you live, kid?"

I smiled because now I knew the answer: "Steam and Soak!" I replied. "Oh, I also heard Mr. White sometimes talk about a place called Oak..." I couldn't remember the word. "Oak my home."

"Oklahoma?" he said.

"Yah! Oklahoma! That's the word. It's fun to say."

"Well good job, kid. That's this entire city. You haven't really narrowed it down much." He paused for a moment, then said, "Wait, did you say you live at the Steam and Soak?"

I nodded.

"No one lives at a Steam and Soak. It's a place where you go to sit in saunas and hot tubs. Does your daddy work there or something?"

"Mr. White isn't my daddy. I told you, I don't know where my parents are."

Just then, my stomach let out the loudest gurgle I had ever heard. The man driving the truck looked down at me angrily. "You hungry, kid?"

"Yes," I said. "I ate my Pop-Tarts which are better than Pop-Tarts and that was a long time ago."

"Okay, kid. I'll get you some McDonalds and then take you to the police." He looked at his watch again. "I can't take you to the police," he said very quietly, like he was thinking really hard. He turned the truck off the street next to a building. He yelled into a black box and then drove around the building. A woman opened the window and handed him a bag of food which smelled so good. It was warm and delicious. I had never had food like this before! I felt my mouth watering.

He handed me the bag and drove forward. I opened it and pulled out the warm food. After the first bite, I couldn't stop eating it all, and before I knew it, I had eaten everything.

"Wow, you put that down!" said the man. We had been driving for a few minutes and he was talking to himself the whole time. He had a bunch of papers on the seat between us and would occasionally flip through them. Sometimes, I don't think he even spoke the same language. He said things like, "Sick semper tirannis," but I didn't want to ask him more questions.

He reached over and opened up a hatch right in front of my legs. He pulled out a small black thing that looked just like the ones the men in the Steam and Soak had! I knew those things made loud sounds, so I covered up my ears.

"What is that thing??" I asked him.

"It's a gun, kid," he answered. "Don't worry, I'm not going to shoot you."

I took my hands off my ears.

"McVeigh is going to kill me," he muttered.

"Who?"

"Kid! Stop asking questions!" He thought for a moment. "My friend and I—my friend Tim—are on a...a mission. And if we run out of time, the mission will fail."

"What is the mission?" I asked.

"We...There are some bad people and we have to...uhh...stop them. Negotiators don't know what they're doing."

"Negoshiaters?" I asked.

"Nevermind, kid. You won't understand. I...I have to blow some people up to put a little fear back in the government...return the power to the people."

I didn't understand. "Is that what the barrels in the back are for?"

"Yah, kid. Thirteen barrels of ANFO and acetylene. Direct delivery to the Federal Building."

"You're going to put people to sleep just like Mr. White?"

The man was silent and looked over at me, trying to think of what to say. "Who is Mr. White?" he asked me.

I smiled. "He took care of me! He brought food and books to my room!"

"At the Steam and Soak?"

"Yah!" I answered. "But now he's asleep with red water coming out of him because someone used a gun to poke holes in him and he won't wake up."

"Well, I—I'm sorry, kid," the man said. Then he was quiet for a long time.

5. Burning Tears

As I thought about Mr. White, I felt a blob in my throat. I got nervous because I felt like I was going to cry, and Mr. White always told me not to cry. I bet that this angry man also doesn't want me to cry.

But then I thought about him getting angry at me for crying, so that made me want to cry more. Apparently my face gave it away and I looked like I was about to cry.

"Aw, kid, don't cry," said the angry man.

As you know, when you say that to someone it makes them want to cry more. My lips pulled back really tight and my eyes squinted closed as tears started to pour through.

"Ahh, kid..." he didn't know what to say. He didn't know what happened when I cried either. It's the reason Mr. White always told me not to cry.

I leaned forward in the seat of the truck and put my hands on my face. Tears began to pour through them and down my arms to my elbows. They burned holes in the blanket which was still wrapped around me and little clouds came up from it.

"Wh—" the man looked at me and slowed the truck down. "Kid, what the hell—?"

He was getting angrier at me which made me cry harder and my tears kept burning through the blanket. I felt them dripping down through the blanket to the seat I was on. The man had stopped the car and reached over to unbuckle the strap around me.

"You're gonna destroy my—AGHHH!" he yelled and pulled his hand away from me. I looked over and through my tears I could see the skin on his hand melting away and heard a small *sssss* as clouds came up from his hand. My tears were burning through his skin and he stared at it in shock.

After a few seconds of staring at it, he opened his door and ran out of the truck, angrily screaming a bunch of bad words. He bent over and tried to wipe my tears off his hand. Finally he got them all off by dragging his hand on the ground, but he had already lost a lot of skin. I had stopped crying because his yelling startled me, so now I just stared at him.

I remembered when Mr. White had first told me not to cry. He was holding me, carrying me back from one of our trips and I was having a bad day. I didn't have fun. I started to cry and some of my tears got on his shoe and burnt two of his toes off. Ever since that day, he told me not to cry even if I didn't feel like crying.

The man was bent over outside the truck, holding his own hand and yelling a bunch of bad words, mixed with "kid." I should have told him not to touch me when I'm crying, but I forgot.

My tears were still running down my face and dripping onto the blanket and seat. I heard the little *ssss* sound as they burnt through them and down. I got worried as they went through those things and down toward the tubes the man wouldn't tell me about. I don't know what they were, but they looked important.

"Mi—mister?" I said as I stopped crying. "Mister, my tears are going to get on your tubes."

He looked up from his hand and looked into the truck by my feet, where the tubes were. His eyes got big. "Kid, get outta there!"

I pushed the blanket and the strap off of me and opened my door. I heard the hiss as my tears hit the tubes and burned through the plastic.

"Run away, kid!" I didn't know why he was telling me to run, but I suddenly got nervous again. I looked around me and saw a lot of green grass and trees. I ran toward them as fast as I could. After a while, I looked back and saw the man still bent over next to the truck, holding his hand.

"Mister!" I yelled, but he was too far away to hear me. He probably knew what he was doing, so I turned back and continued running for the trees. I felt the crying lump come back up my throat, but pushed it back down this time. I was almost to the trees when I heard the bang.

I actually didn't really hear it. It was so loud it blocked up my ears and I couldn't hear anything. A second later a big, hot wind blew me off my feet and I hit a tree. That's all I remember before I woke up later, and I still couldn't hear.

6. Ten Years

When I woke up, I was lying in the grass with a man in a black uniform leaning over me. He was touching my neck and talking to me, but I couldn't hear anything. He squeezed a box on his shoulder and talked into it. I looked around, but it hurt my neck to move.

Back where the man and his truck were, there was only fire and burning black ruins.

The next thing I knew, I was on a bed being carried into the back of another truck. More people in uniforms were leaning over me and putting tubes in my nose and touching me. I still could not hear anything, but The people seemed nice to me, just like Mr. White was.

Mr. White had brought me in because no one wanted me because my tears hurt them. He said he would put me away where I wouldn't hurt anyone anymore, and he would take care of me. And he did, until he died.

Ten years later, I began to understand what had happened that day.

Mr. White had kept me in the Steam and Soak to keep me safe and keep everyone else safe. But the day I escaped, I had accidentally done something else. I had stopped potentially the largest domestic terrorist attack in American history.

The angry man in the truck was on his way to the Federal Building in Oklahoma City and those barrels would have blown up the entire building. Instead, it blew up on the side of the road near a park and killed the angry man and three others, injuring 14 other people nearby.

Eventually my hearing came back, but I wear a hearing aid on my right ear and sometimes get dizzy.

They found the angry man's friend who was supposed to blow up another truck at the same building. But when my tears blew up the first truck, he started driving away from the city. The police caught him and arrested him and put him in jail for life.

They found a lot of books and papers in the mens' homes about words I don't know what they mean: anarkee and neat-chee and restoring the power to the people. They also like to read in Latin a lot, but I don't know why they don't just read in one language.

Speaking of reading, I have been in school and learning to read, even though everyone my age is way ahead of me.

I haven't cried for ten years though, because I don't want to be put in the basement of another Steam and Soak.

14. One Big Meth

Tim swung open the loose glass door to the diner in the slow summer afternoon. He paused once inside as the creaky hydraulic compressor welcomed the door to a close. His eyes slowly adjusted to the restaurant as he scanned the booths that lined the diner like train cars that had derailed and lay scattered over the linoleum ground.

Tim had come to meet Joy, whom he had met two summers prior. Joy was often found scooping syringes out of compost piles behind Old Man Jaken's shed, where, if timed correctly, could still hold some potent product. Joy had lost twenty pounds in the two years Tim had known her, though there was not much of her there to start with. Her eyes had shrunk back into her skull and her arms dangled loosely by her thighs as she walked, as if someone had stapled deflated balloons to her shoulders. Today she sported her typical attire: a decades-old grunge rock band tee with the sleeves ripped off and some washed out jeans that should have been burned up with her breakfast cigarette.

She sat in the diner across from her friend Mitch, whom Tim had come to meet. Mitch was a rising star among Indiana's drug dealers and managed to sift Blue Rhinos full of anhydrous ammonia for making methamphetamines through hardware stores to the correct customers without getting caught. Tim oversaw the production and distribution of the drug, which he thought made him famous and powerful. In reality, he had forty friends on Facebook and two songs on Soundcloud with twelve plays.

The trick to propane tanks is two fold: careful handling and timing. The imbalance of the chemical makes it incredibly unstable; often to the point that a bump or jostle could send fleshy fragments of the carrier into the next zip code. And of course, any leak in the nozzle (which is bound to happen sooner or later) is going to turn the bronze valve blue, which would give him away.

So far, turnover had been good for Mitch, with only one mishap earlier that year in March. One of his clients had gone to create product with the anhydrous in the Blue Rhino, but the idiot forgot about the cigarette smoldering between his lips. Neighbors picked up pieces of him two blocks away.

Tim saw Joy's greasy dirty-blonde hair in the far corner and slid over to the booth with his hands in his pockets. He slumped down into the seat beside Joy and talked to her while looking over Mitch.

"You sure he's clean, Jo'?"

"Yah," Joy leaked lazily while snapping gum in her open mouth. "One a' his tanks shredded Blister over in Fishers a couple months ago, but the police traced it back to the Rhino and couldn't trace it. They questioned tha delivery company, but they said they wa' clean."

"You know we can't work widd any snitches, or anyone 'boutta get lazy on their tracks, Joy," Tim said to her, still staring at Mitch.

Mitch extended his hand in an awkward greeting gesture, but Tim only looked at the outstretched palm and then rubbed his nose while snorting. Joy craned her neck toward the diner's kitchen and muttered an impatient curse about the slow service of the place.

Mitch retracted his hand, "Yah, Tim, I know you run clean business, but I figured that someone like you, workin' with Joy, scooping needles out of Jaken's yard in the afternoons," he paused and nodded at Joy with a sympathetic shrug in his eyes, "I figured you'd be a good partner to work with. Easy, y'know?"

Tim eased back in his seat and crossed his ugly arms in front of his chest. His greasy hair desperately needed a clean and a cut, and his tattoos were clearly the result of too many shots of Jack in one night and a couple stupid dares. He still thought they made him look tough instead of stupid, but no one really tried to convince him otherwise. No one cared.

Despite his serious facade, Tim did not take nearly as much care as he should have when it came to his work. His métier was essentially to middleman the relationships between heroin dealers and high schoolers on the edge of dropping out. If no one else did, at least they found him cool; a washed out thirty-something who drove a convertible (but rusty) Corvette and smoked. His job was to find the rich ones looking for party tricks. Once the relationship was established, he practically drilled a hole in their parents' bank accounts and watched the money pour out.

He had always been sloppy, though for a while, seemed to be getting better. Mostly due to Joy's aid, Tim had established communication as far north as the suburbs of Chicago, and things seemed to be going swimmingly until January.

Tim always triple checked anything he used himself, but when dealing, his care was far from airtight. Joy had been out of town that week, in Memphis with a lover she met on the internet. Tim had a shipment to take up to Indianapolis, which he wrapped before finishing the properties check. Tim joked a lot about bad yams, but this was a catastrophe.

Two days after he dropped off the slip, he heard from his contact that three kids at the party had died after using. Apparently, the opiate had become infected during the cooling and Tim's oversight led to three deaths. Possibly more. Joy cut her romantic Memphis trip short to come back and help him dust up his tracks. He owed her more than he realized.

The meeting with Mitch was to help him branch out from just dealing H.

The waitress brought Joy her food, a ham sandwich dipped in gravy, with bacon cheese fries and a cola. Joy replaced *thank you* with a glare and a nod and began drawing the fries one by one to her limp mouth.

Mitch and Tim had slowly been talking about their businesses without making much progress. They seemed to be subtly telling the other why they were better at their job than the other, rather than seeking to invest in a potential partnership.

Joy sat by idly gnawing at her food, lazily staring at the table below her plate. The silences in their exchange were filled with Mitch's tapping fingers and bouncing leg.

"So how far north do you get?" asked Mitch with genuine curiosity.

"I have a buddy in Logansport. Actually one a' my best customers," answered Tim. Joy snorted. She knew that his 'customer' was a sixteen-year-old drop out whose parents funded his addictions to both computer games and horse.

The two men stated a few more questions at each other, but it was clear to Joy that they had gotten nowhere. She wiped her nose with her napkin and dropped it on her half-eaten sandwich and pile of fries.

"Well," she said, "I gotta go. I'm working a double tonight at Kroger, and I gotta drop Kenny off at the house." Tim and Mitch nodded and the three stood up to leave.

"Bye," Mitch said to Joy, and then nodded at Tim. They accidentally made eye contact, which they both immediately ended and Mitch walked out the door.

"I don't know about him, Joy," said Tim confidently, still staring at the creaking door. He brought his arms up into another unquiet crossing.

"And next time, don't make us meet in a diner. It felt like forever we had to sit there 'n talk while you ate." Without looking at his friend seated beside him, Tim quietly shook his head, stood up, and walked toward the door.

Alternate Ending:

"I have a buddy in Logansport. Actually one a' my best customers," answered Tim. Joy snorted. She knew that his 'customer' was a sixteen-year-old drop out whose parents unknowingly funded his addictions to both computer games and horse.

Before Mitch could react, the sound of a motor revving well into the red zone sounded just on the other side of the wall. Suddenly, the bricks next to the booth where they sat flew across the diner and a '92 Chevrolet Caprice slammed through the wall. The wheels kept spinning as the vehicle pointed its hood upward and finally came to rest where their table used to be. Mitch was completely submerged in the rubble, below the driver's side wheel, and Joy had been battered by the impact of the bricks. The jolt had knocked Tim to the floor next to the booth and he lay there, breathing, bleeding, and unconscious.

Minutes later, sirens sang their piercing song into the humid summer air as EMTs rushed seemingly in slow motion into the diner, hauling oxygen, AEDs, and stretchers through the creaky glass door. The driver had been lost in an early afternoon fade, hammering a bottle and a half of Jage and blazing down the road. When paramedics strapped the old man to the stretcher, he kept asking about the empty orchestra in his lungs.

Tim was loaded into the back of the ambulance, Joy into a bag, and a few parts of Mitch were found, but not enough to identify the body.

15. The Misymphomiacs

The truck tossed and jolted as we made our way up the unkept Thai terrain. Everywhere we looked was green, green, green and we had been on this same steady weaving incline for hours. We had left Chiang Rai and gone west 9 hours ago, driving straight into the mountainous jungle. The last village that had running water or electricity was about 7 hours behind us. This was uncharted territory.

I'm the "medical assistant" on this voyage, which basically means I am the gopher. Reggie says 'go fer' this, and I do it. Reginald Smith and his student Anne were commissioned to visit this colony of people in rural Thailand and they brought me with. And we have a translator named Pornchai.

The people in this tribe have what the doctors call *misymphomia*, which is a fancy word for, their bodies never heal. The Thai people call them *wah-see-how*. If they get a cut, they're stuck with it for life. If they hear something too loud, their hearing is irreparably damaged.

And so on.

Apparently no one has ever gone and done a proper medical evaluation of their condition, so we're going to take a look. I've been wondering how we're going to do blood tests if the needle holes would never heal.

"We ammost there," said Pornchai over his shoulder.

The motion of the truck driving over the mud road could have been that of a boat tossed by the waves of a small storm. From the passenger seat, Reggie looked determined to arrive, slightly anxious at what he might see. The jaw beneath his peppery temples had been tensed this entire trip. He wasn't quite middle aged, but it was dawning quickly on his horizon.

Anne was in the back seat with me, curled up the past four hours trying not to puke for a fourth time. Partly from the truck's motion and partly from nerves. We had been assured that these people were entirely peaceful, but I guess anxiety always accompanies mystery.

"Arright," muttered Pornchai as he shifted the truck into park on the flat dirt path. The three of us looked up and saw the jungle as it had been before, but now, almost as if intentionally hidden among the trees, were bamboo huts scattered across the acres before us. As I continued to scan the foliage, I realized that these were not like the huts we had seen in the tribes before. They were far more intricately crafted. It almost seemed as if different woods had been imported just to adorn the exterior of their cottages, giving the entire village a very prestigious feel.

"Did they know we're coming?" I asked Reggie.

"I doubt it. How would anyone have communicated with them? They haven't even heard of electricity," he answered.

Reggie and I were the first to open our doors. We emerged slowly, so as not to alarm any onlooking tribespeople.

But the village seemed abandoned. I looked through the window at Pornchai and nodded my head for him to get out of the truck too.

Now all three of us had our hands out below us as if petting fragile, invisible dogs to show we meant no harm. Much of this trip hinged on whether or not Pornchai could adapt Thai to their tribal dialect.

He began to call out in Thai, probably something about us coming in peace and meaning no harm.

Flies buzzed.

A door opened in the hut nearest to us, directly in front of the truck.

The first thing we saw was a white umbrella. It preceded a small figure wearing smooth robes that covered nearly every inch of skin. The figure seemed to weightlessly drift toward us beneath its embroidered dome, and very soon it stood before us.

At once I realized the figure was a small boy with the smoothest skin I had ever seen on a human. It seemed to be an ivory piano key that grew into a small human being. His eyes were beautifully shaped and as he pointed them at things, he seemed to be seeing *into* whatever he observed.

Pornchai approached him and bent down. He spoke softly. The boy nodded, replied and turned to walk back to the hut. Pornchai turned and nodded for us to follow. Anne was out of the car by now and the four of us followed the small boy. I almost had to jog to match his swift and graceful gait.

As we approached the edge of the woods, I could now see beyond them into a valley that fell beneath the path we walked on. The valley was filled with huts and homes just as beautiful as the boy's, but these were connected by a web of covered pathways. In that moment I realized the sun would have damaged their skin; even in short bursts it would add up over years. I wondered if they had ever felt a ray of sunlight anywhere on their flesh.

As we approached the boy's hut, I also realized how quiet the town was. No doubt they kept it this way to prevent damage to their eardrums.

He gracefully pushed open the door to his hut and we followed in single file. The interior of the building was just as beautifully intricate as the exterior. Smooth bamboo laced walls of oak. The decoration was minimal but brilliantly executed with sections of stone and brick splashed into the walls, with combed sand gardens in several of the corners.

The boy turned and muttered something to Pornchai and walked down a stairwell on the far side of the hut.

"He's going to bring us the tribe leader," Pornchai informed us. Apparently the tribal dialect was close enough to Thai for him to communicate.

In place of windows, the bamboo poles were further spread out so they could overlook the valley before the hut while letting in the evening breeze. I walked over to them and looked once more at the web of walkways and huts in the valley. There must have been over one hundred homes, each one as ornate as the one in which I stood. I couldn't help but thinking, for a colony of people who have a terminal disease, this village was incredibly beautiful.

After about ten minutes the boy returned, followed by a middle aged man with equally smooth and pale skin. His voice was smooth as he bowed and addressed Pornchai, who informed us that we were welcome. The chief spat a quick yet gentle command to the boy, who turned once again to descend the stairs and return a moment later with four white umbrellas in his arms.

The chief turned to the three Americans and bowed to each of us with a smile pressing into his cheeks.

"My name is Ahn. We will prepare a place for you to stay," he said through Pornchai.

He and the boy led us down a series of stairs and ramps which opened to the web of pathways on the valley floor. The sun had dropped below the rim of the surrounding hills and lights in the huts were beginning to ignite. We saw several villagers slowly pacing the paths between the buildings, none using their umbrellas now that the harmful rays had disappeared, each one with skin like fresh candles and the slow and the graceful gait of ballet dancers.

We followed the chief and boy around several turns until we were ushered into a hut. It was not quite as large as the one from which we had come, but it had the same blend of woods and ornate designs. Ours had only one combed sand bed in the corner.

Soon the boy entered holding two mats and set to laying them out for us. I wandered through the first chamber into the second, where the other pair of us would sleep.

Birds sang in the evening.

I saw fireflies dancing in the colorful dusk through the slatted bamboo window. There was certainly an idyllic atmosphere to the town. I was exhausted from the trip and was slowly beginning to let some of the questions in my head drift away as I turned my mind to sleeping.

Several minutes later, the boy entered again with two more mats and lay them out in our room. I would share a room with Anne. We helped lay out our mats and before I knew it, I was flat on my back drifting away into a dream.

The dream was—as most dreams are—a blur of images and plot lines that bowed and weaved through and over one another like double dutch jump ropes. The resounding theme of my dreams were a screaming chorus. People gathered beneath a king standing on a litter as he whipped those beneath him, carrying him on their shoulders. His family stood behind him on the platform, watching in silence.

Disembodied arms digging their way into the earth.

And of course, white piano keys sounding out discordant tones.

I awoke feeling oddly renewed and calm despite the distressing imagery of my dream. It was one of those things where, when you're in the dream, it's not that strange, but when you describe it to your friend you sound drooling mad.

The town was oddly quiet for a group of people gathered in the center of the jungle. Only a few birds chirped and the song of the insects was present but somehow muted and distant.

I was the last to rise, so I walked to the entrance of the hut. I saw more villagers beneath their domed umbrellas, staring at me as they passed on the maze-like walkways.

One of them saw me standing there, looking awfully aloof, and pointed a smooth finger to a nearby hut. I walked in the shade of the terrace. As I passed over an elevated segment of the walk, I could see clear to the edge of the village, where the huts and walkways met open forest and fields.

I noticed part of the walkway that strayed off around the corner of the valley. It was the only part of the walkway that wandered outside the clear boundary of the rest of the village. No one was walking on this section. I assumed it was for disposing of trash or some other utility and quickly forgot about it. I entered the hut where Reggie, Anne and Pornchai were sitting on the floor with Ahn eating breakfast.

"There she is!" said Reggie with a surprising amount of vigor in his tone. "Morning, Princess!"

Ahn pointed to the food as an invitation for me to eat. We ate a very wet bowl of rice with vegetables and spices boiled in. Previously, I would have thought this a strange breakfast food, but after a few bites I was convinced to the contrary.

Ahn spoke through Pornchai again, "Today I will show you all around our village. I am happy to answer any questions you have." Ahn held a genuine smile on his face as Pornchai spoke for him.

"I have one," said Reggie. "Do you have any young men who would be a good match for our Anne?" He laughed at his own joke as Anne shoved him, also smiling. Apparently I had missed part of the earlier joke.

Ahn led us through all of the village, showing us several of the huts, all of which were kept in impeccable order. There seemed to not be a crumb or clump of dirt that made it past the doorway of any of the huts.

We saw the infirmary, where pale skinned nurses attended elderly villagers who barely seemed sick at all. They lay so peacefully in their beds and their skin had barely given way to wrinkles that the only way I could tell their elevated age was the tiredness in their eyes and the slowness in their movements. They looked at me and gingerly moved a hand or nodded to us to acknowledge us.

We saw the school, where today the boy and many other porcelain children sat still before the lecturing teachers in the various classrooms. Ahn showed us the library, which was not large by any means, but contained several shelves and eager readers who sat carefully scanning the pages of handfuls of books. It was evident that precautions were taken to prevent loud noises and any kind of abrupt surprises. Everyone seemed to move slowly and patiently, never in a hurry and never in a sloppy manner.

When Ahn was about to conclude the tour of the village, I remembered the stray pathway I had seen earlier from the high pass. I asked him about it.

"What pathway?" he replied through Pornchai.

I explained how I saw a pathway that went away from camp

around a fold in the valley.

"I don't know of any pathway except those in the village, connecting our homes and buildings," he said.

My stomach growled and I figured I must have been misremembering from my morning haze.

We returned to Ahn's hut for lunch and two women brought in trays of bamboo cores, garden vegetables, and steamed chicken.

Suddenly I realized Ahn had not shown us any place to prepare food. We had seen nearly every building in the colony, but I had not seen a single area for preparing food, much less killing a chicken. Little mounds of curiosity began to pile up within me.

After lunch, I passed again over the high walkway and paused to look for the stray path I had seen earlier, but a giant curtain had been hung across most of the walkway. It was a rich shade of red which complemented the wood of the huts in a very elegant manner. It was positioned perfectly so as to prevent anyone from seeing out to the edge of the camp.

"Sun," said a voice suddenly behind me. I jolted and turned to see Ahn standing inches from me on the walkway. He pointed to the curtain and motioned the sun coming at them from an angle and being blocked by the curtain. "Sun," he said again, and pointed to his skin. He was not smiling now. He walked away, seemingly irritated by my curious staring at the curtain.

I deemed it best not to pry, so I walked to my hut. Reggie and Anne were lying on their mats talking.

"Isn't this place great?" asked Reggie, looking up at me. I suddenly realized they were unaware of the odd day I was having.

"It's so beautiful," answered Anne before I could speak. "We were just talking about how this is nothing like what we had expected."

"Yah," I muttered, still jarred from the strange encounter with Ahn on the walkway. "Did either of you notice the pathway I was talking about?"

"What pathway?" asked Reggie. "There are literally hundreds...Okay, maybe not hundreds. Dozens! There are dozens!" Reggie was getting to that age most middle aged men reach where they laugh at their own jokes which are in no regard *funny.*

"I didn't see it," said Anne, "but I wasn't looking for anything. Why?"

"Well, it just seemed strange that Ahn avoided my question earlier and now, there is a curtain blocking our view."

"Eh, you just need to relax," said Reggie as he stretched and repositioned himself on the mat.

Ahn had simply told us to enjoy ourselves until dinnertime, when he would gather several of the notable villagers for a special feast with us.

I spent the afternoon wandering around the maze of pathways, half-heartedly looking for the way down to the stray ramp around the corner, but it seemed to not exist anymore. Or perhaps it was hidden or blocked. I was also keeping my eyes open for a kitchen or pantry of any kind, but saw nothing of the sort. There were no structures that contained so much as a chopping board or oven. I guess that made sense though; Why would they want to risk getting burned? Then again, how was our food prepared? And where?

Dinnertime arrived and Ahn led us to his hut where about a dozen villagers and some children were already seated on the ground around a large table. They all looked at us as we smiled and nodded with a warm welcome spread across their faces. I was seated next to a middle-aged man named Samhyup. He knew no more English than I knew his tribal language so we smiled and nodded to one another as I sat down.

The servers soon came out once again with large platters of steaming meat and perfectly spiced vegetables, all alongside bleach-white sticky rice. Without thinking, I loaded up my plate and took a bite of some of the rice with pork. Immediately my mouth was seared and I inhaled quickly to try to cool it down.

"Oooh, hot!" I abashedly exclaimed as I realized everyone at the table was looking at me. No one laughed. I fanned my hand at my mouth to make light of the fact that I had burnt my tongue.

At this, one of the young boys laughed. He then took a heaping bite of the hot pork and rice and then fanned his mouth. After about two seconds, the pain set in on his mouth and his eyes widened.

Immediately, Ahn stood up and pointed at the boy, yelling something in their dialect. Two men who had been standing outside the door to the hut rushed in and ran to the boy while Ahn continued holding his finger straight at him. The guards grabbed the boy from either side, one on each arm and stood up with him. The boy's face turned from pain to shock and fear and he began screaming.

He tried to wriggle from the arms of the guards as they easily picked him up and carried him to the door. The boy's screaming slowly faded as he was carried farther and farther from us until we could hear him no more.

Ahn turned to Pornchai and urgently spoke to him. "Ahn says that he is so sorry you had to see that and would like to know if there is anything he can do to make up—" Ahn cut him off and spoke to him some more. "He would like to apologize for the loud sounds you had to hear and would like to know if he can do anything to make it right."

"Where did they take him?" I asked Ahn directly. Pornchai translated.

"It was taken care of," Ahn answered through Pornchai.

"Yes, but what's going to happen to him?" I persisted.

Ahn was silent for a moment and then said perhaps we should all get some rest. I looked at Samhyup, who still wore his pleasant Thai smile. I tried to communicate with him to ask where they took the boy. He simply continued his grin and shook his head, as if to say either he didn't know or he was not allowed to say.

I looked at Reggie and Anne, who looked as shocked and confused as I was. We all agreed with Ahn that perhaps some more sleep would be good. The table was still overflowing with plates of food as we left the hut and walked to our own.

"What was that about?" asked Reggie once we were alone in our building.

"I told you there was something strange about this place!" I told him.

"Eh, it's probably just something cultural," he replied. "Like us taking our kids out for a spanking. We're just missing something."

I realized then that Reggie still did not perceive anything unusual about the village like I did. I started to get upset with them for being so blind, but rather than belabor the point, I retired to my mat.

"Tomorrow we're going to start running some tests on the villagers," he said. Gonna figure out how to get some blood out of them. Hah! Maybe we'll just have to settle for urine."

Once my body was on the mat, I realized how exhausted I still was from the travel and cultural adjustments. Before I knew it, my mind had let go of its concerns and I was deep into a rich sleep.

In my dream, a hand poked my arm.

It persisted.

It grabbed my arm and shook me.

I faded back into reality and saw Samhyup's wrinkled face leaning over me in the darkness. Slowly I crawled from my dream and gave the small man an inquisitive look. He waved his hand to come with him.

I pushed myself up, rubbed my eyes, and stood up to follow him.

He led me out of our hut and weaved through the many turns of the maze-like walkways. We went down the gentle slopes in the direction of the outer edge of the village. He ducked under some of the railings and left the safety of the covered walkways, which of course did not matter in the quiet moonlight. We cut across some of the courtyards and fields and climbed onto another walkway on the far end of the camp. I realized we were heading toward the path I had seen the first day. My tired head spun with questions, already dizzy from the sudden jolt from sleep. Samhyup had probably caught me right in the middle of my REM cycle.

I looked behind me and saw the rest of the village looming above me, ominous in the pitch blackness. We were presently on the trail I had seen from the overpass. In the darkness I could barely make out the giant red curtain that had been hung across the high central passage to prevent us from seeing this very walkway.

I followed Samhyup around the wide curve of the valley, around the hill where we couldn't previously see. The path curved to the right, so after several minutes of walking, the village was out of view and was replaced by the natural wall. We walked for roughly half an hour as the path turned gently to the left along another turn in the valley, then right again along another. Finally the hills opened up once again and I could see another village. In the darkness, I could soon see that this village was very unlike the other. There were plenty of buildings but no covered walkways between them, only dirt. The buildings themselves were nowhere near as nice as the ones I had come from.

The closer we drew to the village, the more I could detect a foul smell. It was the odor of dead things rotting. Although it was the middle of the night, I noticed that this village was not as quiet as the other. Several fires burned in the buildings. People—or things—were awake and working. Metal clanged. I heard thuds and pounding.

I saw the flicker of a fire in one of the buildings closest to us. As we approached it, I could see a pile of something to the right of the doorframe. I squinted into the darkness against the dim light of the fire through the open door and saw that it was a pile of bones and innards.

Suddenly I realized this is where all the food for the other village is prepared.

Samhyup stood by the building and motioned for me to look inside.

I squinted against the light of the fire, and as my eyes adjusted, I could see a man cooking something. As the bright blurs turned into solid lines, I saw that most of his body was very deformed. Instead of fingers on his hands, he had knobby claw-like appendages. His skin was bubbled and rotten. He was handling hot pots and moving meat around over the fire, preparing it for the next day.

He detected us watching him and turned around. His face was pink and red, disfigured by burns from both the fire and the sun. He appeared young. Possibly even in his late teens. Blots of blood covered his clothes and I wondered if they were from the animals or from unhealed wounds on his body.

When he saw us, he lopped over to us as quickly as he could and fell on his knees before me. His claw hands grabbed my arms and shirt and he yelled in his language. He wept and began screaming. His pulling on my arms grew more violent until finally I jerked my body away from him and he collapsed on the ground, still crying loudly.

I looked at Samhyup and he began walking further into the village. I was unsure about what to do about the weeping man on the ground so I turned and followed Samhyup.

We were walking uphill through a smattering of ramshackle

buildings, many of which were producing staccato sounds of labor. As we passed various windows and doors, I could see children inside, hammering various objects or sitting at desks working on various things. Samhyup walked gracefully but quickly, so I was only allowed momentary glimpses of the figures within the shacks. Some were more disfigured than others, with limbs missing, or infections and rashes spreading across their flesh. Blood was everywhere. The entire village reeked of rancid wounds.

As I was led through the village, I saw that it was much larger than the first one. I followed Samhyup around a corner and down a smaller corridor where he turned into a small opening in one of the huts. A few small candles cast ghostly shadows against the muddy walls. Scattered bodies slept on the dirt floor of the hut and in the corner I saw a figure sitting hugging his knees and quietly sniffling. Immediately I recognized him as the boy from dinner earlier who had burnt his mouth on the food.

Samhyup walked over to him and whispered to him with his hand on his shoulders.

I took another look around the hut and saw that all of the blankets covering the sleeping villagers had dried blood all over them. All the heads poking out the top of the coverings had burns and peeling skin similar to those of the first man I had seen. Years of working in the brutal Thai sun had taken its effect on their unhealing skin. None of them seemed to be very old. Hardly into their twenties, yet their skin reflected many more years of damage.

After whispering to the boy for several minutes, Samhyup stood up and motioned me to follow him out of the hut. We emerged into the dirt pathway again and I followed him around more turns and paths throughout the village. There was no order to this village. The huts were thrown hither and thither without care or planning. How Samhyup knew where he was going was incredible, especially considering the darkness.

He came to a hut several times larger than the others. He came to the door and waved me inside. The entire village stank of putrid disease, but the smell in this building was particularly tremendous. Behind me, Samhyup lit a torch and suddenly, in the dim light I could see a giant floor covered with sleeping bodies. These ones were clearly in worse states than those in the other hut.

A few stirred at the light from the torch. I could see giant gashes bleeding through shoddy bandages. All of their skin was brutalized by the elements, the sun, and other accidental wounds.

We walked through the aisles of bodies and I realized that Samhyup brought me to this building only to show me the sickest members of the village.

This was the infirmary, where the villagers came to die.

As we passed by, one of the sick men grabbed my leg. I looked down at him and saw one eye looking at me through a puffy face. His jaw was missing, so everything south of his nose was a gaping chasm seized by infection. It had reached his other eye as well, which had swollen shut and secreted a black ooze. It looked like he was trying to speak, but only gurgles and gasps escaped his throat. I moved my leg and his weak grasp slid off of my ankle. I felt moist residue on my leg where he had gripped me.

I caught up to Samhyup who looked back at me, looking intently at my face as if to ask, *Well? What do you make of this?*

I looked back and he observed the combination of shock and sorrow that filled my eyes.

We left the infirmary and I followed him back the way we had come. We were heading back toward the first village.

When we were nearly back to the weblike zigzags of covered walkways, Samhyup turned to me and pointed back to the sick village. He then covered his mouth, indicating for me to say nothing about what I had just seen.

When I lay back on my mat, I had trouble sleeping. I had no idea how to comprehend what I had seen in the far village. It was the polar opposite of the village where we were staying, enjoying the clean and quiet comfort of a village made possible by the diseased. Eventually I drifted off into unquiet dreams.

I woke up slowly and realized no one had fetched me in time for breakfast. I could see bright sunlight flooding the world outside my slatted window. I slowly rose and began moving. From a few huts over, I heard the sound of Reggie laughing at one of his own jokes.

I found which hut the voices were coming from and saw that Reggie and Anne had set up an impromptu testing station. A curtain walled off a corner where the villagers were supplying test samples of urine and saliva.

"We can't take their blood, so we're working with what we can get," explained Reggie followed by a chuckle at his 'joke.' He and Anne sat across from each other at a low table on the floor. The surface was covered in a mess of tubes, cups, bottles filled with chemicals, and measuring instruments.

I left the hut to try to find some food to eat. As I wandered the zigzag walkways, I wondered if the episode in the middle of the night could have been a dream. A very realistic dream, conjured up by my paranoid imagination.

"No way," I actually muttered aloud. It was real. I had to find Samhyup.

I found some villagers in their own hut who invited me in for some tea and rice crackers. They smiled and nodded at me, but the language barrier prevented any more interaction.

I spent several hours that day wandering around, looking for Samhyup as well as for the passage we had taken in the middle of the night. However, because it was so dark and I had been so disoriented, I couldn't remember the way.

Dinner time came and once again, we were seated with several of the notable villagers. I walked into the hut, fresh from a bath, and sat next to Reggie. He was quieter than usual, as if something was on his mind. Before I had fully sat down, he began explaining what he and Anne had found.

"Nothing," he said. "We can't find a single difference between their fluids and a normal person's. The enzymes we were expecting to find are not there. I mean, we can only read so much without sampling their blood, but we expected there to be at least some difference! Heck, I even made Annie pee in a cup just to make sure!"

I was literally biting my tongue so I wouldn't burst out and tell my companions about the other village, the village flowing with blood. I withheld because I feared Ahn would somehow know what I was saying. He was very kind, but it was beginning to seem like the same type of kindness and generosity you see in the most evil movie villains. He seemed to understand more than he let on.

I noticed that Samhyup was still missing, but also could not ask about him because it would look suspicious. Had he not woken me in the middle of the night, I probably would have forgotten about him too.

The rest of the dinner was spent in silence.

Later that evening, Reggie, Pornchai, Anne and I were reclining on our mats in our hut. I wanted to try to bring up what I had seen.

"You guys notice anything weird about this place?" I asked, trying to sound as casual as possible.

"Yah, these people never heal and they do a good job of never getting hurt!" said Reggie, once more with the tone of a standup comedian. "Gall, I know I couldn't do that! I fall down the stairs twice a week!"

"But what about that boy the other night?" I replied. "The one who was taken out of dinner? I didn't see him all day today."

"Well..." said Anne, trying to think up an explanation.

"And today, one of the villagers we ate with last night was also gone. Samhyup," I added.

No one said anything, indicating they hadn't noticed his absence. I decided this was not the time to tell them about my midnight adventure.

Soon we were all asleep.

The next day passed the same as the previous. There was no sign of Samhyup or the boy, and Reggie and Anne were finding the same results in their medical tests. They performed every examination possible without injuring the villagers, and found no difference between the Misymphomiacs and a healthy person.

Several more days passed in similar fashion. I kept waiting for an opportunity to tell them about the second village, but no such time presented itself. There were no more odd occurrences, and my brain began to doubt the things I had seen around the curve of the ridge.

Then, three nights later, I was woken up in the middle of the night again. Samhyup stood over me holding a knife. My eyes adjusted as my dizzy head spun and I made sense of what was happening. At first, I jolted away from him, but he remained motionless. Once I realized he was not going to cut me, he turned the blade around and offered me the handle. In the darkness, I could see the quality craftsmanship in the knife. I took it from his hand, still puzzled.

"Ahn," he whispered.

"What??" I blurted out.

Samhyup made a cutting motion over his forearm and again said, "Ahn."

I did not know what to think. Did he really want me to murder the leader of his tribe? I knew that a cut from a hefty knife like this would easily kill a Misymphomiac, even just on the arm.

Samhyup could intuit what I was thinking. He took the knife and held it to his chest, then shook his head. Then put it once again to his forearm and nodded. Perhaps he did not want me to kill Ahn.

I nodded.

Samhyup stood up to leave and I watched to see if he would beckon me to follow. Instead, he just walked out the doorway and was gone. I put the knife under my mat and quickly fell back asleep.

The next morning I woke up and forgot about Samhyup's visit until about five minutes into my morning. I felt the lump under my mat and suddenly remembered everything. I thought for a second and shook my head, thinking about how ludicrous it was that I could cut our host, the leader of this village.

I went to breakfast with the dilemma still heavy on my mind. Every action of the villagers made me suspicious, despite the grace with which they moved and interacted.

The day passed in a blur as the decision weighed so heavily on my mind. Before I knew it, dinnertime had arrived and I was seated one person away from Ahn. I stared at him, watching his every move. I pictured him clutching his wrist, lying on the floor of the hut bleeding out. Would the guards come and take him away as they had the boy?

I had left the knife in my hut, but presently had a small knife for my meat.

Finally, when I was halfway done with my food, I could take it no longer. I would make it look like an accident. I held the knife in my hand and made a sudden reach across the table for a plate that was in front of Ahn. I let the knife hit his arm just above the wrist as I reached over. I felt the blade contact his skin, then slide forward a centimeter as it punctured his flesh. He reacted and pulled his arm away and I did the same.

I apologized, but I was never very good at acting. I mostly just sat there in stunned silence, waiting to see what happened.

So did everyone else.

Ahn held his arm before his eyes, looking at the one-inch rift in his forearm. Three seconds later, blood poured out of it. Ahn looked around the room in anger and screamed something at me in Thai. The entire table then turned their gazes to me as I continued sitting in silence. Still, no one moved. Not even the two guards at the door who had rushed in to carry out the boy.

Ahn suddenly got up and rushed out the door, holding his arm as blood dripped down onto his clothes.

"What did you do?" accused Anne.

I was speechless. I managed to blurt out something about it being an accident, which must have sufficed because Reggie and Anne got up and ran after Ahn, followed by Pornchai. I needed to convince everyone it was an accident, so I got up and walked after Pornchai.

There were drops of blood all along the pathway, some of which had been streaked by passing shoes. We followed Ahn into his hut. Reggie fled back past me, running to get his medical kit from our hut. I approached the door of the hut and saw Ahn sitting on a cushion with Anne holding pressure on his arm.

She looked up at me and said, "You've been acting so strange this whole trip! Did you do this on purpose? There is something wrong with you!"

Reggie came back in and knelt by Ahn, opening his kit. "Make sure and save some of this blood for the tests," he said to Anne, all humor evaporated from his voice. He was in superhero-doctor mode now.

I walked out of the hut and waited.

I walked back up to our hut to wait for the diagnosis and only twenty minutes after that, Reggie and Anne walked in.

"Well the bleeding stopped," said Reggie. "I guess blood clotting is a segregated function from the healing properties, so we'll see how it looks tomorrow. We got some samples we can run tests on too. I'm going to get started on some of those now." He set down his medical kit and left to run the tests in his impromptu lab. I was asleep before he returned.

The next morning, I awoke to Reggie speaking loudly with Anne in the next room. As my consciousness overpowered my sleeping brain, I realized they were talking about the tests.

"I can't figure it out," I heard Reggie say. "What are we missing?"

I stood from my mat and walked to the doorway.

They saw me and looked up.

"It's strange," Reggie started. "Ahn's blood seems to be the same as anyone else's." His serious Mr. Doctor voice was still in effect. It was evident he had not slept much.

I spoke up, "You guys, there's something you need to know."

They detected the gravity in my tone and looked at me.

"One of the first nights we were here, a man came to me in the middle of the night and took me to another section of the valley," I explained. "He took me to another village about half an hour walk from here and it's awful. The people there—"

"Another village?" Reggie cut in. "Of Misymphomiacs?"

"Well," I continued, "I think so. They were horribly deformed. They were making food and clothes and there was blood everywhere."

They didn't know whether they wanted to believe me or not, but they were listening, so I continued.

"And...I've been thinking about it lately, and one of two things is happening here: either the people in this village don't have Misymphomia, or they do and have taken the people in this other village as their slaves. Or maybe some of them have it and some don't? I don't know." My brain was really on the move now. "Remember that boy who was taken away after he burned his mouth? I saw him in the other village! And Samhyup, the man who took me to the village, disappeared the day after he took me there." I paused before dropping the bombshell. "And he's the one who told me to cut Ahn. I think he knew that Ahn doesn't have it. He's faking it. His arm will heal."

Anne and Reggie sat in stunned silence.

"Well," began Reggie, then paused. "If what you're saying is true, we'll just see what happens to Ahn in a few days." He paused to think some more. "Could you take us to this other village?"

"I've tried to go back, but it was pitch black when I went before, and the walkways here are impossible to navigate. I think they may have even rearranged or blocked parts of it so we can't get there. When Samhyup took me before, we climbed over and under railings and bridges. It would be hard to get there again."

"So that's why he wanted you to cut Ahn," said Anne, almost to just herself. "So maybe the best thing to do—if you *are* telling the truth—is to wait a few days and see what happens to Ahn's arm."

We agreed that was the best course of action and decided not to bring it up to anyone in the village.

Two days passed and Ahn's arm seemed to be healing. On the third day we took Pornchai into the hut with us to talk to him.

"Your arm is looking good!" Reggie said through Pornchai, friendly as ever.

"Yes, I must be cured," Ahn replied. He spoke slowly, as if thinking up explanations as he went.

Reggie had taken off the bandages and was examining the wound.

"You know what's strange?" He said to Ahn through Pornchai. "I tested your blood and it is normal. We can't find anything strange in it. It's like you don't have the disease."

Ahn seemed unfazed. Anne looked up at me from where she

was kneeling on the other side of Ahn.

Then something cracked loud behind my ears and everything went black.

I slowly awoke to a throbbing headache and the stench of the bloody village. Night had fallen and it was pitch black beyond the doorway. We were in a small room. A fire burned in the corner and blood was splattered all over the room: on the walls, floor, tables, and I realized that we were in the room where the claw-handed boy had fallen to his knees before me. It was the room where the meat was prepared for both villages. Reggie and Anne were both unconscious near me with blood on their faces and clothes, and Pornchai lay unconscious several feet from us. The claw-handed boy stood on the far side of the room sharpening a knife.

"Hey," I whispered to him. "Hey!"

He turned around and his face was twisted into a combination of fear and sorrow.

"What's happening?" I asked him knowing full well he couldn't understand a word. I pushed myself up onto my hands and the small motion squeezed my head into an invisible vice grip. At best, I only had a concussion.

I grunted.

The boy was still looking at me and waved his deformed hand in front of him, as if saying *I don't want to hurt you.*

My eyes continued to adjust to the dim light and I saw pieces of animals scattered around the room. Some with clumps of fur attached to them, others with feathers protruding from them. I gently shook Reggie's shoulder and then Anne's. She stirred first and began holding her head.

My head pounded as I crawled across the floor to Pornchai and shook him. He did not stir. I moved closer and heard his breathing, but he would not wake up. I noticed that his face was more damaged than Anne or Reggie's, and blood flowed in several thick streams through his hair and down to his neck. I left him and pulled myself back over to the doctors.

"Where are we?" asked Anne, still lying down and holding her temples.

"This is the other village," I answered, "the one I told you about."

Reggie began moving as well.

"This is where they handle the meat," I explained. "I was here before."

From outside the hut we heard voices approaching. Then Ahn was in the doorway with several guards behind him. He growled some commands at the boy with the knife, who bowed his head and walked out the door.

Ahn then turned his attention to us on the floor and yelled some things in his tribal dialect which no one understood. Pornchai remained unconscious. Ahn walked to his body and kicked him twice in the stomach until Pornchai began to move, curling onto his side and holding his stomach.

Ahn yelled some things to the guards who then left and returned a minute later with some chains and cuffs in their hands. They first went to Pornchai, putting one of the cuffs around his neck and then his hands and feet. They dragged the chain from him to us and did the same. The guards first came to me and forced the cuff around my neck, then shoved my hands through the smaller cuffs. They did the same to Anne and Reggie so the four of us were bound to one another and unable to do anything but shuffle our feet.

By this point we were standing in a straight line. There was a chain connecting our necks, another connecting our hands, and one on each foot. The guard in front of us jerked on the neck chain and we lurched forward. My head felt like it had just cracked in half.

They led us out of the hut and up a trail leading outside the village. We left the line of buildings and were now walking through the forest. It was still black out, save a few torches carried by the guards and Ahn.

I leaned forward and whispered to Pornchai, "What are they saying?"

"I donno," he answered. "I only hear them talking 'bout their secret and not let us—" he was hit in the back by one of the guards, who yelled something in Thai.

We continued walking in silence with only the clinking of the chains to disrupt the chirping of the nocturnal insects. We walked for about fifteen minutes, though it seemed much longer because of the pain from being bound and only taking very small steps.

Finally there was a small opening in the path and the familiar stench of death graced our nostrils again. Eight poles surrounded an enormous tree stump in the clearing. The waist-hight stump was at least ten feet in diameter. The guards put the torches atop the poles and made us stand facing the stump. One of them walked behind us and kicked our knees, forcing us to kneel before it.

From the ground, I could see bones and other pieces of human surrounding the stump. Body parts covered in dry blood lay scattered, all rotting, some clearly older than others.

Reggie vomited.

All four of us were now shivering despite the warm Thai night.

Anne began screaming for them to let her go until Ahn walked directly in front of her and screamed something in Thai, presumably telling her to be silent. When she wouldn't, he spat on her head, then pointed to Reggie and gave a command to the guards. Two of the men approached him and removed his cuffs. Reggie sobbed and yelled for them to 'Please, please don't...'

The guards walked on either side of him, both holding an arm, and took him to the stump. They shoved his torso over it so he was bent at the waist, his feet still on the ground and his stomach on the wood. He was looking back at us, still crying out.

Ahn yelled again to silence Reggie and kicked him in the side, which knocked the wind out of him. He heaved for air. Ahn then turned and called another command in Thai and the young man from the kitchen came from behind us. He still looked sad and fearful as he approached the stump. He held the blade he had been sharpening, and was clearly shaking as well. Ahn yelled at him and pointed at Reggie. The boy hesitated, so Ahn snatched the weapon from his hand and began hacking at Reggie's back with it.

Anne shrieked, then forced her jaw to close over loud sobs.

Reggie's back was lacerated repeatedly until streaks of skin began to hang from his body. After about half a minute of chopping at his back, Ahn stepped directly behind Reggie and ran the sword through his torso. Reggie's shrieks had turned from yells to breathless gurgles, which presently fell silent.

Immediately after pulling the blade from Reggie's body, Ahn spun around and pointed it at Anne. She screamed again and fruitlessly jerked against her binds. The two guards silently started walking from Reggie's body to Anne. I saw Ahn step to the young man who brought him the blade and whisper a few fierce words to him. He raised the blade and slowly sliced the side of the boy's neck, right above the shoulder. The boy shrieked in pain. Ahn yelled and the boy turned and ran back up the trail, knowing the wound meant his imminent death.

The guards had undone Anne's cuffs and gotten her to her feet.

Then I heard rapid footsteps behind me and in the next ten seconds, it took me a moment to realize what was happening.

I saw the guards turn and then fall.

I saw several of the mutated Misymphomiacs running from the woods holding makeshift weapons into the flickering torch light.

I saw Samhyup run from the tree line of the clearing and chop with a fire poker at the two guards holding Anne. I heard the wet sounds of stabbing behind me followed by the dull thuds of bodies hitting the ground.

The entire ambush took about ten seconds, and ended with Ahn surrounded by four of the villagers and his left hand cut off. It appeared they had wanted him alive, but needed to disarm him.

Now the four Misymphomiacs were backing Ahn against the stump until he could not back up more. He backed right into Reggie's corpse and stood there holding his bleeding wrist. The two other villagers and Samhyup joined the semi-circle around him and the eight of them began a heated but brief debate. Then they stopped and one of them turned over his shoulder and yelled. The claw-handed boy who had brought the blade came back from the trail, holding a rag onto his bleeding neck.

More of the tribal dialect was shouted and I watched as the villagers grabbed Ahn's arms and legs and held him against the stump, spread like a gingerbread man. The younger man walked to Ahn's severed hand and took the blade from it.

Ahn began talking to him, his tone portrayed a false, pleading sort of kindness to the boy. The boy moved slowly and specifically as he walked right up to Ahn and began slicing up his stomach. The gashes were not deep enough to let his intestines out, but he sliced and sliced with the tip of his sharpened blade until the membrane that divided skin from innards was no more. He then began to slice Ahn's arms with the same kind of shallow gashes until one of the older villagers said something to him. The boy then stabbed Ahn in the chest, pinning him to the stump. Ahn's screams, like Reggie's, turned to a gurgle and then silence as his body slumped against the stump and relaxed onto the sword.

Samhyup and the seven villagers with him then turned to us and hurriedly found the keys to release us from our binds.

Samhyup spoke to Pornchai who told us, "He say he is very sorry he di' not get here sooner to save our other friend. He invite us to his hut to explain errything."

We were led back to the bloody second village, apparently into Samhyup's hut. His wife was already making food with some assistance from some other women in the village.

After we had cleaned up a bit, we sat down to eat and Samhyup began explaining everything through Pornchai, who held his bleeding and bruised face.

"The Misymphomiacs lived here in this village for as long as we know," he began. "But twelve years ago, Ahn came and discovered them. When he and many of his tribe realized how fragile they are, they made the Misymphomiacs their slaves. They made the Misymphomiacs build that entire beautiful village for them, and many of them died in the process. No one who lives there has Misymphomia. They simply act like they do in order to live in comfort and act peaceful when anyone comes to the village. The sick make all their meals, do all the cleaning, all the construction, everything. They do everything.

"I came to the tribe and soon saw exactly what was happening. I decided to act like everyone else while secretly building relationships with the people in this village, the Misymphomiacs. That's how I met my wife. She is Misymphomiac.

"When you arrived, I knew we had a chance to expose them to the world. That's why I brought you here the first night," he pointed at me, "and now you all know. You all can help to bring justice to our tribe. To these people who are now my people."

We agreed. With Ahn dead, it would be easier to bring justice to this group of people who had been pushed down for so long.

Or so we thought. I had underestimated how violently people will hold onto their way of life. And hold onto comfort. We rallied several dozen of the Misymphomiacs to march to the other village and demand equality.

By the time we arrived the next afternoon, the other villagers had heard about Ahn and taken up weapons of their own. They killed over half of the villagers that had walked with us, and because of their condition, even the Misymphomiacs who had minor cuts or broken bones were doomed to die quickly.

There were less than twenty of us when we finally surrendered. They had us surrounded.

They then took Pornchai, Anne and I away from the others and deliberated what they should do with us. Overhearing the conversation, Pornchai told me they were worried about us leaving and telling the rest of the world about their village. I realized that with most of the fighting men from the second village now dead, the Misymphomiacs would return to being slaves working for the healthy and comfortable villagers in the first village.

Finally the guards near us stopped talking and one approached us. Taking the sword from his sheath, he first stabbed Anne in the chest, followed by Pornchai. He then came to me and pushed the blood-covered sword into my stomach and everything faded to gray.

16. Stitches Cactus Farm

Marianne drove through the dry Arizona day to the small middle school where her two boys were just being released. Her old green van showed spots of rust on every corner and rattled as she approached the school. She rode through the desert with the windows down since the air conditioning broke years ago.

Marianne was one of the oldest mothers at the school and her kids knew it. They knew the other moms who came to pick up their children were younger, healthier, and had fewer gray streaks in their hair. Marianne was on the southern border of fifty but already used a cane to cross the parking lot to the school.

Children flowed out of the doors seconds after the final bell sounded. Marianne politely smiled and nodded at some of the other parents standing on the cusp of the sidewalk, not wishing to engage in any trite conversation.

"Mom, let's go!" commanded her oldest, Leo, as they burst out the doors.

"Hi, boys—" she began to reply.

"Hurry up, mom," shouted her other son, Roy, "you're so slow and pathetic."

Marianne said nothing and turned to walk back toward the van. She seemed to lean more heavily on her cane than a minute before. The boys sprinted ahead of her while she limped across the blazing asphalt.

As she approached the van, the boys had already climbed inside. Roy hopped back out and ran to her. "Here, ma, let me help you," he said, putting his hand on her shoulder. Leo Giggled from the vehicle as Roy proceeded to kick Marianne's cane from under her. As it rattled across the scalding pavement, he picked it up and began smacking her on the back of her thighs and lower back. Her hands and knees seared as she fell to the scalding concrete of the lot.

"Come on, mom!" he yelled. "Faster!" Leo joined in the taunting from the van.

Marianne said nothing, but fumbled for her cane once Roy tossed it to the ground. She circled the van to the driver's side and climbed behind the wheel.

"Roy, are you buckled?" she muttered.

"Shut up and go, mom," he replied, "I have to get home for my shows."

The engine burped to life and Marianne steered out of the lot while the boys whispered cuss words to each other in the back seat.

She drove for several more minutes before Leo erupted from the rear, "Mom! Are you stupid? This isn't the way home!" Roy laughed and added more insults. "Take us *home*!"

Marianne did not reply.

"Mom, where are we going?" asked Leo after a few more minutes.

"I have something to show you boys," Marianne said quietly, adding, "I think you'll like it."

"Are you taking us to dad's grave?" piped Leo.

"Hah! Yah, I have to pee," said Roy. "You're probably just so lonely you want to look at it and cry for an hour, don'tcha?" They both laughed and Marianne said nothing.

Afternoon crawled behind the low Arizona hills and evening crept in. The boys continued asking questions, but Marianne said nothing.

Finally, when most of the day's light had vanished from the road and a glowing violet remained beyond the rounded peaks, Marianne turned the van onto a dusty, unpaved driveway that wound into the dark bosom of the hill.

"Mom?" said Roy in a tone that had turned from a taunting jeer to the scared concern of a boy. "Where are we?"

Marianne remained silent.

As they continued down the road, the boys could see what looked like acres and acres of twisted and thorny cacti. They were not the usual straight and cylindrical shape of cacti, but misshapen trunks that painted silhouettes of horrifying figures against the dim desert sky.

The van approached a dark shack as the last threads of light disappeared. By the dim illumination of the headlights, they could see a small sign hung by the door which read 'Stitches Cactus Farm' in crude handwriting.

The door burst open and a tall, thin scarecrow of a man stomped out toward the van. He wore beat-up cowboy boots which were evidently too large for him, making his skinny legs look even skinnier.

Without looking up, Marianne turned off the engine and managed to whisper, "get out." The boys were silent.

The man's boots crunched the warm gravel as he approached the sliding door of the van. He said nothing, but simply peered through the middle window into the dark interior.

"Boys, this is Mr. Stitches," Marianne said, "and you'll be staying here from now on. I believe he has plenty of work for you."

As she spoke, the man circled the vehicle to the driver's window. Marianne pumped at the inside of the door to roll down the dusty window. In place of a greeting, the man grunted and handed her a small roll of cash wrapped in a rubber band.

The boys cried in protest as the man slid the door open, slamming it into its rear rubber stoppers. He grabbed them both by the hair with his bony yet strong hands and wrenched them from the van.

Marianne sat in silence, watching her sons dragged away by their hair until they disappeared into the dark shack hedged in by the warped forms of monstrous cacti.

She silently thumbed the wad of wrinkled bills for a moment, relishing the slow feeling of freedom that was filling her entire body. She felt thirty pounds lighter as she shifted back into drive and slowly began driving back down the warm dirt driveway.

17. The Rope In Our Yard

There's a rope in our front yard
which hangs from the tree.
Sometimes the rope is up in a loop
but sometimes it's untied and free.

Sometimes the rope is gone for a day
but it's back when I look out at night.
Sometimes I see it, but to everyone else
the rope is just nowhere in sight.

Sometimes the wind comes and rips through the hills,
but the rope doesn't move, not an inch,
it just hangs there as if it were perfectly still
like a line painted straight on a fence.

Sometimes it's long and sometimes it's thin,
sometimes it's frayed from the outside on in.
Sometimes it's strong and sometimes it's short,
but I'll never touch that rope again.

18. Love and The Birds

So there's this airplane. And the engines of this airplane caught fire and sure enough, it went down.

Everyone dead.

Now, married to the man seated in 16A was this woman. Not too young, but not yet very old. At the exact moment her husband and all those nearest him were either screaming, speechless, puking, or unconscious; she was gardening.

It has been said that when a loved one is in trouble, people sometimes get the sense that something is wrong. They somehow have a feeling of loss or disconnect between their heart and the heart of their loved one.

This was simply not true of North Dakotans like them.

His lovely wife was in her garden, whistling and sweating on this humid July day. And as the people on the plane began to have less and less skin thanks to the flames from the engines, she went inside for lunch.

They had been married a while—the not-too-old woman and the not-too-young man—and two days before he was driven to the airport by his beloved wife, they were playing Scrabble in the dining room. She was winning. He ended up losing to her and this meant dish duty. He pretended to be disappointed by this, yet he had quite the smile on his face as he turned on the water in the sink and grabbed the dishcloth. As was tradition between the two of them, she couldn't stay away for long. She was his dish drier; his *Lave-vaisselle.*

They had met in college against the will of their respective Catholic and Lutheran schools. Yet their meeting was far from covert. He was not the football captain, or the prom king, but his smile was bigger than St. Louis and his eyes sparkled. During her first conversation with them, she knew she was trapped.

He was her bacon bringer.
Her bed warmer.
Her dish scrubber.

It took a few "chance" meetings until her feelings were reciprocated, but it happened. At the time, she weighed twenty pounds more than she did at graduation, but he warmed up to her, decided there was simply more to love that way, that he loved her how she was—with a little extra cookie dough—and then she went and lost it all. North Dakotans tend to be mostly blind when it comes to irony, but he quickly moved past her figure and proposed.

The two schools soon found out about this and the two were expelled three months before graduation. And that is why they lived in North Dakota, where the days are long and the nights are cold. He became a vacuum cleaner cleaner, which made people mistake him for a stutterer, which caused the two of them to not get invited to many cocktail parties, which was okay with them.

When they were together, no day was too long and no night was too cold. They had hands and knew theirs were meant to be connected.

Life was good for a while until this day she went out to garden. She came in for lunch and just then there was a knock at the front door. It was the little boy from two doors down selling popcorn. She signed up to receive some and went back to her sandwich.

After a few bites, the phone rang.

Her husband had died near the border of Minnesota and Wisconsin.

19. Bury the Bear

I first saw the face in the window of a passing car.

I was walking on the sidewalk when the minivan passed me by and I happened to look up when it did, right into the driver's side window. I didn't think too much of it when I saw it for the first time. It was an older woman, probably in her sixties, driving a minivan in Bryson City. It wasn't that irregular and I gave it no second thought.

It was fall in North Carolina, which is arguably the best season for the region. The leaves yellowed and fell en masse while the air around them was a perfect crisp which was still warm enough to enjoy being outside.

The next day, I was at the grocery store picking out gourds for the fall celebration at my church. I was squeezing and knocking on some squash when I noticed her again, browsing by the bananas. I didn't give it too much thought, as seeing someone in your small town twice in two days is not that irregular. In fact, I wouldn't have even noticed that we'd passed by each other twice, except for one thing: she never once took her eyes off of me. The previous day, she had panned her neck to keep staring at me as she drove past, and today she unblinkingly observed me as I picked through the gourds.

I quickly made a selection and moved to another aisle. I was able to finish my shopping and leave the store without seeing her again. Even those first two encounters would not have been memorable had her face not begun to reappear more frequently over the coming days and weeks.

For the first few days, it continued to be random encounters like the first two. At a bus stop, in the window of a neighbor's house, at the library. I saw the expressionless, aged face staring at me. When I glanced at her, I couldn't tell what color her eyes were. The pupils seemed to expand into the entire iris, looking like nothing more than gigantic black spots in drained white retinal beds. Her gray hair probably would have been shoulder length if she let it down from its pins and curls. Her neck was longer than average, but not freakishly so.

The more her face appeared, the more I began to feel shivers pacing my spine every time I met her eyes. Those black eyes which never blinked were always monitoring my own.

I began to think I was going insane.

One day, as I stood before my classroom teaching, I blinked, and in that split second every student in my classroom became the woman. My blood froze inside my veins and I tried to continue teaching as usual. I stuttered. Dozens of pitch black pupils were all locked onto me. I tried to get a sentence out and blinked again and when I did, the faces of my eight-year-old third graders were back to normal. Some were staring around the classroom, while the good ones were looking at me, patiently waiting for me to continue.

I resumed my lecture while the back half of my brain nervously paced the edges of insanity, wondering when I'd snap out of it and these episodes would cease.

After school that day, I waited for the bus to pick me up at the bus stop while the gentle autumn rain drizzled around me. I was almost used to seeing her face everywhere. Every couple minutes, her face would drive by me as the driver of a sedan, or a passenger on a passing bus. Every time, the black pupils would lock onto my own and her long neck would crane to maintain contact with me as long as possible.

I decided I needed to see someone about it. A psychologist? A detective? A neurologist? I didn't know where to begin, so I opened the phone book when I got home and called the first name I saw—Barbara Green, PhD. It didn't say much about her, just that she was a psychologist.

I expected to leave a message since it was well past business hours and the sun was nearly gone for the day. Instead, the phone was answered halfway through the first ring.

"Hello, this is Barbara," came a friendly voice on the other end.

"H-hi," I stuttered, not expecting to talk so soon. "I need to talk to someone."

"Sure," she replied. "What has been going on?"

"Well, you may think I'm crazy—"

"I won't," she cut me off, now seeming slightly colder.

"Okay, well...I've been seeing this person everywhere I go. Every day. Multiple times a day."

"Well, we live in a small town. Maybe it's not that unusual?" she replied.

"No, it's not like that," I continued. "Can we talk in person?"

"Sure! You busy right now?"

I wasn't sure what to say. Scheduling anything with anybody was always done days out, especially with someone as professional as a psychologist. At the same time, I thought about how nice it would be to figure out what was causing these hallucinations. Maybe she could prescribe some drugs to get my brain back on the right track.

"I guess not," I muttered. "You want to meet now?"

"Sure! I'm still at my office. Can you be here in twenty minutes?"

"Yah, I'll come over."

"Great!" then the line clicked to the dial tone without a goodbye.

When I walked back to the bus stop near my house, the sun was gone and the last traces of its light were trickling down the horizon. The streets had quieted down and the only sound was the wind rustling the drying leaves. After several minutes I saw the headlights of the bus down the road. I closed my eyes as it eased to a stop before me; I was hoping I wouldn't see that wretched face driving the bus when I opened them.

I heard the doors open and forced my eyelids apart. I was relieved to see Francisco, the usual evening bus driver. He grunted as I stepped on without even turning his head toward me. His indifferent demeanor normally irritated me when I rode the bus late at night, but tonight, after being stared at for days, it was a welcome relief.

I swung around the pole and plopped into the first seat on the right. The bus was mostly empty except for two other passengers scattered around the seats. My stop came quickly and I exited the bus, walking quickly across the sidewalks of our small town to get to Dr. Green's building. As I got close, I noticed a sign above an otherwise nondescript door which, in faded maroon lettering on a white background, simply read "Green Psychiatry." I double checked the paper on which I'd written her address and pulled the door. It opened directly to a staircase, so I went up and looked for Suite 202.

The hallway was dark so it was not hard to see the one door with light peeking out underneath. I took a moment to catch my breath, then approached the door and knocked.

A few seconds later the door opened and I saw her.

Doctor Green was the woman.

Or maybe the woman had taken over her face, just like she had taken over the faces of drivers, passengers, and my students.

"Hello, come on in!" she said with a smile. "I'm Doctor Green. Please make yourself comfortable.

Something was different this time though. It took me a moment to realize the difference as I walked in and sat on a couch across from her chair. It was a typical counselor's office—small coffee table with a box of tissues on it, couch with pillows, and her academic plaques hung on the wall behind her desk.

"So tell me more about what you've been seeing," she said, sitting down across from me. Her black pupils seemed to crawl under my skin as she examined me.

The only difference between all my other sightings and now, sitting across from her, was that now she seemed slightly more human. Her eyes were not locked onto me, but freely moved around the room, around my body. I tried not to let her face distract me. I couldn't help thinking that she knew about it. Was she the reason I had been seeing these faces? Did she do it and now she was enacting some sort of cruel joke?

"Well, it was about a week ago," I began. "I first saw her driving a car."

"So it's a female face?"

"Yes."

"Can you describe it at all?"

I was worried she would ask that. She held her pen over her pad, ready to write.

I decided to lie. "Yes, she's a young woman. Attractive and blonde. That's probably why I noticed her—"

Before I could go on she cut me off. "You're lying."

I paused. I had no idea how to reply. *How did she know??*

"Okay..." I thought through how to tell her that it was *her* face I had been seeing all along. "It's your face. It's exactly your face that I've been seeing." I studied her face for a reaction. It didn't change.

"I know," she said, still with a blank face. I was shocked. Out of all the possible responses she could have made, that was the worst.

"Wh— How do you...?" I trailed off, unsure of what to say.

She simply smiled, soaking in my confusion and enjoying it. I felt like a mouse being toyed with by a cat.

She began to speak in what seemed like metered prose, trancelike. "Find the roads that lead to nowhere, the bridges without ends. Find the paths that cut through mountains, the bear without a den."

This time I cut her off: "I'm sorry, Doctor Green, but this is not helping." I went to stand up, but she jumped to her feet before I could get up from the couch. She repeated the same line, but this time louder.

> "Find the roads that lead to nowhere,
> the bridges without ends!
> Find the paths that cut through mountains,
> the bear without a den!"

She plopped back onto the couch as if reciting the verse had utterly worn her out.

"Doctor Green?" I asked.

Her eyes were closed. She wasn't moving. I saw her sweater rising in quick, short breaths.

"Doctor Green? I'm going to leave now," I said. I slowly stood up and walked to the door. As I touched the handle, I heard her speak from the couch without moving:

> "Find the roads..."

I turned the door knob and rushed out of her office. I intended to wipe the episode from my mind and chock it up to a lack of sleep and a vivid imagination. The bus came slowly and once again, the indifferent bus driver was a welcome relief back to the world of normalcy. It was nearing 10 when I exited the bus and walked toward my front door.

I kept expecting something to happen to me, now that I had met—and possibly angered—the owner of the face.

But nothing did.

I went into my home and passed out, not looking forward to the early morning of teaching ahead of me. The next day I made it to my classroom without encountering the face again. No students morphed into a terrible old woman, nor did any drivers or coworkers. It seemed that the hallucinations had come to an end. The mystery had been solved: I probably caught a glimpse of her face in passing and something about the eerie creases in her face or her dark eyes adhered itself to the inside of my skull. Case closed.

But a week after meeting her in her office, I couldn't shake her words from my head. Her face had stopped haunting me but it was replaced by those four lines echoing in my mind.

> *"Find the roads that lead to nowhere,*
> *the bridges without ends.*
> *Follow the paths that cut through mountains,*
> *the bear without a den."*

Something about it refused to stop bouncing around my skull, so as much as I tried to fight it, I found myself walking to my school's computer lab to do a search. It had been over a week since the strange appointment, but the words still rang in my ears clear as a bell.

I sat down at the keyboard and after looking over my shoulder several times, turned on the computer tower. The whirring sound seemed to spin forever as the CPU booted up.

After waiting several minutes I opened a search page of the internet, looked over both shoulders again, and typed in the first line: "roads that lead to nowhere."

The first result was a classic rock album. I scrolled down, and after a few more clicks, found an article which shocked me. I felt trickles of gooseflesh trace down my spine as I read past the headline and scrolled down through the paragraphs. *How did I not know this earlier??*

The article recounted the start and abandonment of North Shore Road in 1948. It was a 6.5 mile road which wound through the Smoky Mountains, but the road was never finished. It ends in the middle of the forest.

a road that leads to nowhere…

The part which was even more frightening to me was the fact that it was so close to me, yet I had never heard of it before. The start of the road was only about a 20-minute drive from my house, then it was 6.5 miles to its termination in the woods. In that moment, I resolved to get out to the edge of the 'road that leads to nowhere' and see if I could discover what Dr. Green was talking about, putting her and her cryptic words behind me once and for all.

I sat back and thought for a moment, deciding what method was best for getting out there since I didn't have a car. Then I leaned forward and searched on the computer for a taxi service in Bryson City. I found the nearest one had a base on the main street of town and tingles raced down my spine once again as I realized it was basically across the street from Dr. Green's office.

No big deal, I told myself. *What can she do? I'll be across the street and won't even have to see her. Won't even look at her building.*

The next day was Saturday, so I took my normal bus ride into town from my home in the late morning. I stepped off the bus and approached the taxi station, trying desperately not to glance toward Dr. Green's building.

Finally my morbid curiosity got the best of me and I glanced across the quiet main street at her building.

Wait...is that the right building?

I was sure I was looking at the same building I had entered only a few nights before; it had the same door leading to a staircase visible through the window. And I'd lived in this tiny town for decades. It didn't change that much, and I knew where I was.

But the sign was missing.

There wasn't even a darker rectangle of red in the brick wall where the sign would have blocked the sun for years. I looked closer, trying to find an indication of "Green Psychiatry," but saw nothing. I squinted from across the street at the tiny list of residents listed by the door buzzers. I couldn't make out every one, but I was fairly certain there was no "Green."

I tried to dismiss this from my mind. *It must have been a different building.* As much as I tried to convince myself of this, I was fairly certain that this *had* been where I was a few nights prior.

Eventually I yanked my attention back toward the taxi service. I was only two buildings from it, so I forced my feet to resume their walking. They were waiting for me in the small office room which was more like a closet than a reception area.

After exchanging a few details, my driver, Freddy, walked me out back to where the taxis were parked. He was a brown-skinned man with an unplaceable accent. I immediately sensed that he was not interested in small talk, which was fine with me.

My brain was pacing at an incredible rate through all the events of the past few weeks: I had seen a woman's terrifying face for days on end, encountered the *real* version of her, and now was on some scavenger hunt to hopefully put an end to the mystery surrounding her.

I sat in the peeling pleather back seat of the taxi as Freddy whipped me through the yellowing forest outside of Bryson City. I watched the leaves whip by in a warm blur of fall colors, breathing in the stale air of the cab which smelled like plastic and ancient cigarettes. I wanted to roll the window down but had a feeling Freddy wouldn't appreciate it.

About 20 minutes later, we were on North Shore Drive. From here it was just over 6 miles to the end of the road, where the abandoned bridge passed over the location where the concrete trailed off into overgrown forest.

> the road that leads to nowhere,
> the bridge without its ends…

Anticipation rose in my stomach like an anxious flower blossoming in fast-forward. What would I find? What was I even looking for? The four lines she had spoken to me were emblazoned on my mind. They seemed to get hotter like a searing iron in my brain the closer we drew to the end of the road.

What was the bear without a den?

The paths through the mountains seemed pretty simple—it described the road Freddy and I were on. If my thoughts weren't so focused on the mystery at hand it would have been an incredibly beautiful drive to soak in.

The butterflies in my stomach grew more lively the closer we drew to the end of the road. It wasn't more than a mile now.

Freddy tapped the brakes as the arched stone bridge came into view. The road passed through underneath the ancient structure, but it was clear that the drivable road ended several yards before it. Beyond the stone arch, the road crumbled into stones which were swallowed by green weeds and lichen.

"You just want me to wait here boss?" he asked.

"Yes, if you could..."

"How long you gonna walk around for?"

"I'm not sure."

"Meter's running," Freddy said as he reached for a magazine from his passenger seat. I winced as I felt the sting of his words dig into my meager bank account. I wanted to hurry so I'd save money, but had to find what The Face was talking about.

The door's staccato thump barely broke the ambience of the forest as I closed it behind me. I slowly walked forward, looking for clues on the bridge, the ground, and the trees. *Would I find a bear? A stone that looked like a bear?*

I approached the large stone overpass, examining every inch of the construct as I drew closer. I looked for carved symbols or a note stuffed between the cracks. There were plenty of teenage love proclamations. "EL+GD 4EVER" carved inside a rough heart. More initials. Other hearts.

Nothing jumped out at me from the dizzying wall of etchings and graffiti. I walked through the arched overpass, pausing to look back at Freddy in his taxi. He was either sleeping or focused on his magazine. Either way, he was paying no attention to me.

I continued out the other side of the tunnel and that's when everything happened.

My feet had only begun to toe the area where the road began crumbling into nature when I heard voices. It was a woman's voice at first. *Doctor Green's?*

It chanted in metered rhythm. Initially it was unintelligible groans. I couldn't tell which direction the voice came from. It sang from the right, but when I turned, it was suddenly behind me. The voice of the forest surrounded me.

Slowly the babbling moans morphed into words I could understand.

> ...bury the bear, bury the bear
> she's rotting in the open air...

Shivers ran down my spine, but this seemed to confirm that I was close to...something. I managed to stop spinning in search of the origin of the voice. I continued taking slow steps down the 'road' which was now simply a stretch of weeds cutting through the forest.

A dozen steps later I went to step but couldn't pull my right leg forward. My shoe had caught on something.

I looked down—it wasn't caught on something.
A hand was holding my ankle.

Someone was lying on the grass in the weeds, grasping my ankle. I traced the arm to its owner and there in the grass lay Doctor Green. She looked awful, like her flesh had begun to decay while she was still living in it. Her eyes had sunk into her skull and once again, they were locked onto mine. I gazed into those massive, dead pupils as the forest fell silent around us. Then she whispered those four lines once more,

> "Find the roads that lead to nowhere,
> the bridges without ends.
> Follow the paths that cut through mountains,
> the bear without a den."

Suddenly the forest resumed its chant of those terrible words, and Doctor Green whispered them again.

I tried to kick my ankle free from her grip as I yelled back, "Doctor Green! It—it's me!" I shook my ankle free and stumbled backward until my shoulder was caught by something else.

I turned and there, inches from my own face, were Doctor Green's eyes. Her decomposing face inhaled a raspy breath and joined into the chant. Her warm breath burned my nostrils with its horrid odor.

My world began to spin.

The other Doctor Green on the ground crawled toward me in a wretched lumbering motion. One of her arms was clearly no longer working.

The one standing beside me squeezed my shoulder tighter and bellowed the four-line chant louder and louder. I tried to pry my shoulder from her grip but her finger strength was surprisingly tight. I finally jerked my body free, but my motion propelled me away from her. By then, the Doctor Green on the ground had crawled behind me so that when I tore myself away from the other, my heel went right into her splintering ribcage and I fell to the ground.

When I hit the grassy soil, my head connected with a rock and I heard and felt a loud *crack* ripple through my face and down into my neck. The pain streaked like white fire from the back corner of my neck to my forehead and back.

My eyes crossed and then uncrossed as I lay on my back.

A few seconds later, when I regained my focus, the voices chanting in the forest had fallen still. I saw a figure standing over me. Then she was joined by another, then another. More and more Doctor Greens arrived to stand over me, looking down.

Then, in one unified chorus, they droned in a gross monotone,

> *Bury the bear, bury the bear*
> *she's rotting in the open air.*

When they had finished their couplet, they leaned down toward me. I squeezed my eyes closed, unsure what miserable fate awaited me. I clenched my entire face and covered my head with my forearms.

But then nothing happened.

I waited a second. And then another one. But no rotten fingers touched my body. I peeked out from behind my arms and the forest was empty. I slowly sat up in a motion that sent pain streaking through my head. I made my way up to my feet with the pressure squeezing my head into a vice grip.

There were no more voices. No more Doctor Greens anywhere. Except—

I was looking around the forest again and getting a grip on my surroundings when I saw the patch of white up the trail a bit.

During the hallucination, I had wandered several yards down the trail away from the arch. It was barely visible around a bend in the trail, and Freddy's yellow cab was completely gone from sight. I couldn't tell how long I had been away from the taxi, but the sun was still up, so that was a good sign.

I approached the white patch to the side of the path and found that it was cloth. It was clothes.

It was stained with blood and dirt, but appeared to have been there for a while. The blood was long dried and faded. The body lay face down, but I knew who it was from the mid-length brown hair which lay bunched around its head.

The body must have been there for at least a week, maybe two or three.

I stood there staring at the body of Doctor Green for a long time, realizing I had met with a ghost.

I had been haunted by a ghost.

I had spoken to it and run from it.

And now I knew why.

Doctor Green was not alone when she died. She had been murdered in some gruesome way which I did not intend to learn

—that was a mystery for the police to solve. I'd contact them, let them bring her killer to justice, and put her underneath the earth.

I would bury that bear.
I would deliver her to her den for the long hibernation.

I keep having this notion that when we die we become a cloud. Or maybe we don't become one, but we fly through them, in and out and above and below. We feel the icy cool specks of cloud matter stinging our faces as we soar through cotton puffs.

"You can never have too much sky," wrote Sandra Cisneros. And it's true. And I think that if you are sky, then who can really damage you? Clouds mete out a great deal of punishment, but who punishes them? A plane flies through them and the cloud opens right up to create a passage for them.

20. Tom & The Cloud People

"There's Tom again," she sighed as the bum walked by. "He always tries to convince me that we become clouds when we die and he wants his face to burn from the floating ice drops while he flies through them."

I looked up as I walked along the sidewalk and saw the man zigzagging around the street. He brushed past me and his torn jacket smelled so bitter it was nearly sweet. It was a very human smell—every material the body produces, all bundled together and simmered beneath an old Broncos jacket for months.

Tom needed a shower.

He turned and ran diagonally across the street away from us, screaming, "There's too much sky! There's too much sky!"

It called to mind something Sandra Cisneros once wrote: "You can never have too much sky."

Apparently Tom can.

My new girlfriend, Cindy, and I were making our way along 16th Street Mall in Denver as summer was finally beginning to concede to fall and the day was picturesque. Problem was, Cindy didn't like homeless people. They creeped her out and made her nervous. She saw them less as people and more as stray dogs which probably wanted to bite her. It was a little flag for me, but as someone who didn't do much about homeless people to begin with, I could overlook her insensitivity.

Tom had circled back now and was bearing straight up the sidewalk toward us. He was screaming at the sky, so he was looking up and not where he was going. The distance between us was closing—20 feet, then 15. Cindy and I slowed down and her fingers clenched harder onto mine.

"The mooooon," Tom yelled at the distant white satellite. "Why are you out now? It's still light out! Go back to bed!" and then he proceeded to curse the moon at the top of his lungs. Several parents bent down and covered their children's ears, or yanked their little hands in the opposite direction of Tom.

He was now right in front of us. He managed to look down and stop his screaming two feet in front of us. He seemed shocked to see two humans before him, on a public crowded sidewalk in the afternoon.

He stared into Cindy's eyes for several seconds, white gunk resting on his lower lip as he caught his breath from screaming. As he stood, he swayed closer to her, then further away, then closer.

Cindy squeezed my hand so hard I grunted.

"They're in the th—th—ckllggg," Tom muttered to her with his blue eyes staring straight into hers. He drunkenly leaned toward her again, caught himself.

"What?" whispered Cindy, coiled into a standing ball. Her left hand held mine and her right was tucked around her head, but she couldn't take her eyes off of Tom.

"They're in th-th-thhh," his speech turned into blowing raspberries through his lips, spraying saliva and white gunk everywhere. I suddenly had an overwhelming feeling come over me. It was not pity or sorrow for this man, but an actual interest in what he was trying to say. Like the prophets of the Old Testament, he seemed to have an important message for us—or the world—but no one gave him the time of day.

Cindy tugged my hand, "Let's go. Come on."

Now it was I who couldn't take my eyes away from the sidewalk messenger.

"What?" I asked him.

He yanked his gaze away from Cindy and narrowed in on me. Then it was as if he suddenly sobered up and spoke several complete sentences, directly to me: "They live in the moon and they have told me," he wheezed, coughed, and continued. "When we die, we become clouds. NO! We fly through the clouds and feel the frozen water particles stinging our face."

"Okay..." I replied. I didn't really know what to say. I never talk to homeless people. I wanted to know why this mattered, because Tom made it seem like it really did.

"Have you seen the cartoons?" he asked.

"The cartoons?" I responded. "Which cartoons?" By this time Cindy was adamantly yanking on my arm with both hands, but I had to hear what Tom said.

"The cartoons with angels on clouds? The people in heaven. The line outside the golden gates." Then his voice lowered a full octave and finished with, "All of the departed live in a silent country in the clouds. You don't see me as I am, you see me as you are."

Suddenly, as if a rope was around his neck, he yanked himself away and ran down the sidewalk away from us, still shaking his fists at the sky and taking swings at the low tree branches.

That night I could not shake what Tom had yelled into my face through his rancid breath and remaining teeth. I assumed most of the talk about clouds and sky and the moon was the substances talking, but what about how I saw him? How did he know?

Cindy and I had retreated back into an alleyway and ascended back into the clouds. I sat pensively on the edge of some mammatus formations when Cindy flew over to me.

"How did he figure it out, do you think?" she asked.

"I honestly have no idea. I thought we were doing a great job of blending in."

"Well," she said as she reclined next to me on the cool surface, "at least everyone thinks he's crazy."

"Yup," I said and I smiled as we watched the lightning dance over the badlands, illuminated by a beautiful autumn sunset.

21. Lordsburg, NM

Lordsburg, New Mexico. Population: 3,379. The absolute middle of nowhere. It's seven in the morning November 15, 1995, and the air is still. Mark rose at four to greet the smoky gray dawn with a cigarette and black coffee. He only ever drinks half of it, but still makes too much. His hair is getting long now, as is his patchy beard, and the greasy strands are starting to fall in his face.

His battered boots crunch the gravel under his feet as he walks slowly toward his truck. His denim jacket is torn around the edges and smells like old liquor. Mark spits to the side as he reaches for the door handle, tosses his cigarette butt to the gravel as he slides onto the drivers seat.

The town is only now beginning to stir as the sun makes itself known above city hall, and Mark's truck revs itself to life. After a quick top off of his gas tank at the run down Conoco, he made his way to the edge of town.

Scrawled on the chalkboard of the second grade room of Lordsburg Elementary is the repeated phrase:

This is really happening.
I see the children but I can't touch them.

This is really happening.
I keep having this dream where I'm a giant.

Over and over and over again, in a child's handwriting, this phrase covers the board. Miss Lacey came in one morning and discovered it. To her knowledge, no one had been in the room before her that morning. She shuffled to her desk and dropped her papers and purse, muttering under her breath about the "high school dropout bums."

Miss Lacey prodded at her face a lot, worrying about loose and saggy cheeks. She wore a lot of makeup for an upper-middle aged single school teacher, and she always smelled like a cool garden breeze. She made sure of it. She read a lot of romance novels, often out loud, and secretly took pain relieving pills when she didn't need them.

Without a moment's hesitation, she dutifully picked up the eraser and began wiping the board clean.

& & &

"It never snows in Lordsburg," said Anne. She and Macy walked toward their houses through the couple inches of white powder that had fallen during the afternoon. Their parents had only recently allowed the two girls to be out of the house on their own, and they intended to take full advantage of this newfound freedom.

They had met up with a couple of boys behind the drugstore, but now it was getting dark and they had already missed dinner.

"It makes everything quiet," observed Macy. "I can't believe how quiet everything is in the snow. It's beautiful!"

Anne was silent as she ran possibilities through her head. It really was quiet. A man bundled up in all black walked on the sidewalk opposite them. The town grew darker and darker, but no houselights were on. They had reached their neighborhood by now, but still saw no one but the man across the street, walking parallel with them. A few porch and driveway lights were on.

The town was silent.

They bade each other goodnight and nervously walked to their separate houses.

22. The Tall People

It was nearing the end of August when things began to get strange on Cape Cod. The summer heat kept the beaches occupied; families still lay scattered across the white sand for miles along the Eastern coast, but tourists were beginning to pack up and leave.

Residents of the Cape know that this time of year moves more slowly than the rest. Schools begin to reopen their doors across the spit of land, and sailing teams reunite to conquer the still-warm Atlantic in their dragging sloops and wider hauls.

One particular day before my 8th grade school year began, late in the afternoon before the sky began to yellow, I was on my bicycle with my friend Emily and a swarm of gulls flew over us. Not a normal pack of gulls, but a group so vast it blocked out the sun for nearly a minute. We looked up and overhead saw the motion of thousands of wings in staccato motion. The dark cloud was accompanied by a chorus of squawks and sighs from the airborne vermin. Once the birds had passed, we hurried to the docks.

Emily and I pedaled up the trail along the bay to the Barnstable Harbor where her father worked. He was a thin, leathery man who had spent his life on the sea. The sky was golden and darkening as we slowed up to the bay. He waved to us from a distance and made his way back up the dock. He usually bought ice cream for us girls, so my hopes were high.

"Hey, gihls," he called to us with a smile as me made his way across the boards. "Wheah wah you today?"

Emily and I explained that we had been a mile West down on the bay and saw a cloud of gulls flying overhead.

"Is that what that was?" he asked in his thick New England accent. "I sawr that from heah but couldn't tell what it was."

We didn't see gulls again for days. No one on the entire Cape saw birds of any sort—a fact which may have been missed if the cape weren't such a major birdwatching hotspot .

I returned to school the following week and a couple of my classmates noticed the absence of the fowl in the area. We thought little of it until the second week of school.

Emily and I were biking again, holding tightly onto the last warm days of September. This time we were South by Hyannisport. The wealthy folk live around here, and we liked riding through their neighborhoods and looking at the tall white houses shooting up from the sand by the sea. We had made our way along the coast again, following the trail between Hyannis and Centerville, when we saw it again.

The birds swarmed over the ocean, coming North from Nantucket. They flew just to the East of us and settled on the yellowing branches of the trees. They rested on the limbs and became still and quiet as if they had never left.

Emily and I watched for under a minute as the enormous swarm was broken up and the birds chose trees on which to settle and remain. It was over before we realized it was happening. We were silent for a moment before hopping back on our bikes and pedaling back to my house a few miles away. The sun was going down and the sky was done showing off her colorful displays and began fading through various shades of gray.

As we biked down my driveway, Emily and I were buzzing with excitement.

"What if no one else saw it?" she asked me with bright enthusiasm.

I giggled. "Maybe we shouldn't tell anyone," I said. "Let's just wait and see what happens."

I paused for a moment and Emily and I seemed to have the same thought at the same time.

"Do you want to go back there tonight?" I asked her. "Maybe we can figure out what's making all the birds leave and return."

Emily nodded as a menacing smile spread into her cheeks.

We ate dinner and waited until my parents went to bed. I could hardly focus on our conversation because of the adrenaline pumping through my veins. We were both so excited to go back to the beach.

Emily and I waited half an hour to be sure my parents were asleep before slipping out the side door and pushing the front door open just enough to roll our bikes out. Rubber tires crunched atop the cool pebbles on the drive. It was dark. Summer stars still hung in the sky, white pockets of punctuation across the pitch black sheet, and we rode to the trail.

The trees against the moonlight were still dark, rising as conspicuous silhouettes before the glowing sky. The Cape can be a scary place at night, but our prepubescent curiosity outweighed our fear of the dark.

As we drew near to the beach, the air shifted. A breeze picked up for no more than a second and then it was warm. It suddenly felt more like July than September, as if we had passed through a barrier.

The beach came into sight and it happened again. It seemed like every bird on Cape Cod flew to that beach. As we slowed our pedaling, we heard rustling in the bushes at our wheels. We realized it was not just the birds now, but all sorts of animals congregating at the beach. Rats and snakes flitted across the path before and behind us. We slowed our pedaling to a crawl, not wanting to run over the vermin, but not wanting to put our feet down either.

Over the sea, the birds began to gather and swirl. This tornado of aves lasted about a minute before they all suddenly flew back to the trees peppering the coast. They were lined up on the trees nearest the water, as if expecting the waves to put on a show for them.

Emily and I came to a stop behind a cluster of holly and looked South to the water. Shivers were slowly beginning to crawl along my skin.

The night was still.

Then out of the water, past the buoys and the bay, something emerged from the surface of the water. It was white and very far away. It could have been just another buoy bobbing up from a swell. Then another near it rose up and moved toward the coast.

Emily let out a breath as quietly as she could, and I realized I had been holding mine as well. We continued watching as the white shapes were joined by more and more white shapes, approaching land and rising out of the water. There must have been hundreds of them.

The first ones reached the buoys and in the darkness we could distinguish the rough shapes of heads and shoulders. They were not bobbing. They were walking.

As the forms got closer, we could see that they were enormous. They were as tall as the trees and moved with a gentle grace as they emerged from the water until the waves lapped at their ankles. Their pace was slow and steady. Their long pale limbs swayed gently like beach grass in the ocean breeze. The whole thing seemed like a dream.

We continued watching as they made their way ashore and across the cool dark sand. Their arms continued swinging lightly as they made their way from the sand to the tree line, lumbering across the marram grass.

The ones in the rear were still emerging from the deep when the first ones reached the trees, one hundred yards from the water. There was an army of them.

> *The Tall Ones came so late at night,*
> *we barely would have known*
> *that they had wandered up to shore*
> *and brought with them Shalom.*
> *They have no eyes, but we all know*
> *when they're looking at you;*
> *they have no mouths, but we can tell*
> *that what they know is true.*
> *They wear no clothes, but never seem*
> *exposed among the trees*
> *they have no faces but we know*
> *they have identities.*
> *They whisper to the living things,*
> *the plants and animals;*
> *our heads are at their knees and yet*
> *we seldom feel too small.*

The following weeks, we saw the Tall People spread across the Cape. More of them wandered in from the sea and dispersed among the towns of the peninsula, bringing with them a strange peace. They seemed to love living things. Initially, my father was worried about them. But then he saw one in his garden and let go of his fear. The garden blossomed a few days later.

They seemed to soothe and cultivate everything they came in contact with. Emily and I would hike through the woods by our houses and see them, standing near the trees as if having discourse.

It seemed like everyone who came in contact with them was mystified by these ethereal beings. They carried such an immense feeling of innocence and purity that they wordlessly convinced us to not tell anyone off Cape about their existence. And no one did. It was as if we were under a spell.

My father told me how one day he came home and saw one standing near the side of our house. It wasn't touching the house, but it was inches away. He told me about how his gut rose up within him, but the tall person turned his head and then my father was calmed and entered the house.

Not more than a month after they appeared, I was at the lunch table with some boys at school. They were the ones who let their lips fly and didn't care where their words landed.

"I heard the homos up in P-Town have had sex with them," said one boy with a scowl.

"Yah," added his friend, trying to top his cohort's statement. "And I heard weird stuff happened to them when they did!"

This caught my attention. Since I had first seen them, I had wanted to touch them. To see what they felt like. To see if they had skin or some sort of ghostly membrane. No one I had talked to had touched them. I hadn't even seen them touch each other.

The first boy lowered his voice and we all leaned in. "My dad told me that the homos went crazy and died a few days later. He says he thinks the Tall People didn't want to be touched in the first place. I mean, you've seen them. They don't have weenies or.... You know, they don't have genders. They don't touch!"

I was so curious about this news, and even though I was repulsed at the thought of some dirty men grabbing a Tall Person against his will and forcing him to do...stuff, I wanted to know more. After school, I asked Emily if she had heard about the men in Provincetown, and what she knew about the sex of the Tall People. She knew as much as I did, but did not seem to share my intrigue regarding their skin and feeling.

I sat with those boys the next day to see if I could glean more information, but they also did not seem to want to divulge more.

The weather had begun to sink to a skin-chilling crisp. It was the time of year when, after sunset your fingers grew stiff from the cold, but the air was still walkable. After school that day, I went out on my bike alone. I biked to a forest near my house to try to get a closer look at a tall person. I didn't tell anyone where I was going when I left, worried my parents would disagree.

I went to a familiar grove two miles away and started walking my bike once I reached the dirt. It was only about ten minutes before I happened on a Tall Person standing near a tree. It was inches away from the tree, facing its bark. The tree was full of singing birds who would occasionally leave their branch to circle the Tall Person and land on a different limb.

I leaned my bike against a trunk by the path and slowly approached the back of the Tall Person. When I was ten feet from it, I saw the shoulder turn and the head faced me. I stared at the faceless figure for a moment before realizing myself.

I cleared my throat. "H—hi," I got out.

In lieu of facial expressions, the figure's posture changed. It hinted a feeling of welcome but caution. I imagined that this Tall Person knew about what had happened in P-Town.

I stared up at it, my head just below its thin pale knee. "What's your name?" I remember asking it. There was no answer, but I suddenly understood that they have no names. I looked down in embarrassment blended with confusion.

After a moment, I took a step closer to the person. It stepped back, ready to retreat. I wondered if it was trying to protect me by not touching me. I remembered the boys mentioning that everyone who touched them had died.

I decided to walk away. It was difficult to take my eyes from the form of the Tall Person, so tall and pure before the tree. I stepped backward until I was back on the path, then turned and ran to my bike.

I found you in the forest
and I caught you by surprise.
You seemed to speak in silence
without lips and without eyes.
I wonder if I love you,
if I see you as a god.
I wonder if it's possible
for perfect to be flawed.
And we would love to touch you,
to let your skin meet ours,
but contact is forbidden
like a lover behind bars.

Three days after I spoke to the Tall Person in the woods, my mother and I were eating dinner together. My father burst in and shouted, "They've gaht one!" He slammed the door behind him and strode to the table, sitting as he explained. "Just today, I heahd that tha' police put one in theyah cah and took it to prison!"

Questions flowed through my head like a river. "What did it do to them?" I blurted out.

My father shrugged and brushed his hair back with his palms. "They wah uneasy about two of 'em standing by the Dennis Post Office. Took 'em to prison fah loitering."

I sat silently. I knew my father was as conflicted about the arrest as I was because he too had a quiet affinity for the Tall People. In fact, everyone I knew did. No one seemed to mind their quiet presence here the past month.

The next day, the Tall People were digging.

We were let out of class early because of how stirred everyone was. In the past month, we had never seen them do anything except stand and slowly walk around the Cape. They seemed to communicate with living things. They even had a gentle way of placing thoughts in your head when you stared at them long enough. This was the first time they were actively engaging in work or activity.

I saw them on my way to school several yards from the road, two of them, digging with their hands. It was peculiar to see them hunched over and pulling up ground. When I passed by after class was let out, the hole was nearly as tall as they were and about ten feet in diameter. They clearly hadn't rested while I was in school. Emily and I tried to look away as we walked by, but we were mesmerized by their activity.

We walked to my house and my mother sternly told us not to leave the house. "Your father will be home soon," she explained. And then we waited. No news had come regarding the Tall People that had been arrested, but I was sure my father would have some when he returned home.

The afternoon passed and my father had not returned. My mother chewed her fingernail and Emily and I drew with charcoal.

"Mother?" I finally muttered, "I think I could go to the hole and maybe try to talk to them again. Maybe they'll remember me."

My mother was silent and continued chewing her nail.

"Emily could come with me," I added.

She tucked her hands into her lap and toyed with her skirts as she turned to look once more out the window. "Okay," she faintly muttered. Her eyes batted back tears.

Emily and I biked to the hole we had seen earlier. As we approached, we found that it had grown substantially wider. Now it was at least thirty feet in diameter, but the same depth as before. From a dozen yards away, we could see the heads of the Tall People, who seemed to be scraping dirt off the walls of the hole. My stomach hurt.

One of them saw us coming and suddenly the thought entered into my head.

"Maybe we shouldn't be here," Emily and I said simultaneously. I stared at her, both of us realizing that the Tall People had placed the same thought in our heads at the same time.

We slowly continued toward the hole, walking now. Once we could see over the edge, we realized the Tall People were not the only ones in the hole. Many men were in the bottom of it. Some were speaking, some were walking, some were sitting. There were at least twenty men in the pit, but something was strange about the way they moved. Each one groped around, feeling his way forward.

I realized none of them could see. Many of them seemed not to know where they were, and cried for help. The silent Tall People were no help, and none of the men seemed to speak to one another.

Emily and I stood in shock at the edge of the hole. We couldn't look away. The Tall People continued pulling dirt from the sides of the pit as if the men were not within. I looked once more at the men and saw my father, near the far side of the pit. He was sitting against the wall of the hole, moving his head back and forth as if looking for angels above him. He muttered to himself constantly. His arms and legs rested limply on the ground, as if they had been hung on him this morning.

I ran over to the far side of the hole. "Daddy!" I cried out, falling to my knees on the grassy lip. "Father, up here!"

He seemed to hear me and looked up. I called again, and he directed his face toward me. "No," he called up once he recognized my voice. "No, Sweetheaht, go away from here! Run! Get out!"

As he was yelling, one of the Tall People gracefully strode toward him and bent over. It reached down to him, grasping his torso with one hand and his head with the other. In one move, the Tall Person supplely removed my father's head from his body with a snap, the way you pick an apple from a branch. The Tall Person placed the body and head back on the ground, turned, and strode back to the wall he was working on.

I screamed. I was on my hands and knees in the cold grass, and I felt my arms quake beneath me. Emily was behind me, stunned by what was happening. We couldn't speak. Saliva fell from my gaping mouth and my nose ran onto my shirt.

I continued watching as some of the other men heard the commotion and blindly wandered over to where my father lay. One of them tripped over the head and when he landed forward on his hands, the right one snapped off. He rolled over, holding his wrist in pain. His hand was on the ground next to him.

Not long after that, another one of the walking men appeared to stumble. When I looked at him, however, I realized that his foot had broken off. It was as if their limbs were rotting while still on their bodies. They were breaking apart.

"Let's go," cried Emily through breathless sobs. We started backing up, when Emily screeched.

I turned around. She had backed right into the leg of a Tall Person. He bent down and put his hands on her shoulders. I crawled away backward, shuffling away from between the hole and the Tall Person.

Emily screamed as the Tall Person picked her up and turned, walking back into the woods with her in his arm. I could feel tears flooding my cheeks, blurring my vision. I tasted mucus rolling from my nose. I ran back to our bikes and pedaled away from the hole.

> It's a quiet kind of violence
> when you touch 'em til they're dead.
> And it's an awful kind of coward
> Who pulls a father from his head.

The next day the Tall People were gone. Some people said they walked back into the ocean. The Dennis Police decided to release the two they had incarcerated, and a few hours after, all of them were gone.

Riots broke out across the Cape on every Main Street. People raided police stations, wanting retribution for arresting the Tall People. They claimed that the arrests were what had led to the Death Holes, which led to over a thousand deaths across Cape Cod.

From my understanding, the Tall People were corrupted by humans. After the P-Town Rape, they realized that touch was harmful. The boys at school said they thought that once the Tall People saw how harmful touch could be, they hurt people with their touch. People's bodies rotted after touching a Tall Person. They went blind and many of them went mad immediately, killing others or themselves.

And when they saw that humans locked each other up in prison cells, they made their own out of the earth.

I don't think the Tall People were stupid; I think they acted according to their purity.

Many people were swayed by the Tall People. Women longed for their touch, and walked around Main Streets dressed in all white, crying out for their return. People chanted to the Tall People. These religious folk would be seen for years to come, sitting on green summer grass in circles, singing songs to the Tall People and raising their arms. Others were adamantly against them. Tall People Support Groups were formed, mostly for those who lost loved ones in the Death Holes, or saw what occurred.

We never found Emily.

My father's memorial was on a Thursday morning in November. It was cold and wet, but there was no burial. The Death Holes vanished as quickly as the Tall People themselves.

I looked at old photographs of my father on the docks and his boat, consistently smiling through patchy scruff. My mother wept bitterly, as did I and we held each other.

After the service, I walked alone out of the tall white church building and looked up. A dozen gulls drifted overhead, cawing casually to their friends.

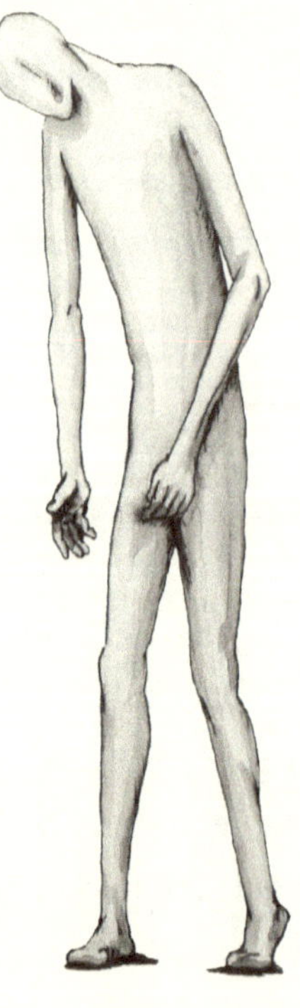

23. The Trainman

Act I: Trainman

The Trainman tells me not to whisper,

but I whisper anyway

because I can.

He says that sometimes, when a Train

comes around a curve,

it tips over and comes off the track.

I used to ride the Subway.

They had good peanuts,

but then they stopped making good peanuts,

so now I sit with the Trainman.

He says that someday, the Train will

come for us, and take us out

of this desolate wasteland.

I think I believe him.

He tells me not to listen

to certain people because they're bad.

Sometimes I do anyway

because I want to and I want to hear

what they are saying.

I don't believe them,

Just the Trainman:

He says that the Train will come

someday. And take us away.

The Trainman gave me more peanuts.

He says they're good for the head.

He says they clear the mind

for pondering and mind-wandering.

I eat them.

They taste pretty good.

He says the Train will come soon.

We've been waiting here for so long.

He says it's getting real soon now.

The Trainman said not to go

down the really long, dark tunnel.

I've never been down there.

I wonder what it is.

He said don't go down there

because Government is down there.

Act II: Government

He says Government is huge and

terrifying. He says

it'll hurt me and put me in

a room with seats.

I won't be alone there.

I wonder if it's really bad

to go down the tunnel and see

the Government.

The Trainman says it's bad.

I think I believe him.

The Trainman wouldn't hurt me.

I don't think I'll go down there,

where Government is.

I'll stay here with the Trainman

and wait for the Train to come.

He says it will come soon,

that we won't have to wait

very much longer.

I did some of the things

that the Trainman said not to do,

like whispering

and listening to people

who The Trainman says not to.

So far, these haven't hurt me,

and neither has the Trainman.

But I don't think I'll go down

the long, dark tunnel

where Government lives.

I like waiting with the Trainman,

even though he says

a lot of things not to do.

I think I believe him,

and I don't want to go to Government

where there are seats and others like me.

The Trainman says it's bad

and I think I believe him.

I've heard of the Train

that he talks about, even before I

came here.

It's got a huge light in the front

and a dead man watches from the back.

The Trainman knows him

so he won't hurt us.

And I think I believe him.

The Trainman tells me not to whisper

and a bright light fills the shaft.

Act III: The Train

It's a loud noise.

The Trainman puts his hand on my shoulder

and he says not to whisper.

Don't whisper.

I see the Train and look up

at the Trainman. His eyes widen.

I looked over at the Train.

It was on fire.

The dead conductor hung out the window

with flames dancing on his back.

The Trainman staggered back

and sat on his bench where he always

waited for the Train to come.

I stare at the back,

at the dead man

who is now on fire.

I ask the Trainman what to do.

He says one word.

Wait.

For the next Train.

I sat by the Trainman.

This is the kind of day I've had.

I would ask him a question,

but the Trainman tells me not to whisper.

I would normally whisper anyway

but he missed his Train. Forever.

Now we have to wait for the next one.

I want to know what Government is,

but the Trainman tells me not to go down there.

It's dark in the tunnel.

I want some of the Trainman's peanuts,

but the Trainman tells me not to whisper.

There are screams coming from the long, dark tunnel

where Government lives.

I've heard them before.

Another question I wont be able to ask.

The Trainman still sits there, motionless.

We're still here,

waiting for the next Train to come

and take us out of this desolate shaft.

No one knows we're down here.

I'm thirsty and ashes still hang in the air.

The Trainman says not to drink.

I've only drank a few times,

but water hurts my throat.

I guess the Trainman warned me.

The Trainman told me not to whisper

but I whispered anyway

and nothing bad happened,

but now I have to ask him for some peanuts

Act IV: Whispering

My dry lips part.

Breath comes up through my throat.

The Trainman told me not to whisper

but I had so many questions

to ask him.

I asked him for some peanuts

and what the Government looks like.

He sharply looked at me

And raised his voice to a yell.

Are you trying to wake the Government?

he yelled at the top of his lungs.

The Government only hears whispers

passing through the lips of young children.

He sat down and resumed his waiting

for the Train we already missed.

He said there will be more

Trains that come through the tunnel.

I wanted to scream.

I wanted to run,

but the Trainman told me not to go down there.

I've been down here so long,

sitting with the Trainman.

He didn't answer my questions

but he handed me a little flask

of liquid fire.

It soothed my throat as it went down

and started a fire in my chest.

I nod my thank you and hand back the flask.

The Trainman tells me that sometimes

a Train comes off the track

when it comes around a curve.

Maybe that happened now,

and thats why the Train's not coming now.

This shaft is getting darker

as the lantern burns out.

The Trainman got up to relight it.

I wonder how he can see

in this pitch blackness.

Minutes pass and I hear nothing.

Minutes turn into hours.

I got up and walked over

toward where the lamp was.

I wanted to whisper,

but the Trainman tells me not to whisper.

I felt around for him

and only bumped the creaky lantern.

Act V: Alone

The Trainman tells me not to whisper.

I wanted to whisper

and ask where he was.

I felt around in the pitch blackness.

The Trainman was nowhere.

I find the matches and straighten the wick.

The tunnel is illuminated

when the match strikes,

but there is no Trainman.

Only a dark tunnel,

and no way out.

I wondered where he went.

Maybe Government got him.

There is no fear in me.

There is a spilled sack of peanuts

over by the bench.

They are better than the Subway's peanuts.

That's why I came down here with the Trainman.

The Trainman would tell me not to whisper

or to talk to certain people

or to go down the long, dark tunnel

if he were here.

He just went to go get some more peanuts,

thats all.

Just more peanuts.

Because he dropped his bag.

I don't have any fear.

Why would he go down the long, dark tunnel

if he tells me not to?

The Trainman wouldn't harm me.

He'll be back soon.

Maybe he's looking for the next Train

because sometimes, when a Train comes around a curve,

it comes off the track,

so he's looking for the next Train.

I whispered.

The Trainman told me not to whisper

and I whispered.

Thats why he's gone.

It's my fault the Trainman is gone.

I whispered and Government got him,

and put him in a room with others like him.

No it didn't.

The Trainman told me

that Government only hears Children's whispers.

And Government only takes children.

He's getting more peanuts.

This is the kind of day I've had.

Act VI: Abandoned

The Trainman is not here.

If he were here,

he would tell me what not to do,

like whisper,

or go down the long, dark tunnel,

which is looking very tempting right now.

The Trainman gave me good peanuts

to get rid of the voices,

the ones that said to me,

Don't kill us. The Trainman's peanuts will kill us.

I fought with them

and I killed them.

They're coming back.

There's a sack of peanuts over by the bench.

Don't eat them!

They fell on the ground!

They don't work anymore!

I crunch on the dry peanuts.

Silence follows.

I think the voices are gone now.

Theres a chinking noise,

behind me, where the light doesn't reach.

There's no fear in me,

so I walk toward the noise.

As I get closer,

the noise moves farther from me.

I stopped.

Maybe it's Government,

luring me in.

I turned around

and started to run.

The gravel crunched as I sped over it.

Then I fall.

There was a rock bigger than the others,

and my foot hit it.

I fell and my arm hit the glass

from the bottle broken by the drunk.

The Trainman had beat him up

with his own bottle,

and then he told me never to drink alcohol.

My arm hits the glass.

The skin slides across the sharp edge,

and the fluid flows out.

I would have screamed,

but the Trainman tells me not to scream.

I rolled over

and feel more glass go up into my back.

I opened my mouth

in a silent scream,

and didn't permit any sound to come out.

Even a whisper would awaken Government.

Blood flooded from my arm

and stained the ground crimson.

Blood was coming from my back,

because my shirt was wet.

There was a red stain where

I had just rolled from.

Act VII: Bleeding

Blood is all over the ground.

I suddenly feel very tired.

My eyes try to shut,

but I jerked them open.

The Trainman is still gone.

He would know what to do now.

Maybe the peanuts would help.

They are only good for the voices.

They wont heal my cuts.

I try to push myself up,

but my arms are too weak.

I try pushing up again,

but collapse and send more glass

into my shoulder and chest.

The drunk man must have had a lot of bottles.

I don't know how many he had,

because the Trainman told me

to turn around and shut my eyes.

I passed out,

then forced myself to wake up.

I must have been out for a long time,

because now the blood was dry,

and it cracks when I move.

My arms are sticky

and stiff from the dried blood.

I can't move because there's glass

all around me like a pool.

I blacked out again.

I try to wake up, but I can't.

Theres a good dream playing.

I jump on the Trainman.

He laughs, then stops,

and tells me not to jump on him.

Suddenly his face dries up.

I froze in the dream.

He fell to his knees

and then onto his back,

and an eagle swooped down

and took his body,

and I was all alone in the dark.

My eyes opened to see nothing.

The lamp had burned out.

I hadn't moved in hours.

My eyes could have been open or closed,

I wouldn't have known.

I hope they are open

so I don't black out again.

Then the floor drops out from under me

and I fall, and hear the Trainman's voice

telling me not to whisper.

Then he laughs

and laughs and won't stop.

The ground is getting near.

I hit it and jerk my eyes open.

There is a light from the lamp,

and a figure sitting on the bench.

I can't tell if its the Trainman,

or someone who could be bad.

Act VIII: Stranger

I still can't move.

I hope that's the Trainman sitting

over on the bench.

He starts mumbling to himself,

complaining about the Subway snacks

and the Badger in the Subway tunnel.
It's not the Trainman,
because the Trainman wouldn't complain.
I want to ask who it is,
but the Trainman tells me not to whisper,
or to talk to some people,
so I try to crawl closer to the bench,
then freeze in my tracks.
The Trainman is running down the tunnel,
toward the stranger.
I know it's him because of his big coat
and his scarf waving off his shoulders.
He tells me to look the other way
and to shut my eyes.
I want to ask him where he was,
and why the Train was on fire,
and who the man on the bench is,
but the Trainman tells me not to whisper.
I turn around and shut my eyes.
Tight.
It hurts to move.
I try to cover my ears,
but I can't move my hands fast enough.
I try to think about other things,
but I can't shut out the man screaming,
and the crunch of gravel as he runs away,
and the smell of blood

coming from their direction.
The Trainman ran over to me
and picked me up and took me over
to the bench. Lays me down.
He went in his pocket and pulled out
a pack of peanuts and tells me to have some.
I thought they only worked for the voices,
but I feel my wounds healing.
He tells me the salt heals wounds,
and that's why they help my cuts.
He sits down at my feet,
and sits like he has
ever since I came down here,
as if I never fell,
and he never left.
I look down at my arms.
The cuts are still there,
but the bleeding stopped
and they don't hurt at all.
I hear the chinking noise again
and look up at the Trainman.
He sits there
staring straight ahead, straight into nothing.
I don't know if he hears it.
I would ask him,
but the Trainman tells me not to whisper.

Act IX: Chinking

The Chinking is getting louder

and the tunnel is getting lighter.

I look up at the Trainman

and he looks up at the Train.

It's getting closer

and slowing down.

the conductor is dead,

and his body is burnt to ashes,

but the Train is still stopping.

The Trainman told me that the conductor

would wave as the Train came close,

but now he is dead

and the fire is almost out.

The Train stops right in front of us,

but the Trainman hesitates,

because the conductor is dead.

Finally he gets up

and walks toward the Train.

He's been waiting for a long time

and the Train is finally here

but the conductor is dead.

He walks over to the door

and slowly opens it.

One of the dead passengers falls out

and the Trainman steps aside

and goes into the Train.

I hold in my cough

from the ashes of the dead man.

I followed the Trainman

into the Train full of dead people.

I saw the terror in his eyes

as he looked at all the dead passengers.

He would have sat with them

and talked and laughed with them,

but now they're all dead.

The Trainman doesn't cry

and he tells me not to cry,

but I'm more confused

than I am scared.

There is no fear in me right now.

The Trainman sat down in a seat

that the former passenger had fallen out of.

I sat down, too.

And the Train started to move.

We were going down the dark tunnel

that the Trainman told me not to go down,

but he said it's okay,

because we're in a Train.

I don't want to see the Government,

so I don't look out the window

Act X: Leaving

I stare straight away from the window

and it's very dark in here.

I think we're going very fast,

but I don't want to look out the window.

Suddenly, the chamber gets very light,

like we're outside,

or in front of the Government.

The Trainman still looks the same

as when we were in the tunnel.

I still won't look up,

because I may see Government.

Suddenly the light stops,

as if we went back into a tunnel,

or finished passing Government.

The Trainman nods to me,

telling me its okay to look up.

I looked out the window

and only saw a dark tunnel wall.

We rode in silence

surrounded by dead, charred people.

The Trainman tells me not to whisper

because Government will get me,

but we're past Government,

so I asked the Trainman how much longer

until we're there.

Right then the Train went around a curve

and I heard a metal screech

and the Train shook and went

off the Track.
The Trainman jumped to his feet,
and reached into his coat.
He got out a bottle of gasoline
and a packet of matches.
As he started taking his coat
and scarf off,
he yelled at me for whispering.
He dumped the gas on his clothes
Which were piled in the middle
of the dead Train.
Then, the Trainman threw the empty bottle
out the broken window.
Then the Trainman lied down
on his soaked garments.
He tells me not to whisper,
and lights a match.
He says that sometimes, when a Train
goes around a curve,
it tips over and comes off the track,
but he never told me
it would happen if I whispered.
So the flaming Train will come
to the next station
where the passengers wait
for it to come and take them
out of their desolate wastelands.

24. Maverick The Cleaner

It was minutes before the first traces of daylight began weaving their threadlike fingers through the black sky. Mav checked his watch again and took a final puff of his cigarette. He stood next to a road stretching into the darkness on the dirt path before a gate. The path wound through the gate and up to a house that had not yet woken up.

The house was large and gothic. It had been built near the beginning of the 20th century and barely stood till this day as Maverick stood at the end of the driveway.

The morning was still and silent. Even the birds and chirping insects had not yet stirred. It hadn't been two minutes, but Mav checked his watch again and slowly paced his 4-foot route. He was calm but evidently growing impatient. Mav shivered. He smothered his cigarette underfoot and patted his pocket to extract the next from the box when finally it happened.

A scream rose from the house.

It was not a full-length scream, but seemed to be cut short midway through. Maverick let his hand rest on the latch of the gate to make sure no more sounds left the building.

He waited.

Then pressed through the gate and walked the incline up to the front steps. Although the morning was still silent, he looked around him—left and then right—before ascending the stair. The sky had birthed a faint glow in the east, but there was plenty of time left.

Inside the house, violence had painted the walls with fresh crimson and an odoriferous aura that reached out and tapped Maverick's sinuses immediately. As he stepped into the front room, he could count one, two bodies, almost fully intact on the floor. He stepped over them and proceeded to the stairs to check the upper bedrooms.

It took him a full forty-five minutes to locate the third body. He had been doing this nearly 23 years, yet always neglected to look under the beds.

Two hours later, he walked out the front door and quietly pulled it closed behind him. The house had been cleaned. By now, the morning had come into full vibrance and the tall weeds in the fields surrounding the house seemed to join in a unified chorus with the birds and the chirping beasties to give fresh life to the day and welcome its newcomers. There was a mere prick of cold in the air, left over from the blackness of night, but it was the kind of cold that promised to give way to warmth in the coming hours.

On the front step, Maverick brought in a breath of the satisfying country air and held it in, letting the taste linger in his lungs before pulling out his box of cigarettes. He walked down the hill and out the gate to his car parked on the dirt beside the road.

Maverick's apartment was small and messy. It clearly had not been cleaned once since he moved in six years ago. It probably smelled, but he could no longer notice. Or care.

He slumped down onto the couch, not bothering to move any of the takeout containers or clothes beneath him.

Mav woke hours later and grabbed for his wrist. It was 20 till five. He stood up and paused as the blood rushed to his head. He rubbed his eyes as he walked out the door.

He drove to the small cathedral on 17th in downtown Little Rock and slid into the side of a rear pew just as the vespers was beginning. The words of the priest slid into the background of his mind as he pulled the Bible out of the pocket of the pew in front of him. As he held it in his lap, he paused for a moment before opening it up to roughly the middle. Written across Psalm 138 in yellow highlighter was an address. He shut the book, stood up and walked out the building.

That night as Maverick slept his usual two and a half hours, his dreams turned to the violence painted on the walls from the morning before. He saw their faces. He heard that half of a scream again. But this time, he was in the house as it was happening. His brain filled in the places where there were gaps. (He never knew if he was better or worse off because of this.)

Maverick was a cleaner.

He didn't know for whom. He had never seen them. He had never talked with them. He received all of his assignments the same way: An address written somewhere unexpected. One time he heard the location in a dream, so he went there upon waking and found the aftermath of the violence. The damage done to the victims could barely have been done by humans. It was not the markings of gunfire, knives, or even blunt objects. It was unlike anything on television or in films. Maverick had long thought he would eventually become used to the violence, but 23 years in, he still had not adjusted to the gore.

The morning was still and dark. The streetlights were still on, scattering their intermittent luminescence down the long, straight city street.

Maverick was smoking his second cigarette and thinking about how he despised these urban calls because so much more could go wrong. He slowly paced on the sidewalk, swaying one foot about in front of the other, in small circles. He stayed in the dark space between streetlights, waiting for the sound.

This morning, it was yells that came to his ears. He heard sentences, urgent sentences, and then a series of thuds. Sounds of large pillows hitting walls. One of the windows popped and rained glass on the sidewalk 20 feet from where he stood. A screaming gurgle and then stillness.

The sun resumed rising. The streetlights clicked off a moment later. Mav was more on edge this morning, and the mysterious aligning of the streetlight darkness seemed to be too perfectly timed. He looked once more to both sides of the street. No lights turned on in the surrounding homes, despite how closely they were packed. He opened the gate and ascended the stairs.

He smelled the bloodshed before he opened the door.

An hour later, as he was finishing cleaning the second body, he heard someone walking on the sidewalk outside. He heard the glass crunch under their sneaker. He heard their pace slow and his heartbeat raced. The pedestrian crunched back and forth on the glass twice more before Maverick heard him open the gate before the house.

Mav slowly rose and went to the kitchen to fetch a knife. From the kitchen window he could see the daylight was not yet in full radiance, as if some tinted window still sheltered the earth from the heavens.

"Hello?" a man's voice cracked from behind the front door.

"Everything alright in there?"

Maverick silently crept to the front door and waited to see if the man would persist.

"You alright in there, neighbor? I saw the glass..."

Maverick opened the door and for a brief second the man smiled and readied to speak again. Maverick stabbed him in his chest. The man stood, utterly confused for a moment and slowly looked down at the blood running out of his sweatshirt. Maverick was not a large man by any means and likely weighed 100 pounds less than the stranger. Before the man reacted further, Mav wrapped his arms around him and pulled him inside. The man fell to his hands and knees.

Maverick had never killed anyone before. He had never been so sloppy as to leave glass on the sidewalk either.

He finished his job, now cleaning the body of the man as well. An hour later, the job was completed and Maverick pulled the door closed behind him. He tapped the cigarette box on his palm until the first volunteer emerged. Today his fingers trembled as he drew it to his lips and teased with the lighter. He walked the sidewalk toward the lot where his car was parked. Under his wiper was an envelope. He opened it and was surprised to find a thick card with silver engraved lettering. It was simply a number: 34.544876, -92.176556. He looked at it for a moment and then drove to the library. He went to the row of beige boxy computers and typed the numbers into a mapping program. He scrawled the directions onto a receipt-sized paper with a golf pencil and drove home.

That night his dreams were worse than usual. He had killed a man. And then cleaned him. In his dream, Maverick saw the man's momentary smile as it turned to confusion and then terror.

He barely slept an hour.

He rose long before sunrise and drove to the location designated by the coordinates. It was south of the city, in the middle of farm country. Mav was pleased that he did not have to do another clean-up downtown.

He neared the location, but saw nothing on the horizon. He double-checked his handwritten note and slowed the car. There was nothing but wild grassland in all directions. He stopped the car and lit a cigarette. The morning was still dark, and it was evident there were no traces of civilization nearby.

He waited and smoked nearly an entire package of cigarettes. The sun was well into its trek across the heavens and Mav's stomach released a small growl. He looked up and down the road once more. He had not seen another soul since yesterday. In the distance to the east was a collection of trees, and he finally decided to walk to them, to make sure he had missed nothing.

He crossed the field which was partly muddy due to the dew left from the morning. He crossed 300 of the 500 yards to the trees when a sudden darkness crossed the sky. He looked up, assuming a cloud had momentarily eclipsed the sun.

But there was no sun to be seen. Or clouds.

Darkness seemed to be overtaking all the land within sight. Maverick stopped walking. He froze as he considered running to the trees, or back to his vehicle. In the halflight, he could see all the grass on which he walked turn brown and shrivel before his eyes. One of the trees in the grouping fell from no apparent cause. He started jogging to his car and immediately felt his years of cigarette smoking grab hold of his lungs. A sound somewhere between rolling thunder and a high-pitched scream splayed across the land. It was so piercing that Maverick fell to his knees and slammed his palms to his ears.

His pants soaked in the mud and dew. His knees chilled.

He looked up and from the horizon behind his car came what looked like a swarm of black birds. As they flew closer, he noted that they were flying very low to the ground, and were much larger than birds. Their shape was impossible to identify as they seemed to be slipping through the air the way black dye slips through a clear stream. They moved fast.

Maverick looked over his shoulder and saw several more trees falling down, their vibrant spring green evaporated into a deathly rotten gray.

Expletives fell from his mouth in a steady stream. The airborne shadows drew nearer. Mav screamed as they closed the final yards between them.

Their speed ripped his jaw from his head. His clothes were lost in the fury, and soon his skin was being pulled from his bones.

Before he died, Mav fell to his knees and then to his side. He heaved his final breaths, mere expletives at an invisible employer.

No more than a few seconds later, the daylight returned. A hawk glided overhead as a car approached and parked next to Maverick's.

A man emerged and looked around as he lit his cigarette. He scanned the horizon before he noticed the clod in the dirt where Mav lay, halfway to the fallen trees. He opened the trunk of his car and removed the necessary cleaning equipment.

He was glad this was a rural location because less could go sour.

25. Agent Blake Sees A Ghost

I am wildly good looking and I always know what to say.

Women swoon and touch my elbow when I slip out a smooth joke and my cheek pulls the corner of my lips back into a trademark grin. My tailor is Italian and my cobbler imports his leather from Turkish bulls.

The best part of being Max Blake, however, is what I do for work: I've made it a habit of saving the world, over and over again. I think I have a total of about 8 world-saves under my black, full-grain Gucci belt.

My high-tech phone watch rang as I was sunbathing beneath a cloudless Bermuda sky so I held my wrist to my ear.

"Blake," I said, never taking my gaze from the sharp blue horizon.

"Agent Blake," I knew the voice well.

It was the Queen of England.

Again.

"What do you need this time?" I asked while winking at two nice young ladies passing by on the sand.

The voice on the other end remained serious; it was not time to joke around. With her, it never is. "Are you familiar with Embassy 33?"

I quickly ran through my rolodex of secretive names and locations and recalled the secret Georgian base after a second of thought.

"Of course I am."

"It has been compromised."

My blood seemed to sink within my veins for a moment as I pondered the implications of this event. Embassy 33 was the safe house used by many in my profession. It also housed volumes of classified information which, if it fell into the wrong hands, could mean imminent danger for all of us. And not just those in my profession—the entire human race.

If the codes for the nuclear arsenal fell into the hands of another bitter billionaire nerd, that could spell the death of the planet.

These guys are always nerds. They never got ladies in high school so they're taking their revenge on the world which apparently wronged them.

When I spoke again, I tried to remain cool despite the implications of this news. "That's not good, ma'am."

"No it's not," the queen remained serious. "Agent Blake, I need you to find the ones responsible for this compromise and recover whatever has been taken from our safe house. I don't need to tell you the consequences if you fail."

"Ma'am," I said and tapped the face of my watch to end the call.

Suddenly Bermuda wasn't feeling quite as sunny.

This was supposed to be a relaxing weekend off, but duty called. I jogged back to my hotel room and threw my belongings into my bag.

At the lobby, I threw my ticket to the valet and waited as he brought my pitch black 1963 MG to the front. When my car pulled up, however, it was not the valet seated in the driver's seat.

I popped open the passenger door and stuck my head in.

"Hello Max," said a wickedly familiar voice.

It was Neville Chambers.

Physically inferior to me in every way, Neville was the picture of a nerd who became rich and powerful and now used his resources to exact revenge on the popular and attractive folks of the world, as well as everyone else. He sat there in a gray

Barney's suit (two sizes too big) complete with a black tie, yanked up to his Adam's apple.

"Concerned about Embassy 33?" he asked in a polite tone. Before I could answer, he instructed, "get in, Max. Let's talk."

"Alright, you old goat chode," I said, "but you'll never pull this off."

I pulled the door of the tiny car closed while throwing my duffel into the backseat. As I predicted, he wove my beautiful car through the flat Bermuda landscape while revealing the ins and outs of his scheme. He must have rehearsed his timing, because just as he was wrapping up his yarn, he eased my car to a stop before a hidden helicopter pad where a private Blackhawk was waiting for him.

"Remember, Max," he said as he exited my vehicle, "the plan is already in motion and there's nothing you can do to stop it. All you need to do is sit back and watch." He smiled and winked before turning to run into the cabin of his helicopter.

Now I was mad.
Winking is my thing.

In a flurry of dust and wind the helicopter was gone, leaving me sitting alone in the passenger seat of my own car. I didn't have time to think, so I hopped over the console and whipped my car around, retracing the road we had taken to the pad.

& & &

The flight from Bermuda to Scotland was slow. My legs bounced while I sat in First Class, wishing the plane would fly faster. Sometimes the world just moves too slowly for me.

Shortly after takeoff, Lewis, my technology provider, had emerged from the back of the plane and given me some new gadgets to fiddle with. In addition to my phone watch, I was now equipped with shoes that shot poison darts and a tin of mints which was really a bomb (though it also had 2 real mints, in case the occasion for wooing presented itself).

The most amazing new piece of gear was a belt which was woven in such a way that it could be unfurled into a 1,000 meter thread which could hold my weight—and if I tap the belt buckle, the electrical currents in the thread instantly pull it back into the fully-woven belt.

Afterward, I slept my nightly hour and a half, so the rest of the flight was spent thinking about how to stop Chambers. He told me his entire plan in the car, and I knew there was a crack in it somewhere, I just had to find it. I always do. You would think he'd stop explaining his entire plan to me after a while, since I've found a way to stop him every time.

Perhaps he just likes the game.
As do I.

I was on my way to storm his private castle in the highlands of Scotland. His plan didn't involve his castle—the Embassy was in Georgia after all—but by invading his headquarters, I was sure I could interrupt his scheme and throw a wrench into the outcome. He wouldn't end the world *this* time. Embassy 33 was too important to lose to a joker like this.

On the descent, I saw a black convertible Jaguar driving onto the tarmac, meaning my British lover Esme had come to give me a lift.

The plane landed on the runway and before it taxied up to the terminal, I dropped out the emergency hatch beneath the plane's bathroom and tuck and rolled onto the concrete.

I popped to my feet and coolly jogged to her car. I tossed my tactical duffel bag into the back seat and jumped over the door into the passenger seat.

Esme's head was wrapped vertically in a scarf and adorned with oversized round sunglasses. She had bright red lipstick on her zealously plump lips.

"Hello, my love," she said as I dropped into the seat.

I didn't say hello. I never say hello when a dramatic kiss will do the job. I leaned over the console and planted a passionate smooch onto her lips.

Rather than kiss me back as I'm accustomed to, she pulled back and yelled '*Wowwww!*'

I couldn't believe my eyes. I had thought her voice sounded funny, and suddenly everything clicked together at once as she removed her sunglasses. She was now hideous!

That's because it wasn't Esme at all.

"Chambers!" I yelled in shock. I resisted the urge to gag as I realized I just tried to make out with my arch nemesis.

"Hello, Blake," he said as he undid his bonnet and smiled wickedly. "Let's go see what's happening at my castle, shall we?"

He had gotten me good, I'll give him that. I settled back into my seat as I realized he may still be a step or two ahead of me yet.

"Wait," I suddenly blurted. "What happened to Esme, you sweaty ox gooch??"

"I haven't touched her, dear boy."

"But this is her car!"

At this, Chambers threw his head back and laughed an annoyingly wicked laugh. "This is my own automobile!" he said. "I have one of every car, so of course I selected the one which would fool you into getting in. Don't try to jump out, dear boy. This car has more booby traps than a Mayan mausoleum."

We were now leaving Glasgow and heading into the high country of Scotland. The crowded urban streets gave way to winding, smooth roads which cut through gentle green hills. It would have been a lovely ride had it not been for Chambers' cryptic bragging about his plan the entire time. I did my best to tune him out of my thoughts.

Finally, his medieval headquarters rolled into view from behind a massive, sheep-covered hill. I had to give it to him—it was a beautiful castle.

I made a mental note to look into the cost of a castle.
I bet women love a man with a good castle.

Chambers pulled the Jag up to the wall of the fortress where a gate rose as soon as we approached. Directly inside the gate were several armed guards who surrounded the car.

"Hello sir," one said to Chambers.

"Yes, good evening gentlemen," replied Chambers as he stood from his vehicle. "Please take our guest down to his quarters and make sure he is...comfortable." A nasty smile crossed his face as he said that last word. I felt a guard behind me pull my wrists toward him and slap some cuffs on them.

I knew that trying to reach for my duffel bag would be disastrous, so I resigned to walk with the men with just the gear I had on—my belt, shoes, and watch. The exploding mints would have been nice, but sometimes I like to get creative.

I was led by the guards down a musty hallway which led to a narrow staircase dug into the earth hundreds of years prior. The warm humidity of entering into Scotland's soil was a strangely homey feeling, even though I was a prisoner surrounded by armed guards.

The room they led me to was just as I expected—the size of an average closet with no amenities and a dirt floor. A small amount of light came in through a small, barred window in the top corner. It was really just an opening to outside with some rusted iron bars set across it.

Three of the guards left, leaving me alone with the fourth. He turned to face me. I braced myself for a cloying speech on how I'm fighting for the wrong side, etc.

I was, however, pleasantly surprised.

"You know," he said, turning toward me at the door. "Mister Neville is not after the codes."

I felt my ears perk up and my guts twist into some sideways sort of surprise. "He's not, is he?" I successfully masked my surprise. "Let me guess—he purely wants revenge on all the agents named in the roster?"

The guard shook his head and stepped back into the room with me—the last step of his life.

"Do you know what is really at Embassy 33?" he asked me.

One thing I hate more than anything is when people are condescending to me. I can't stand for it.

I curled my toes and found the trigger in my left shoe. After taking aim at his leg, I squeezed it with my pinky toe and a small dart shot from the sole of my shoe and punctured his shin through his pants.

He yelped in surprise and looked down at the tiny dart sticking out of his pant leg. Before he could grab it and yank it from his skin, his limbs began seizing violently. He sprayed a bloody foam from his mouth like a volcano until his body sank limply to the floor. He continued heaving out gulps of red-streaked vomit until he finally lay still on the dirt.

He had turned the ground around him into a soggy, muddy mess with his projectile liquids and I didn't want to go near him. I had to give it to Lewis though—those darts were certainly effective!

I tried not to let my leather shoes touch the blood, but by then they were already completely destroyed. I stepped toward his corpse and bent down to retrieve his keyring from his belt.

That's when I noticed a strange tattoo on the back of his neck. It was right under his shirt collar, so I hadn't seen it before when he was standing. It was just two vertical lines next to one another:

II

I tucked it away inside the pocket of my mind and continued reaching for the keys. Once I had freed myself of my handcuffs and taken the guard's gun, I retraced my route back to the staircase and then the hallway. I heard voices behind a door, so I kicked it in without trying the handle. Ornate 500-year-old doors splinter so easily.

I saw three nerds sitting before dozens of screens, chattering about diagnostics and coordinates.

"What is Chambers trying to do with Embassy 33, you hog-licking beaverholes?" I roared, swinging the pistol back and forth. They all froze and put their little hands up.

"We can't tell—" one of them started, but that was all I needed to hear. I blasted a hole clear through his sternum.

The other two tensed up even more and one began babbling. "Okay okay, I'll tell you, but you won't like what I have to say!"

"You have ten seconds to make me like it," I snarled back.

"Embassy 33 doesn't have nuclear codes," he began.

"I know this already. Tell me something I don't know."

"And—and what he's after is not even related to the database of agents." This was similar to what the guard had told me. I began to think Chambers had intentionally misled me when he told me his entire plan back in Bermuda. Maybe he's smarter than his 46R suit makes him look.

"Well what is it then? Four seconds."

"It—it..." he took a deep breath, knowing I wouldn't like it. "It's called the soul eraser."

"I don't believe you." I shot him too.

There was one nerd left and he started babbling.

"It really is! It's the soul eraser."

I had the gun leveled at his chest but wanted to hear him out. Maybe I shouldn't have shot the other two.

He went on. "Your government has been developing something which doesn't just kill people, but wipes them *and* their soul from every possible dimension!"

It sounded too far fetched so I pulled back the gun's hammer for dramatic effect.

"Here," he said in a panic, "look at this study on the screen and I can show you what it's supposed to do."

I stepped forward as he bent over the screen, frantically typing in codes and pulling up visuals. I kept the gun pointed at his chest in case he tried anything funny like pulling an alarm.

Windows popped up on the screen as he scanned through them, looking for the plans for this project. He opened one window which played a video recording. In the video, a female patient in a white hospital gown was seated on a cot in a plain white room.

A scientist entered the room and approached the woman. He then began to bat his hands around, like there were swarms of invisible bees assaulting his head. His lab coat flapped around as if a violent wind had blown into the room. He reached in his lab coat and pulled out a small object which I couldn't make out.

He held this over the body of the woman, then waved it over her like a metal detector over a beach. When he passed the small object over her waist, she collapsed onto the bed and fell still. Whatever was bothering the scientist was now gone too. His clothes fell still and no longer blew around.

Then he exited the room and the woman remained lying on the bed, looking dead but faintly breathing.

Then the nerd beside me began to explain more.

"The Russians were the first to experiment with haunting tactics." I was skeptical but decided to hear him out. After all, he was the last nerd left.

"What is a haunting tactic?" I asked, losing my patience.

"You know, ghost agents. Sleeper cells."

"I think you and I have different definitions of these terms, bud," I said, making sure to puff out my chest and further intimidate him.

He continued on: "Is your organization really not familiar with these tactics? It began with a question—how do we build a soldier who cannot be killed? The answer turned out to be somewhat simple. We kill them ourselves and they enter into the afterlife prepared to communicate with the living. They turned out to be less of *soldiers* and more of *spies*, but they're still wildly effective."

"This sounds like science fiction," I told him, still holding my finger tightly against the trigger.

"Agent Blake," he continued, seeming less intimidated than I would have liked, "you have heard tales of ghosts from biblical times until now. Did you really not believe a single one was real? The only question was, how do we harness this phenomenon for our benefit? The researchers at Embassy 33 have been working on this for decades. It may even have roots in Nazi experimentation."

Now I was beginning to get curious. "What sort of things did they do?"

"Well, the operatives who died for the sake of the study were able to communicate with the living...for the most part. They had set up every conceivable method for the dead to communicate with the living—Ouija boards, dolls, candles, and so on—in hopes that the operatives would speak back."

"And did they?"

"Forty-seven participants were put to sleep—killed, that is, voluntarily; hence, sleeper agents—for the study, and the scientists reported hearing from forty of them." Then his eyes lit up as he expounded. "Think about it, Agent Blake! How can you keep a ghost out of top secret rooms? What could stop a phantom from overhearing all of your confidential information and reporting it back to their home government? You can't stop them!"

"So you're telling me that this is an old practice and countries have been doing it for years?"

"Oh yes, Agent Blake. I'm surprised your organization hasn't looped you in." He was beginning to sound condescending again and I didn't like it. But he had piqued my curiosity so I decided not to kill him yet.

"So tell me about this soul eraser then."

"To be honest, Agent Blake, it is what it sounds like. How do we stop a phantasmic threat to our nation? You erase the phantom; you take away the soul. That's what you saw in the video. The woman's ghost was assaulting our scientist, so he erased it."

"What happens to the soul?"

Right then, before the nerd could answer, a voice from behind me spoke. "Wouldn't you like to find out?" I didn't have to turn around to know the voice belonged to Neville.

"It took you long enough to come around," I told him as I turned.

"The guard came to get me as quickly as he could," replied Neville.

"The gua—" I paused as I began to put the pieces together. "Did he...?"

"Yes, my boy," said Neville with his trademark grin spilling like acid across his face. "He told me about how you killed him with a poison dart and were on the loose in *my* castle."

He just had to rub in that he has a castle and I don't.

"He told you..." I began and let him finish my sentence.

"His ghost came to me shortly after you killed him. I believe you saw his marking? The tattoo?"

I recalled the two lines on the guard's neck: ||

"Two vertical lines," continued Chambers, incredibly pleased with himself. "The two realms, the land of the living and the dead. Always hovering alongside the other. Everyone who has volunteered themselves for this project has been marked in this way. Our mission is to open a door between the two realms, while at the same time stopping those who would use this against us. I believe Roger here was explaining to you how the soul eraser works?"

"He was just about to get to it."

"Oh, well I'm sorry you'll never get to hear the full explanation. I guess you'll have to settle for experiencing it!"

I saw what Neville was hinting toward, and by this time three new guards had trickled into the door behind him and stood ready to grab me. They took a few steps toward me.

"Sorry, ya limp-wristed milquetoasts," I said as I reached down and pulled a small tab on my belt which unhooked the thousand-meter thread. "I only let the ladies whisk me off my feet."

I quickly hurled the weighted end of the thread over the shoulder of the guard on the right. Before they knew what was happening, I took several quick steps to my left, so the thread now lay over the shoulder of the farthest guard from me and across the front of the rest. They were halfway wrapped up in my thread and began grabbing for it.

"This may sting, you wrinkled yak taints," I said as I slammed my fist into my belt buckle, which recoiled the thread instantly back to the belt. As it did, it cut a straight line through the three guards like a wire through soft butter. The first guard's head tumbled to the floor and the second was cut diagonally from his shoulder to his opposite ribcage. His top half slid from his hips onto the dirt.

The third guard was cut clean in half at the waist. His torso tottered for a moment before he fell to his knees, then his top half seemed to leap off of his waist.

I stepped back while the closest guard fell to avoid splashing more blood onto my already-muddied oxford shoes.

Neville's jaw slacked open for a moment before he hid his shock at seeing his three guards sliced in half with a tiny thread right before his eyes. Now it was just Neville, me, and the nerd whose name I forgot, in the room. Or so I thought.

"Well, are you going to take me in yourself?" I smirked.

Neville usually had surprise gadgets of his own, so I knew not to completely underestimate him. He made a lunge to grab me with some sort of bionic arm shooting out of his sleeve. I jumped to my right and used his momentum to shove him to the ground behind me. I ran past him, jumped the guards' bodies and ran back out the door I had kicked through.

I wasn't sure where to run, but I figured Neville must have a stockpile of vehicles somewhere in his castle so I could get out of here.

As I ran down the hallway away from the nerds' room, I heard Neville shouting after me, "Yes, Blake! This is exactly what I wanted you to do!"

Sure it was.

I couldn't stand to hear another lecture on how Chambers was going to save the world by blowing it up or some nonsense like that. I kept running down the hallway in a direction I hadn't been before. One of my favorite inspirational posters popped into my head:

> *If you don't go down new roads,*
> *you'll never get to new destinations.*

So good. I love a good inspirational poster.

The ancient stone hall turned right, so I followed it around the bend and suddenly cursed out loud. More guards had cut me off. I heard footsteps behind me so I knew I'd have to fight my way out no matter which direction I went. I stepped toward the guards and they didn't move.

"Alrighty then," I said to myself, rolling up my sleeves. I charged at them but they remained still. *This will either be really hard or really easy,* I thought as I tucked my shoulder and braced to slam into the middle guard.

But then I tumbled forward. I had charged so hard that my inertia threw me to the ground instead of hitting the guards. I must have missed them. My shoulder was wet.

But that's impossible!

I turned behind me and saw the guards all facing me.
Then I realized it.

They were the same ones I had just sliced into pieces. But...

It slowly clicked together.

They had been killed, so now these were their ghosts. They had been part of the project and now here they were, continuing their postmortem duties. I stood up and began running away from them, further down the hallway. It was lit only by faint electrical lanterns spaced every fifteen feet.

The damp dirt beneath my leather shoes absorbed most of the sound of my running down the hallway. The large stones which had been pasted together centuries ago with cement and clay contributed to the ominous atmosphere of the castle.

I made more turns and found myself at another staircase which spiraled downward, deeper into the earth. There was no other option here except to go back and face the ghosts, or go down into the dark. As I stood atop the stone stairs, I could see nothing below them except darkness. They seemed to descend into a pitch black abyss.

I clicked the button on the side of my watch which activated a dim light and descended into the depths. The watch light was next to no help, but it was better than nothing.

I couldn't run down the stairs due to the lack of light, so I slowly made my way step by step, checking what was before me by swinging the wristwatch back and forth to illuminate the next two feet before my eyes.

The temperature dropped as I walked lower and lower into the humid darkness of the castle's bowels. A trickle of icicle pinpricks made their way down my spine.

Finally the ground leveled off again and I was walking straight through another corridor. It was walled in by medieval stones and the dirt ground seemed soggier here. I heard the echoing sound of water droplets falling all around the hall, but other than that, it was silent.

I held my wrist up to the wall, hoping for a torch of some kind so I could see what else was in the tunnel with me. Nothing but wet stones and moss.

As I slowly made my way along the wall, I soon detected a faint glow around the corner of the hallway. A shiver ran from the base of my skull down my back. *Were they expecting me to come this way?*

I continued along, trying to be as quiet as possible so they wouldn't hear me coming. I turned my watch light off and kept my hand on the stone wall, feeling my way along. When I reached the corner's edge, I peered around and my heart dropped into my nuggets at what I saw.

It was the guards again.

They were facing me as if they were waiting for me the whole time. They emitted a faint glow which gently illuminated the hallway around them. I instinctively pulled back around the corner, hoping they hadn't seen me.

Hundreds of questions rushed through my mind at once: *Did they see me? Can ghosts see in the darkness? What can ghosts do to living humans?*

This couldn't be real.

I had lived my whole life never believing ghosts were real, much less seeing any. And now I saw three who were working for the nerd Neville. What did they want with me?

I felt frozen against the corner of the hallway. I glued my back against the wall and squeezed my eyes closed. When I opened them again, the room seemed slightly brighter. I didn't dare look around the corner. I felt like the phantom guards had moved closer.

Without consciously thinking about it, I felt my feet begin to step back the way I had come, away from the guards. My hand slid along the wet rocks as my feet clumsily slopped through the mud.

Suddenly I heard a whisper.

"Max," it said. It was gentle but clear. It wasn't loud, but seemed to fill the entire tunnel.

It wasn't a man's voice, but a woman's.

I stopped running and paused.

The darkness seemed to lift from the tunnel, as if a thick black filter were suddenly slid off of an old film.

A woman and a little boy materialized in the tunnel before me. The little boy was several feet further up the tunnel and they both had their backs to me. I froze and watched as a strangely familiar scene unfolded before me.

The woman was calling for the little boy while he sat on the dirt ground, playing with his back to her.

"Max," she said again.

The boy turned and looked at his mother. She stepped toward him and knelt beside him, bringing her head level with his.

I realized why it was familiar.

It was me.

I was the little boy.

I remembered this as the last time I had seen my mother.

I watched in horror as the woman, still with her back to me, knelt before the boy and whispered to him why she had to leave. In sixty seconds, she tried to make a reasonable explanation for her disappearance from his life.

Then she stood up and the little boy looked confused. She didn't hug him goodbye or tell him she loved him.

I couldn't contain my emotion. I heard myself whispering under my breath, "No....no!"

I watched as the woman rose to her full height and turned to walk away from young Max.

But when she turned toward me, I saw her face for the first time. It was not the face of my mother I recalled, but a grotesque and twisted face. Her eyes had sunken into her skull and didn't seem to have eyelids. The skin of her cheeks had holes which swelled and stretched apart before my eyes.

She walked toward me and I recoiled in disgust and fear. Even though she barely looked human, I felt like she was still my mother and I wanted to make things right. Her face started to melt. One of her eyes rolled out and fell to the ground and her jaw sank down to her neck, then past her breast. Her mouth gaped open a full foot, and I watched as her teeth fell out one by one.

"Maaaaxxx," the creature groaned, no longer sounding like a woman, but a growling demon.

I stepped backward, away from it. She extended a bony hand which no longer had much gray skin left on it.

"Maaaaa—" it groaned again without a clear 'M' sound, as its jaw now hung like a puppet on strings from its cheekbones. It sounded more like, "Wahhhhhx."

It was lurching toward me now. Each step seemed to cause her incredible pain. Half of me wanted to turn and run but the other half needed to stay and connect with the mother I lost so many years ago. Despite my sophomoric longing for nurture and affection, I felt myself taking a step backward with every step she took toward me.

I stepped backward until it felt like I was back at the turn in the hallway, around which waited the three ghosts of the guards, but I couldn't take my eyes from my decaying mother.

Finally I took a quick glance back me to see where I was retreating to, but rather than a corner, ten feet behind me was a dead end with a faded white door.

I looked back at my mother, then at the six-year-old Max beyond her. My horror had turned to grief and for the first time in decades, I felt tears dribbling from my eyelids.

"Goodbye, Mum," I managed to get out in a frail voice, and turned to grab the handle of the white door. She continued lurching toward me, her legs seeming to crumble and fall apart beneath her as she stomped toward me.

I pushed through the white door, not knowing what I'd find on the other side.

The door held itself open as I passed through, but as soon as I was inside the room, it slammed closed behind me. Somehow I figured that I couldn't reopen it if I tried, so I carefully continued forward.

The room was small and dark and it took my eyes a moment to adjust, and when they did, I wished they hadn't.

Something metallic clicked in the darkness before me. It was the pull string of a lamp, and the bulb sparked to life. The lamp sat on a desk, and at the desk sat a hunched-over figure with his back to me. His hand pulled away from the lamp and from behind, I could see that he was writing something on a piece of paper.

I quietly approached from behind and peered over his shoulder to see what he wrote. In the sloppy handwriting of an old man seized by tremors, the paper read,

> Mother's in a well
> and Father will be soon
> the children all are coming
> to join them in their tomb

As I got closer to the man, I heard him muttering the rhyme to himself. Then he chuckled and began writing the dark lines again, and I watched as his shaky hand scrawled the words across the page.

"and Father will be soon..." he muttered as he wrote the line.

"Eh—Excuse me," I said, tapping him on the shoulder. He stopped writing and spoke to me without turning to look at me.

"Max," he stated. "It's been so long."

I was expecting it to be Neville again, playing tricks on me and disguising himself. But this voice was certainly not the voice of Neville. It was strangely familiar, so I continued speaking to him.

"Who are you?" I asked.

He turned and looked up at me from his wooden seat.
It felt like every organ in my body dropped to the floor of my being.

It was me.

It was me as an old, old man. He didn't say a word, just looked at me, slightly shivering. Then under his breath, he continued his mad rambling which didn't make any sense.

> "Mommy's in the basement
> with a bat stuck in her hair
> but Daddy won't come help her
> when his shows are on the air."

"What?" I asked him. His face was like mine if I never moisturized it for the next forty years. Or shaved. He was covered in wrinkles and missing a few teeth. He was not rotting or decaying like my mother was, but it was still haunting to look into the face of my future self.

"How are you here?" I asked.

Suddenly, the future version of myself stopped his rambling and seemed to click out of a trance into a state of coherence.

It was silent. I heard a laugh from a child in the hallway. Then the old man spoke.

"We've been here for a while, Max."

"We? Who is we? What are you talking about?"

"Oh Max!" He let out a wheezy laugh and seemed to get distracted by uttering another haunting rhyme.

> "Mommy and Daddy
> and Neville make three,
> they're a-waitin' downstairs
> for a-you and for me!"

Suddenly he snapped back to his sober self and looked straight at me. "You never left the dungeon, Max."

"What? Yes I did. I chopped the guards in half and found out about the soul eraser from the nerd..."

"Not that dungeon!"

"What?" I muttered under my breath.

"I mean the one in here," he raised a twisted old hand and pointed to his temple. "You're trapped."

"What are you *talking* about?" I spat, not wanting to hear this.

Before he could answer, the older version of myself needed to get another verse out.

> "Mommy took a star
> and she put it in her pocket
> where Daddy couldn't see it
> so he beat her like she lost it."

Then, something strange happened. In the seconds between his poem and his next words, everything clicked together. His strange didactic verses had opened my eyes to what I had been suppressing my whole life. My relationship with my mother *was* locked away in the basement of my heart.

His soliloquies had opened my eyes in a way no one could understand but my own psyche; the older version of myself had spoken wisdom into the ears of my younger self. My ears were open to new melodies and my eyes opened to new colors. The dark castle cell was now illuminated by a rainbow of life and light.

The epiphany hit me all at once.

All of my philandering was a race to patch up the hole left by my mother. All of my violent rage was a vicious attempt to get back at my father!

All of this clicked together inside my mind in a matter of seconds and I suddenly felt weightless.

But then the light dimmed and the colors lost their saturation. The room with the old man spun and then faded away.

I was on the dirt in the hallway again, lying down on it. My shoulder was wet from passing through the ghostly guards—some sort of disgusting ectoplasm.

But the guards were now nowhere to be seen.

As I stood to my feet, I was thinking about everything I had just experienced. Seeing the past version of myself, followed by the old version had sparked emotions and thoughts I'd tucked away for decades. I didn't want to think about my mother leaving, or my father a few years after her.

Something about this castle brought to life things which should have remained buried.

I sniffled and realized that during the strange, supernatural episode, I had quietly been crying. I realized that my cheeks were wet with tears. The tunnel was dark, but my eyes were adjusting. It was silent except for the occasional, distant drip of water.

As I sat there, figuring out which way I had come from and which way I should go, a faint glow appeared around the corner. The guards were coming back.

It was then, sitting on the wet ground of the castle, that I remembered something the nerd had told me earlier. He said that the ghosts were good for spying, but not for fighting. This must mean that they couldn't do anything to me.

I decided to put it to the test. I'd go back the way I came, walking right through the guards and getting the soul eraser from Neville. The glow around the corner slowly grew in brightness as I rose to my feet. The three ghostly guards rounded the bend and I walked toward them.

They drew nearer to me and I walked toward them. It felt strange to walk at someone, intending to walk *through* them, but I did. I walked directly down the center of the hallway at the center guard.

His human appearance was already beginning to fade and be replaced by a ghastly, gory figure with sunken eyes and dehydrated flesh. Apparently, ghosts still suffer from the entropy which assails the entire universe. Even the matter which makes phantoms will shrivel in the coming heat death of the cosmos.

I slowly passed through the ghost, feeling the moist ectoplasm from his glowing effervescence sticking to my skin. I was passing through much slower this time, as last time I charged full speed at the specter. A low hum buzzed in the base of my skull.

The ghost, however didn't react. He didn't even acknowledge my presence at all. Already, roughly an hour after his death, he was detaching from the earthly realm and from his cares about anything on this side of the grave.

Haunting tactics seemed to neglect taking this into account: that when a soul crosses the threshold between the temporal and the timeless, between the lands of becoming and of being, it retains little concern for the affairs of the former. Or maybe they *did* take that into account, and that's why it was an ongoing project.

After passing through the dead guard, I brought my hands up to my face and wiped the translucent slime from my face, trying not to gag. It was scentless and very unlike other viscous fluids I'd ever encountered. I tried to shake it off of my hands, but it seemed as if, all at once, the ectoplasm poofed into steam and drifted up into the humid air of the corridor. I felt around the rest of my body, which seemed to be free of the fluid.

I continued retracing my steps until I came to the stone staircase cut into the earth. I ascended it slowly, letting my eyes adjust as I rose.

I stormed back down the hallway until I came to the door I had kicked in earlier. I was no longer filled with the same eternal rage I had felt before. I no longer yearned for the hollow, quick affection of beautiful women or the painful, slow deaths of my enemies. I knew I had a long way to go, but encountering my mother's ghost in the basement of the castle had awakened things in me which were buried for decades.

I was an emotional mess.

I pushed the scene of my mother from my thoughts, promising I'd return to it later. For now, I had to disarm Neville and return the soul eraser to safer hands.

From down the hallway, I heard Neville's voice talking to one of his associates. I could only catch vague terms as I drew closer: "…soul eraser…details…may feel drowsy…test…men…"

None of it made sense yet.

I clenched my fists as I walked through the shattered door.

Neville fell silent when he saw me, standing there smiling, expecting some sort of snarky taunt. Rather than a condescending joke about his short stature or fishlike eyes, I quietly smiled at him.

This seemed to disarm him more than a hurtful insult. "Well, Agent Blake?"

I continued to say nothing, but smiled down at him.

"What are you doing? Didn't my guards get to you?" He nervously leaned back and whispered something to the nerd, who ran off through a door to an adjacent room to follow an order. "My associate has gone to get the soul eraser, Agent Blake."

"That's fine," I said, smiling at him.

"What are you doing here, Blake?" he said, slowly losing his cool.

"I forgave my mother for leaving," I told him. It was true. In the musty tunnels of his castle—or my mind, or wherever I was—I had encountered the source of my trauma. My womanizing was uprooted and my rage was quelled.

"What do you mean?" asked Chambers.

"I mean, I'm happy for you and your castle," I told him.

Neville seemed to look at me for a long time, seeing when I would break out in laughter and accuse him of being a fool again.

But I didn't.

I meant what I had said. For the first time I could remember, I felt at peace. I felt like a man who was solid and grounded in who he was. I didn't need to impress anyone or earn any cheap sort of satisfaction to plug up the dam of wounds I'd accrued over my life.

The longer Neville stared at me, the more convinced he became. He swallowed. Then he blinked. Then he pressed his lips together tightly and a rebellious tear fell down his cheek.

"Well if you're allowed to forgive," he started, "I guess I can too-*hoo-hoo*." He broke out into full-on sobs and the waterworks rolled.

I relaxed my fists as Neville stepped toward me, sniffled, and reached up to put his hand on my shoulder. "You and me, Blake…We're two sides of the same dime."

Feeling the human touch in his hand sent a warm tremor racing through my entire body and suddenly I was pinching my cheeks back to fight stubborn tears. We hugged, my arms reaching down to wrap around his tiny frame and oversized suit and we wept while holding one another until the nerd came back.

I had expected the soul eraser to be a giant machine, but what he carried fit in a single hand. It was even smaller than a pistol.

Neville looked over at the man and said, "That will not be necessary anymore."

The nerd seemed shocked, wondering what had happened in the minutes he was gone, as he came back to find the two enemies crying in one another's arms.

When Chambers let me go, I walked toward the nerd, acting as if I was well and good and all was forgiven. When I was within punching distance of the nerd, I cracked him one in the side of the neck and his head wobbled side to side and he fell to the ground, unconscious. As he went down, his hand swung toward me, and I smoothly caught the soul eraser from his limp hand.

He fell to the side, so I now faced Neville with his own weapon. It looked less like a weapon and more like a construction worker's stud detector. There was a single button on the top of it, and I presumed that you pushed it while waving it over the victim's body.

Neville put his hands up. "Wow, wow, Agent Blake." He sniffled. "What was all this for?" He sobbed a little bit more. "Was this all an act??"

"No, Neville, it wasn't," I assured him. "What we just felt was real. It was very real. But I can't let you go back out and continue to endanger millions of innocent people!"

At this Neville cried out like a five-year-old throwing a tantrum, "But I don't want my soul era-hased!" He sobbed again.

"I'm sorry," I said, stepping toward him with the soul eraser raised toward his chest.

"Agent Blake, please!" He knew I was stronger than him in every way and he now had no defenses but to beg for his soul.

"I won't kill you," I promised him, "but I will need to evict your murderous soul from your little body." I even resisted my overwhelming urge to call him mean names.

In the minutes which followed, I discovered that everyone's soul resides in a different part of their body. The woman in the video held her soul in her waist, but Neville's was not there behind his small zipper. I first waved the instrument over Neville's head, but nothing happened and he continued crying, awaiting the inevitable relinquishment of his invisible essence. The same happened with his chest and abdomen as I worked my way down.

It wasn't until I got down to his left ankle that I found Neville Chambers' soul. When I waved the soul eraser over that joint, Neville fell suddenly quiet and stood up straighter. His eyes stared off into the distance and the only faint sound coming from his body was the calm rhythm of his breathing.

I had done it. I had erased Neville Chambers' soul.

If it wasn't for the reality I encountered in his basement tunnels, I would have enjoyed erasing his soul and then brutalizing his body afterward. But the new me was different. I no longer took joy in the suffering of others, and now Neville would never suffer again, nor would he harm anyone. In fact, in a new part of my mind, I found myself even liking the little guy.

I read once that angels are souls without bodies and animals are bodies without souls. Humans are the wonderful balance of a body animated by a soul, but Neville's was now erased.

So I decided to take him home as a pet.

I feed him well and he even helps me around the flat. He doesn't do very well with complex tasks, but if I ask him to bring me a glass of cranberry juice, he can usually manage that. When he's not helping me with a chore or fetching me a snack, he will sit quietly on our sofa, staring into the void before his eyes. He seems very interested in it, so I typically let him focus.

Sometimes I'll help him don a new fall wardrobe and we will go for a walk. I'll point out the colorful leaves or the boats dancing on the tide, but Neville will mostly stare straight ahead.

26. Plastic Chair

So there's a chair on the side of Route 28 at the intersection by my road. It's a plastic chair. White. Nothing special about it. And it just sits there and lets the grass grow around it. Or at least, that's how it's been lately.

Late last week when I drove by, a man was sitting in it. Is it his chair? He didn't appear to be doing anything; he was just sitting there, looking at the cars going by. Perhaps he was waiting for someone. And then forgot his chair. Assuming, of course, that it was his chair.

Maybe the person he was waiting for is incredibly wealthy (it is Cape Cod after all), despite the fact that he himself did not appear too well off. It was a beautiful woman, who wore silk bath robes and pink fuzzy slippers in the evening, as she prepared for her lavender scented bath. After graduating from boarding school in the south, she had gone to Paris for a few years—not too few, but not too many either; just a good number of years to go to school in Paris—and had grown tired of the extravagant lifestyle of the Parisians. She began writing letters to her friend on the Cape. Letters of longing, as if she were the tide and he was the moon. They grew more and more intense, and as the time grew closer for her to return to the Cape, back in his arms, she felt as if she could not bear it anymore.

Before long, however, her father caught word of the letters and decided he should intervene. A retired sergeant in the United States Navy, he chartered a ship to France to have a face to face conversation with his daughter before letting her run off with a man who sits in plastic chairs in nothing but his shorts and tank top on the side of 28.

As he was nearly across the Atlantic, the ship came into an awful storm. Navigation was thrown off, the engines shut down and could not restart for three whole days because of the water coming over the sides of the ship. The waves were catastrophic. The proportions were thought only to have existed in movies.

Miraculously, no one was hurt and everyone made it safely to the shores of Morocco, where the boat had been blown during the storm. Now that the girl's father was in Africa, rather than Europe, he had no money to spend. Moroccan Dirham does not transfer very well with Euros, which is all the father had brought with him. He spent what he could on some food that could last him a few days, but realized that what he needed was a job. He earned some money at a local deli right on the edge of the ocean and became quite fluent in French, the national second language. The irony was not lost on him.

After several months of working in the deli, he became quite adept at slicing things, and he could wow the passersby with his quick blade. He ended up quitting the deli because he felt that it was only holding him back from his full potential as a knife-wielding traveling showman. He told a girl he had met named Leila that he was leaving and she told him she was coming with him, so now he and Leila travel the African coastline doing knife tricks and impressing the townsfolk.

He eventually forgot about his daughter, as old age seized his mind and he slowly headed down the path of dementia. Some mornings, he wakes up and doesn't even recognize Leila lying next to him.

His daughter followed through with her plans and moved back to the States. She met up with her lover, who was faithfully waiting for her in a plastic lawn chair on the side of 28. They were in passionate love for several months, but ended up living rather nonchalant lives. Occasionally, they order pizza from the nearest place and watch whatever is good on TV. Other than that, they are rather boring people to be with. She often gossips with the older church ladies. They sometimes inquire about Paris, and she loves to tell them all about it. But that was in the past. As is her father. She occasionally thinks about him and wonders where he went.

And that white lawn chair is still sitting by the side of 28. And as they drive by, some people wonder to themselves what it's doing there.

These gloomy stairs, so dark, so damp, so cold.

27. If you could haunt your house forever

If you could haunt your house forever,
you'd see the drywall fall apart.
You'd see the studs all start to rot
until done in by crane or spark.

If you could haunt your house forever,
you'd see the urban city sprawl;
the government's development
would soon take hold of all.

If you could haunt your house forever,
oh the violence you would see.
You'd be monitoring arguments
for all eternity.

If you could haunt your house forever,
you'd see your home become a house.
It'd be a soulless heap of wood
just like a corpse wearing a blouse

If you could haunt your house forever,
you'd see the people come and go.
You'd see families live and die
until you're only there alone.

28. The Stilt Walker

Supposedly your body hair will grow for over a week after you die, so as I stood beside my uncle's open casket, I wondered who was responsible for shaving him and why they had done such a bad job. It was evident that they had done it a few days ago, as one last 5 o'clock shadow was struggling to burst through, as if to say "I'm still here. I'm not dead yet. Don't sink me beneath the dirt yet."

But he's not still there. The follicles just haven't finished dying and when they do, their cry will be forgotten. They'll be sunk beneath the ground clinging to cheeks which began decomposing a week ago.

Most people, standing next to the open casket of a beloved family member, would not take time to examine the facial hair growth post mortem, but I notice things like that. I notice that there are three shades on the face of my uncle: his signature goatee which is the longest shade, the places the funeral home missed in their shave, and then the places they hit which had already begun their slow, dying regrowth.

I notice things like this because I think about death more than anyone else I know. Perhaps I'm gifted in this area — or cursed, depending on how you look at it.

It may be OCD.

It may be a dark fascination with how time kills all things and nothing escapes the long, twisty fingers of atrophy.

It was there as a boy, standing beside the box where my uncle would sleep for the rest of my life, that it hit me: What I had to do. I began to craft an idea of how I could act out my obsession.

Whatever it is, most kids aren't weighed down by this obsession with death and how all things slowly (or quickly) move in that direction.

I can't remember when it began, but I began compulsively measuring everything. Perhaps measuring isn't the right word. I began seeking out balance.

Everything created in the universe is held in tension between two extremes. Siddhartha called it the Middle Way, but it exists outside of Buddhism as well. Christianity attempts to balance everything between good and bad extremes: You can't be too legalistic or too licentious.

I think that's why God gave us two hands. If you wanted to, you could hold an ice cube in one hand and a lit match in the other and you act as the tension between. You have two eyes, so you can see beautiful things and tragic things and balance each other out. You have two ears so you can hear Beethoven as well as the screams of bodies caught in a house fire.

You have two hands so one can hold the hand of your lover while the other strikes the face of your brother.

It all has to balance out.

Dark and light.

Beauty and decay.

Life and death.

Nothing is more opposite than the last pair, yet how little thought we give them both! We don't contemplate our own lives until we near death and once we die we can never contemplate anything ever again.

"Who can praise you from the grave?" asks the psalmist.

"The body responds well to metaphor," a teacher told me once. I didn't understand it until my uncle's funeral as I stood there watching his beard grow back. Now I get it. Now I embrace the movement of my body as a piece of theater before God himself.

Eastern thought capitulates dark and light forces against one another, but coexisting in the yin-yang. This is too stark. There is no balance when everything is black and white. Where is the grey? Where is the tension?

Jerusalem, on the other hand, is rife with tension. The land itself holds together the global East and the global West like a geographic belt buckle. So should we be surprised that out of this contested location emerged the greatest act of cosmic balance in history?

Picture God.

Berkeley said everything that exists, exists in the mind of God. If He were to stop thinking about it for one moment, the very structure of reality would fall apart.

But Berk, imagine if He were to speak! What would happen then?

We find out in the opening pages of the Bible: God speaks and rather than sounds emerging, galaxies do.

Picture God.

Now picture man.

Now picture war.

Famine.

Genocide.

Riots.

Injustice.

Structural racism.

My hands can only reach so far apart. The tension my little body is able to produce is limited to my four-foot-seven frame. Imagine if I could extend into the sky and my limbs grew grotesquely long like a Salvador Dali painting. Then I could get some real tension going.

What hath God to do with man? The two are opposites like noon and night.

Let's look once more to Jerusalem and ask the ancient city this question: How do you maintain such wondrous tension? How do you suspend such impossible balance?

Their answer: A carpenter from buttcrack nowhere Galilee. Get a load of this guy. Claiming to be God, yet he's as killable as a man.

Talk about tension.

Plato would ask:
How can the Being enter into the land of Becoming?
How can the Form become a Shadow?

Jews would ask:
How can the *I AM* wear skin?
Whose eyes can see the face of God and live to see anything else?

This carpenter — now hanging like a bloody pulp from a tree outside the city — claimed to be able to handle the tension, but I guess his body couldn't take it.

He's trying to hold the tension of a busted world in His chest...a chest now splayed apart between two nail-bitten hands.

That night, after the funeral, I went into the forest behind my family's house and cut down a tree. I worked away in our garage for weeks on end, working to make them perfect. No one understood but me, but that's okay. They don't have to.

Two days later, the carpenter's body was still underground and probably had the postmortem stubble covering his cheeks. His follicles hadn't given up hope, nor should they have. In this case, they would be needed again.

Turns out, this Jewish nobody from buttcrack nowhere *could* take the tension

between God and man,

between

life

and death.

Turns out He wasn't very good at staying dead.

Today I'm getting better at tension. I'm getting better at holding it within my body and acting out the balance. It's how I worship.

I pull my stilts out of the garage and pace down the street. The ones I made as a boy only lifted me a foot and a half above the ground.

Today I fly.

Today my limbs extend meters as I pace above the surface of the world. The ends of my stilts produce massive amounts of pressure, and here I am in the middle — the crux, the one who can take the tension.

One stilt is beauty, the other is time.

One stilt is pain, the other is glory.

And here I am, perched in the middle like a bird in a precarious nest, holding the tension in my body. It's the only way I know how.

This is my dance; the large awkward strides and the magnificent feeling of force pressing into me from my eternal limbs.

One is life, the other death.

29. ABOUT ETHAN

The dating app version of this bio would include a lot of continent hopping, advanced graduate degrees, and the fact that I won a bodybuilding competition in Guatemala.

While those things are true, they miss some of the reality of me as a human and my day-to-day life. It would go against some of the advice of this book, which is present an honest version of yourself. You're not that cool, and neither am I. No one is (Except maybe Adrien Brody).

I live in Denver, pet dogs, and hang out with my roommates. I love to write (it's an addiction, not an accomplishment), run and lift weights. I went to Moody Bible Institute and have written five other books. Follow along wherever this life takes me at ethanrenoe.com or @ethanrenoe. I'd love to hear from you!

www.ingramcontent.com/pod-product-compliance
Lightning Source LLC
Chambersburg PA
CBHW031439160726
47994CB00005B/1804